Red Queen

The Substrate Wars

Book 1

Jeb Kinnison

© 2014 Jeb Kinnison

www.jebkinnison.com

jebkinnison@gmail.com

Library of Congress Control Number: 2014958935

Cover photo: Shutterstock

RED QUEEN

THE SUBSTRATE WARS

BOOK 1

JEB KINNISON

For all of the other kids who escaped by reading.

Contents

Author's Note

Red Queen is a story about the yearning for freedom and agency in a world dominated by bureaucrats and propagandists. The world of *Red Queen* is just a decade or two away, and looks very much like the world we live in, just a few steps worse. In the tradition of Heinlein's *If This Goes On—*, I have extrapolated from current trends and imagined the politics that result. The authoritarian tendencies we see in modern western states will probably be reversed at some point—but what if they just keep getting worse? This is especially true of the US, with its 9/11-justified surveillance and interception of every citizen's email and message metadata, and a penal-industrial complex that imprisons about one in three black men at some point in their lives, often for victimless crimes like drug possession. A more serious terrorist incident might lead to even more restrictions on freedom and privacy. And that's where *Red Queen* begins.

Classic science fiction posits a future society and technology, then tells a story that shows how that new world might evolve. Human nature changes much more slowly than technology, and even amid the strange lands of the future, people remain people, with all their nobility, vices, insecurities, and dreams.

I've footnoted some of the topics in science, politics, and economics that are brought up. Check through the footnotes at the end for topics you may wish to know more about.

Prologue

> There is nothing in this world so permanent as a temporary emergency. —Robert Heinlein, The Man Who Sold the Moon, 1950

Just before midnight Saturday in the Coast Guard's Vessel Traffic Service watch room for New York Harbor, one of the hundreds of vessels being tracked began to deviate from its usual course. The computer noted the discrepancy and buzzed Petty Officer Assante's console. He looked at the transponder info: charter party boat, regular transit in and out from the Skyport Marina on the East River. The deviation from course that had signaled the alert: the blip had moved steadily up the river past its normal turn to dock. It was approaching the sensitive area near the UN buildings. Assante hailed them via radio; while waiting for a response, he reminded himself to leave early for once so he would at least see his wife for a few minutes before she slept. After getting no response to his second hail attempt, Assante sent an alert to the nearest patrol boat to check it out.

Seaman Curtis Jackson on the Coast Guard patrol boat received the alert to check out the vessel, which was slowly encroaching on a security zone. Probably too much partying, Jackson thought; they turned to come up behind the party barge and Jackson began surveying the decks with binoculars. Lights on, party music going, but no one outside, and the people visible through the larger view windows weren't moving as you'd expect. Which gave him a very bad feeling—

Inside the party barge, blood flowed from the machine-gunned bodies of the passengers and crew, ran down the stairways, and pooled on the dance floor. One hijacker remained on board to steer toward the target and activate the device now planted belowdecks. His life had been long enough, he thought, and when they had asked for a martyr he had said yes. Striking a blow at the heart of the American beast would avenge their humiliation of Islam and its people. He noticed a patrol boat coming up fast behind, and decided the target was close enough—he pushed the red button on the box he carried.

The bomb was compact, one of the smallest fission devices made by the old Soviet Union and lost by the Ukrainian government during the chaos. It had made its way through several countries, changing hands at higher and higher prices, until it was purchased by Islamists and had its neutron-reflecting casing replaced with cobalt—which reduced the yield of the device but would spread far more radioactive fallout than a standard fission bomb. The conventional explosive casing was old and went off more weakly than it was designed to, and the uranium quadrants that were driven together to reach critical mass and ignite the chain reaction were a little off-center, but it was close enough: the reaction ignited and generated energy the equivalent of ten kilotons of TNT, and the neutron flux converted the added metal jacket to highly radioactive cobalt-60 dust. Hard X-rays from the reaction created an expanding ball of glowing ionized air. Then the expanding fireball cooled and began to rise into the classic mushroom cloud shape over the East River.

The blast wave tore apart hundreds of buildings near shore, throwing their bricks like missiles into Manhattan. All the windows and interior walls of the UN building blew out first, then the tower rocked backward, and began to melt and sag before toppling. Under the river, the Queens Midtown Tunnel collapsed and flooded. Most of the major hospitals along the river were blasted into rubble. Grand Central Station's roof fell in. The Chrysler Building's aluminum cap began to burn and melt as the upper tower collapsed onto Lexington

Avenue. The New York Public Library caught fire and burned for days. Streets were filled with smoldering rubble three stories deep. Fires fed by broken gas lines consumed block after block.

In Times Square, thousands of people were still walking the streets or in restaurants and bars after Broadway plays had let out. They were jolted first by a dazzling flash in the eastern sky, then the lights went out. The blast wave passed over their heads, shaking loose cornices and showering the sidewalks with debris and shattered glass, and those outside were deafened by the roar. This far from the blast, most people inside buildings survived, but the gentle rain of fallout that began as they tried to make their way west to escape would take many of their lives.

Hundreds of thousands of people on the east side of Manhattan and west side of Brooklyn and Queens died in the first minutes. More succumbed to burns and radiation in the next few hours. In the less-damaged areas, people tried to help the injured and get supplies for what might be days of waiting for rescue—but those who stayed outdoors for more than a few minutes did not know they would sicken and die in agony within days or years from exposure to the radioactive dust. Civil defense preparedness was nil, and convoys from far suburbs driving in to help had to turn back when their radiation detectors showed lethal levels in Manhattan and points east as the dust settled in the prevailing wind.

Part One: Co-Evolution

Chapter One: Activities Week

ALife Simulation, Model 1: Organism 33

Its sensors showed no dangers visible and the scent of Green to the left. Those inputs, fed into its neural network, resulted in outputs for its next action: turn left and move toward the scent. By this generation of its kind this was an instinctive response. Unfortunately it was eaten by a predator before it reached the food three squares away, but some of its species reproduced for the next round.

A-Life Lab

Life is a process which can be abstracted away from any particular medium. —John von Neumann

It was late September on the California coast, and warmer than it had been all summer. The campus was humming with the new term, bicycles everywhere and students streaming to morning classes. Justin Smith pedaled past the Quad, noting the booths set up there for Activities Fair, and parked his bike in the rack in front of Gates Hall, the rough limestone Computer Science building donated by a successful college dropout.

When he reached the Artificial Life lab he could hear Prof. Wilson and Justin's research partner Rasna Kapoor talking. Justin already knew from checking the overnight simulation run from home that something was amiss, and he had a good idea what it was: "We need to check the sex routine. I tweaked it yesterday and from the looks of the stats, I'd guess I made a locking error."

Justin put his backpack down and hovered over the two at the console. In front of them was the impressive machine running the simulation: impressive in size, but the box was a standard cabinet with some blinking lights (the communications ports) and a stream-lined "*Evolve*" logo on the front to look good in photos. Most of the cabinet was actually empty.

Prof. Wilson looked up and pointed at the graph on screen. "That would explain this rapid decline in fitness and the turnover spike."

Rasna clicked the mouse and brought up some code. "Here? This is the problem with multiprocessors, even though it almost never happens, 'almost never' isn't good enough when it happens millions of times."

Justin took the third chair and sighed. "That's what I changed. Yup, see this? I accidentally commented out the locking of the new organism list, so two processors could think they had sole possession of a new organism pointer before it was removed from the stack. Both processors then tried to write into the slots in the structure at the same time and created a horrible mutant child out of parts from two different ones. The environment may be in hardware, but we still have buggy software in the new-generation processing."

Prof. Wilson sat back. "Moving the environment simulation to the DARPA chip sped things up, but now we're bottlenecked in mating and new organisms. Finding bugs faster than ever." He stroked his bushy mustache. "How much time did we lose? If we reload the last generation before you made the change, and restart from there?"

Rasna scanned the directory. "Looks like yesterday at 6:14 PM is the last stored state before the change. We only lost a thousand generations."

Justin went to work at his desk fixing his mistake, recompiled the code, and restored the last good state before his bug had damaged so many organisms. "There. It's restarted."

Turning to Rasna, Prof. Wilson said, "Did you happen to chat up the quantum computing guys about putting up the simulator on their machine? I've been meaning to talk to Friedman about it but he's hard to reach." The latest quantum machine there was supposed to show many orders of magnitude speedups for some kinds of search problems—with the government funding it to find faster ways to crack the tougher encryption methods that remained secure even from the NSA.

"I haven't yet. I usually run into Steve Duong every few days, but not recently." Steve was already well-known around campus as the first grad student admitted solely on the basis of his online course performance, starting with advanced math and physics at 12 in a backwater village in Vietnam's highlands. Recruited at fifteen and put to work in the quantum computation project, he had already been featured in news stories and university PR releases.

"I should probably give Friedman a call first to follow protocol. Steve is really the principal investigator over there, but Friedman is officially running the project so we should discuss a joint paper."

Prof. Wilson got up to leave. "But, on to more bureaucratic concerns. I'll be back in my office. Got some documents to read on the damn hearing."

Rasna's eyes narrowed. "You know, every single person I talk to thinks it's ridiculous. You were just stating a hypothesis which has a lot of evidence supporting it. Why would anyone expect men and women on average to be exactly the same in any characteristic?"

Wilson gave her a weary smile. "You don't know any of the people objecting, because they come from a different tribe. They are not on the science side of campus, and they don't talk to anyone not like themselves. I've seen this Title IX nonsense get worse every year since they first came after me ten years ago, and now almost anyone can make a complaint about anything they claim is offensive and get a hearing."

Justin snorted. "I'm offended by their constant offense. It's to the point where the science is stifled by politics, and you have to watch everything you say or somebody will report you to the thought police."

"Careful, Justin, even saying that now is an offense against the feelings of our social justice colleagues. Your attitude is… *unconstructive*. Like any movement that started out fighting real injustice, it lives on as a tribe even though they already won the equality we dreamed of back in my day. But 'this, too, shall pass.' Just wait patiently and some other religious belief system will grow up to take over from them. The real problem is the evolved human tendency to tribalism."

"So what do you think will happen at the hearing?"

"I'll make a statement about campus freedom of inquiry, the fact my comments were made as part of a speculative panel exploring evolutionary psychology and where it is and isn't proving useful to understanding human behavior, and point out that these five students came as a group apparently looking to be offended so they could file a complaint. All five are from departments known to have little respect for the scientific method or open inquiry, which I will subtly point out. Then the Title IX coordinator will say something mushy about respecting everyone's right to feel comfortable on campus, and probably the committee will vote to affirm the charge."

"But what happens? Do you get a demerit, or what?"

"At worst a reprimand on my file! Scary. That is, nothing but another symbolic scalp for their trophy case. Luckily I'm tenured and that still means something, though not as much as it once did, or this hearing wouldn't be happening."

The Grey Tribe

In his mountain cottage on the other side of the world, Michael McCulloch, leader of the underground Grey Tribe,' noted in the news: an old friend was in trouble. Halfway through the article, he decided: *It's time to contact the Prof.* Professor Wilson's fame from the incident a decade ago—when the university Safety Office confiscated a poster from his office door, leading to a firestorm of publicity about bureaucratic overreach—meant it was very possible he was in danger of being sacrificed to make the political point that enemies of the new regime who had stymied them in the past would be punished harshly now. Michael wanted Wilson to know he had friends, even if they were outlaw friends. Michael had become a dangerous person to have known, and it was possible even someone as far back in his life as Wilson would have his message traffic examined. He'd send an anonymized multi-hop message to a temporary pirate email for-warder... nothing that anyone else could understand, but enough clues to allow Wilson to get in touch, if he dared.

He turned back to scanning the daily digest of items caught by his custom filters. The global stock and bond market crash after the New York terrorist bomb had been followed by a decade of wartime shortage economies, and only a few places in Asia and Europe were anything like recovered. Even his country of refuge, Switzerland, had very high prices and a stagnant economy, but he was relatively safe here in his well-connected cottage, acting as the nerve center of the Grey Tribe and its affiliated bands of geeks and outlaws. Early on in the wars, the Swiss had sensibly decided to enforce countermeasures to protect their Internet from spies and incursions. From here, he could listen to uncensored sources that were blocked from the US, and coordinate encrypted communications between all of those skeptical of the Unity Party government of the US and its tightening control over communications and media.

The Quad

We have now sunk to a depth at which restatement of the obvious is the first duty of intelligent men. —George Orwell

Justin was wrapping up work and getting ready to leave for the gym when he got a text from his friend Wendy: "Drop by the quad? I'm at the hanging tree."

Justin texted back: "I'll be there in 5."

He detoured through the Quad and pushed his bike along the pedestrian path between the rows of festively-decorated booths. After Housing Week and the settling of new students into dorms and frats, Activities Fair was a one-stop mall for enticing the new students to get involved in the dozens of campus social and interest groups. These activities were one thing the online colleges couldn't offer—real human contact with other students who were just as geeky about something as you were.

He could hear a burst of brassy music from the Pep Band booth, mixed with *a cappella* harmonies from the Keytones down the way. The frats and sororities—there was little distinction left since they had been encouraged to accept any sex or gender preference as a condition of being recognized—had their own area and were passing out party schedules. Students stopped to talk with booth volunteers in clusters he had to work around. The religious groups were still active, though having to accept all students made for some mischief, as when the Muslim Students ended up with a non-believing chair. The LGBT group had a large booth and lots of happy people working it; next to them the Buddhists in their mindfulness seemed to offer much less fun. The gamers had several offshoot groups, still divided by platform, and the Redshirts (fans of a long-cancelled TV space opera, *Starspark*) were still notably geekier than most, though of

course many of their more well-rounded members had duties elsewhere in the Fair.

Organizing for All had a triple-sized booth with a lot of students
staffing it, all in blue tee shirts with the red sunrise logo. Since the
Youth Service requirement, the Youth Corps fed new members to the
supposedly independent Organizing for All, which continued to do
service work on a volunteer basis, always with a reminder of who to
vote for in return. Justin had spent his summer in the Youth Corps
when he was 18, in Brooklyn decontaminating soil from the cobalt
bomb attack. He considered it a well-meaning but wasteful effort
crippled by obtuse bureaucracy—much, he suspected, like the con-
scripted armed forces used to be. Days of labor in hot protective suits,
shoveling the top layer of soil into wheelbarrows for removal, all to
allow for the return of community gardens under the President's new
local growing program. Nights spent with other kids from all around
the country in their tent village, with Youth Corps Network movies
interspersed with videos on the value of group effort and the joy of
shared sacrifice for the good of others. The furtive sexual encounters
were impossible to stop, so he learned to ignore the nighttime noises
—and more than once made noises of his own.

Justin pondered detouring as he approached the Organizing for All
booth; he could see Tyler Sheppard out front speechifying for a knot
of younger students. Tyler was an old adversary from his grad dorm,
where he insisted it was his right to use as many washers as he wanted
even if that meant all of them, and his reputation for gaming the
system to get what he wanted was campus-wide. Tyler had led several
campaigns to have students brought up on charges for hate speech
and sexism, including one successful effort to get a student expelled
for posting a list of women he had slept with, with star ratings—
anonymized, but not enough to keep people from gossiping and
guessing, a fun game unless you're the person people are gossiping
about. Justin was ambivalent about that episode, but to expel a 19-

year-old for a lapse in judgment seemed excessive.

Justin decided to go straight through and risk an unpleasant encounter with Tyler. He was almost by when Tyler saw him, turning to point and direct his audience's attention to Justin: "And here's Justin Smith, one of our computer jocks who thinks social justice isn't important. His thesis advisor is up on charges today for his sexist remarks. Let's see if Justin will talk to us…."

Justin smiled back at him. "You know Prof. Wilson is no sexist. The complaint is bullshit. Why don't you tell these folks what happened to your last girlfriend?"

Tyler didn't take the bait, but responded toward the crowd, "More women would go into computer science if it weren't for guys like Justin here. But we're doing our best to make every department a safe place for women and everyone who has been excluded by white privilege and the patriarchy…."

Justin moved on, and found Wendy leaning against the trunk of the so-called hanging tree, the old live oak with one thick branch at just the right height for a noose, though so far as anyone knew, no one had ever been hanged there. She was dressed in a simple black yoga outfit, her hair a not-entirely-natural cascade of varied gold and copper, and her coffee-colored skin contrasted with her California-white teeth. The tortoise-shell glasses made her look like Hollywood's idea of a hot librarian.

Justin leaned the bike against the tree. "Got hassled by Tyler along the way. He's an asshole."

"He's an asshole, for sure."

"He says Wilson's going down at that hearing. Trying to get me mad.

Not falling for it."

"Everybody knows it's just theater. Satisfy the politicals, keep the Feds happy, keep the deans afraid of Organizing for All. Wilson is just collateral damage."

"Well, it's ugly. The Chinese look better all the time."

Wendy turned her head to scan the crowd, then looked back toward him seductively. "You know this is one of the things I like about you. So noble and clueless. You should get with the program like everybody else or you'll end up in some militia in the mountains."

"It's not like I haven't thought about it. But it would wreck my thesis."

"And what will you do after you finish your Ph.D.? There are no jobs."

"Wilson can get me a post-doc. If he gets the new round of DARPA funding."

"You know that's not exactly the lifestyle to which I'd like to become accustomed."

"We've been over this. You know I think you're beautiful, and smart, and I love that we can talk like this. But you need to give up on that particular fantasy. I can't think of you that way. And you can't bear my children. And you have a dick."

"Which could be remedied. I just don't think it's that important. The right guy will want me as I am."

"You're not exactly all-natural. But I know what you mean—I really, really wish I could be interested in you that way. I'm lucky to have you as a friend. You know I'm all for gay people and happiness for everyone. But all I can do is be *fond* of you."

"'I Can't Make You Love Me.' But I can tease you about it."

"So why aren't you over with your people? LGBTQ-et-cetera or Students for Equality?"

"They're not *my people*. I don't need their condescending, do-gooding, privileged-ass help."

Hearing Prep

Back in his office, Prof. Wilson sat down to force himself to look through the file folder containing papers related to the upcoming hearing; the complaints from the student activists, the University's formal notice of Title IX investigation and hearing, the filings from other interested parties. His response to the charges had been written and submitted weeks ago, but he would have to testify and possibly answer questions from the committee, which meant he had better refresh his memory on all the points made by all the parties.

Trying to read the first document, his mind wandered and his eyes went to the poster above his desk. In the overdramatic style in favor in its day, the poster showed a ruggedly-handsome man dressed in tight black pants and a form-fitting leather jacket brandishing an assault-rifle-style energy weapon with a determined look on his face and the caption, "I AIM TO DISOBEY." This was Matt Raley, heroic captain of the *Starspark* and secret leader of the reborn Rebel Alliance, who had a few catchphrases like that covering every situation that came up. They were used often on the ship's five-year mission to recontact the colonies lost during the Rebellion, which had been crushed at great cost. The destruction and loss of interstellar ships left the frontier to fend for itself for a century until the home worlds recovered. In every episode the ship would orbit a lost colony planet and send an away team to check out the state of the colony—they had always survived, somehow, though often mutated into a dictatorship or orgiastic party planet. The latter allowed for much semi-naked dancing, which was good for ratings.

A decade earlier, this poster had hung on the outside of his office door—most doors along the corridor, offices or not, had a variety of posters, photos, charts, graphs, and bumper stickers on them, expressing what those who used that room thought was funny, interesting, or cool. Candidates and causes were well represented, and no one thought much of this free expression.

Until one day a newly-appointed Chief of Campus Safety received an anonymous complaint suggesting that the *Starspark* poster created a sense of threat and, with its oversized gun, violated the new written policy against any representation of violence or tools of violence. The Chief of Security came by herself to check it out while he was elsewhere, and took the poster, leaving a notice of violation in its place.

He had asked for it back and pointed out that every student knew it was a fictional character and a fictional gun from a popular TV show, and could not possibly be mistaken for a real threat of violence— Captain Raley was inclined to disobey a fictional dictatorship! The Safety Office gathered its Threat Assessment Team and pondered a disciplinary hearing. Word got out, and the media had a field day making fun of the administration and its busybody zero-tolerance policies. His story and interviews with him were broadcast around the world. Science fiction writers and some of the stars of the show came to his defense. Finally the Safety Office had quietly closed the matter and returned the poster after he agreed to keep it inside his office, where it remained, a symbol of one professor's victory over brain-dead bureaucracy.

It occurred to him now that in the years following the poster incident, there had been a steady decline in the number of posters and political cartoons in the corridor. He hadn't noticed it happening, but today most doors were empty of all but class folders and information sheets.

The administration had left him alone for a decade. Now here was a new battle because he had mentioned some of the interesting research into innate sex differences, evolved along with humanity's march to higher intelligence and division of labor. In past years the students who wanted such discussions silenced would have been persuaded not to pursue such a complaint, but something had changed. He went back to read their written complaints again...

After an hour of reading, his screen showed an email notification
with the subject: "From an Old Friend." He stopped to take a look:

```
Old friend —

I have heard of difficulties. You remember
how Andres used to stink up the lab with his
clove e-cigarettes? Do you remember who used
to put garlic in them? If you need anything,
get in touch.

Go to a place named after the movie you
called "a critique of the European Project,"
minus the first and last letter. Fetch the
tool with a name that rhymes with your cat's
name when I knew you. Follow the instruc-
tions and enter the color of your favorite
coffee cup plus your cat's name as key. Post
your cat photos to Pictagram account Cute-
Cats4All.

Best of luck and send as many cat pictures
as you need to.
```

Wilson wondered if he should just delete the email and pretend it
never came. If they were watching him, it was too late—it had already
been stored and scanned in HomeSec's servers. Most likely it was too
obscure to draw attention, but since it could only be from the leader
of the underground Grey Tribe, his former star grad student Michael
McCulloch, even their suspicion that he had been contacted could
bring more surveillance.

He thought more. There was nothing in the email that even semantic
scanners could connect with Michael; only an AI with deep knowledge of his records would find a connection to an old grad student,
and he was sure they were not that good, yet. A suspicious human
would immediately pick up on the invitation to clandestine communications, but doubtful there were enough smart humans in HomeSec
to be doing that kind of thing for all of his email.

So perhaps it was safe enough to set up the reply. He went to "ardo" (which a search revealed was an open-source website in Belgium—the movie clue was *Zardoz.*) His long-dead cat was named Victor, so he looked around and found a tool named PicTor, which seemed to have been added yesterday. It had an app for his brand of phone. He switched to his phone and found the app there for downloading and installed it.

A few minutes later, he pondered the text message he would type in and send, encrypted and hidden in the digital noise of one of his cat photos, to his outlaw student, Michael....

Justin and Samantha

The next day Justin walked over to the Student Union cafeteria for lunch, since he had forgotten to pick up his usual brown bag lunch from the fridge at home. The Union was a brutalist concrete block from the 1970s, and the concrete was spalling off the walls and stairways in places. The thick plate glass of the windows had been replaced by plywood in large areas. Many of the outside light fixtures had been pulled from the walls by vandals and hung useless; blowing trash filled the stairwells down to the lower level landing, where water pooled because of the clogged drains. Prosperous people in prosperous times had built the buildings, but maintenance was an easy target when budgetary survival was at stake, and times were hard. Students had tried to clean up what they could themselves, but they had given up over time.

In the cafeteria, he looked at the line for entrees and decided to save time by picking up a foil-wrapped ready-made burrito, which the sign assured him was organic and gluten-free. Water and a cup of coffee were enough extras—the burrito had veggies inside, right?

He put his phone on the checkout box and touched the screen to authorize the $78 charge. At least the food was generally decent. Some parts of the country were short of fresh produce since shipping had become so expensive and unreliable, but California still ate well.

He looked around for place to sit—many of the plastic chairs were broken and the ones that weren't were taken. He considered heading back to the lab to eat at his desk as usual—but then he noticed a clumsy but strikingly pretty woman—or girl, she was probably a grad student but her elfin features made her look much younger. Apparently clumsy, because she had just turned abruptly and lost her drink over the side of the tray; it fell to the floor and splashed an exclamation point of ice and cola that reached the feet of a group sitting at a table.

He put his tray down at the nearest table and went over to where she stood, cursing quietly. "Let's go get some napkins or ask for a towel to clean that up." The students at the table had started to wipe up the spill near them with their napkins, so he ran to the staffed counter and they gave him some industrial grade paper towels. He handed her a wad and used the rest to sop up the mess. Quickly they met in the middle and she laughed as their towels competed to get the last liquid.

"Well, that was a mess. That cola stuff makes good floor cleaner," he said, gesturing to the filthy paper towel in his hand. He noticed her eyes were ice blue and her hair was shoulder-length and auburn. He went on, "Sit here and I'll get you another drink."

"Just water this time. I shouldn't drink diet coke anyway." She took the unbroken chair at the table they were near. By the time he got back, she was checking her phone but had waited for him before eating.

"I'm Justin, by the way. Justin Smith."

"Samantha, Samantha West. And I don't usually drop things."

"The physical world is stubborn—can't waive the laws of physics because you decide to turn. Your drink doesn't. Want to turn, that is." Justin started opening the foil on his burrito.

"I don't study law—I'm in Economics. Working in rational expectations theory with Prof. Yu. We expect the drink will rationally act to avoid being spilled."

"You may be too into your theory. I'm doing A-Life—Artificial Life—

simulated evolution with Prof. Wilson. We'd say that the drink species would experience selection pressure to evolve toward spillage-avoidance behaviors, if they were alive. Which they aren't."

The conversation moved from topic to topic as they ate. Samantha had a habit of moving her food around with the fork a bit before actually picking it up. She seemed to want every bite managed and neat.

"So what do you do outside of studying?" he said, raising an eyebrow theatrically.

She matched his gesture by looking theatrically taken aback. "I am a virgin and study late into the night. No one has penetrated my social membranes. I am pure."

"So am I, mostly, but not by choice. It's a reality that it's hard to find anyone who wants to spend time together." He looked comically forlorn, playing for sympathy.

"Well, I actually have a boyfriend. Dylan, we met hanging out with the Students for Liberty." When he looked surprised, she went on, "Yes, we are still active, though Activities has shoved us back into the smallest, dingiest office they had. Behind the Science Fiction Society and their rooms of musty old books. You can get sick breathing all the fumes from their ancient paperbacks crumbling from the acid. Anyway, I went to a few meetings, met Dylan and the leader, Ben Ramirez—who I know is going to be famous some day—and started hanging out. Before I knew it, I was Secretary."

"Clawed your way to near the top?"

"Which is also near the bottom, since we only have fourteen official members. Most of them useless. The Unity Party has scared people out of any 'subversive' political activity. I wasn't too worried since I'm in Economics! We have saner people in my field. Except for the labor economists, and there are more of those every day."

"I have stayed out of activities. Too busy. Don't like conformism. The OfAs give me the creeps. My Youth Service time was hellish."

"I totally agree. Students for Liberty is just a tiny voice against the tide of political sellouts who know it's a lot easier to get a job in government service than anywhere else, and you don't get picked if you're not a Unity droid," Samantha sighed. "But I might have to be a little less principled when I start looking for a job. Economics research is mostly funded by government, even when it's in academia. Most research places still have some insulation from the commissars in DC, but I won't be showing Students for Liberty on my resume. It's like asking to have your application lost."

They were nearly done but had stopped eating. The last few morsels remained as they talked, unwilling to let lunch be over.

She looked at him carefully. "Ben is inspiring. You really ought to come meet him. Dylan, not so much; I thought he was great when we started going together, but he's more controlling than I can stand sometimes. Texting me to find out what I'm doing, planning things for us without asking, that kind of thing."

"Sounds like a bad boyfriend."

"Well, he can be sweet and thoughtful. But not as much as he was. And I'm tired of being a part of his wardrobe instead of a person. I'm giving it more time—he says he's just stressed. Thesis grind, mathematics I don't understand—manifolds? But I am aware it probably won't last… but come to our office Thursday at 7 for our dinner meeting. Get your tray downstairs and come up to the third floor, north hall, all the way in back. Meet the gang."

"If it means I get to see you… and about that…."

"Time enough to get to know each other. Most likely you smell bad or hang your toilet paper the wrong way."

Justin raised his arm and sniffed his armpit. "Not yet. Got another few days!"

Samantha laughed, then stood up and piled the trash on her tray. "You really have the most refined and charming way about you. And you have yet to pass the toilet paper test—over or under?"

"I'm an 'over.' It's the only way." He stood up and prepared to leave.

"Well, first stage criteria: passed. Let's see how stage two goes Thursday."

He opened his phone's address book. "Samantha. Can I call you Sam?"

"Sam's okay when you know me. Never Sammy."

"Your number?" She took his phone and typed it in for him.

At the door to the outside, Justin stopped and they faced each other. "I'll text you," he said. "And send you my contact info."

"Just what a girl wants to hear," she said, giving him one more smile and a glance back as she walked away, hair gleaming copper in the afternoon sun.

Chapter Two: Justice for All

ALife Simulation, Model 2: Organism 670

He was born hungry and knowing nothing but what his instincts told him—move away from predators, find and eat foods that smelled good but not those that didn't, find and mate with a she who smelled and looked healthy and well-fed. As he moved about and saw and smelled the world, he found foods that smelled good and yet hurt him when eaten, and learned to avoid those by sight—the purple berries evoked a strong reaction of distaste and memory of the days spent recovering his energy; he did not know it, but another species had evolved which spread the seeds of purple berries in its feces and had co-evolved the chemistry to neutralize its poison, so the berries were a weapon against his species. The world was hazy but he could see further than his ancestors who didn't have his marvelously-evolved compound eyes. He avoided predators and learned to combine sensory cues—sight and smell and hearing—to evade them before he could be seen. He encountered a fit female of his species and after a mutual fitness evaluation they mated—they touched organs and their code was intermingled. And quickly their world ended again, for them, and their children went on to dominate their species, which survived for eons before being wiped out by a more successful breed.

Disciplinary Hearing

Doublethink means the power of holding two contradictory beliefs in one's mind simultaneously, and accepting both of them. — George Orwell, Nineteen Eighty-Four, 1949

The hearing room was a standard meeting room in the administration building; walnut paneling, indirect lighting, comfy chairs around three long tables set up as three sides of a square. The fourth side had a raised platform with a desk and three chairs for the Chair and staff. Since complaints against faculty were not public proceedings, there was no need for extra seating for spectators.

The members of the Disciplinary Committee were faculty and deans who had been appointed to this special subcommittee of the Academic Senate, the full faculty acting as a whole who theoretically had great influence in the policies of the school. In practice, the administration ran things, with occasional interference from the faraway trustees, and increasingly followed policy directives from the Feds, notably Title IX, which was originally intended to guarantee that schools receiving federal money did not discriminate by race or sex.

Wilson noticed his friend from Biology, Lindemann. He tried to get his attention but Lindemann was deep in conversation; he finally looked up and noticed Wilson and came over.

"Walter, sorry this is happening. I hear the result is wired in, people in the Title IX Office put on the pressure."

"None of my fine words or the supporting letters meant anything?"

"You know we are all sympathetic, but the times as they are, we have to keep the 'Red Guards" happy or we will have some serious bad luck when support funding is handed out. And we're barely surviving as it is."

"I understand. The usual censure, I suppose?"

"Of course. Everyone's handing those out like traffic tickets, so it no longer means much. But it gives us a way to satisfy them without actually harming faculty."

"There's that. I guess it was inevitable that they'd come after me for something—you know me."

"Indeed I do. So let's get this mummery over with. And keep your head down for a year or two."

Wilson felt a little calmer. This was just a performance, with the result preordained; he could make a few points to salvage his dignity and it would all be over. As in most places in most times, justice was no longer about finding and punishing criminals, but a show intended to provide the desired symbolism for the people who supported the true rulers. If innocent people were punished it was just more collateral damage—more broken eggs for the omelette of Unity.

The hearing opened with an explanation of the offenses ("harassment on the basis of sex" and "speech intended to intimidate or harm.") There was an elaborate recap of the disciplinary procedure to date— the Investigative Officer's report, his rebuttal, the attempt at media- tion, the refusal of the settlement offer. On principle he had refused the offer to plead guilty and accept a censure on his record, which would have spared everyone this travesty of a hearing, but he wanted them to have to live by their corruption.

He was given the microphone for his statement. A glass of water at hand, he started in; never a great speaker, he tried to make himself meet some of his fellow professor's eyes as he part-read, part-ad-libbed: "I address you as a seeker for truth who may not always be aware of the need to soften the truth, or be tactful in seeking it, and for this I apologize to the students who were offended."

"But the ideas I expressed were *hypotheses*—the very heart of the scientific method, where discussion of how the world *might* work is unbounded by dogma and fashionable ideology. Paraphrasing our own faculty rules, 'the purpose of discipline is to preserve conditions hospitable to pursuit of free inquiry and exchange of ideas.' The panel on Evolutionary Psychology and Social Science was exactly the kind of interdisciplinary dialog required to generate new ideas and new ways of testing them. Discussing some ideas like evolved group differences seems to be inherently offensive to some students because of their ideology. I did not say—and no one on that panel would say —that any individual person should ever be assumed to have more or less of any characteristic simply because of their race or sex, and certainly no discrimination against group members because of group differences could ever be justified. Yet the complainants seem to see any discussion of sex differences as too dangerous to be allowed. I would point out that 'Darwin's Dangerous Idea' of evolution was deemed heretical and socially dangerous, yet over time was inescapably found to be correct, overturning much of biology and threatening religious dogma. Freedom of inquiry can only be maintained if even ideas some find offensive can be discussed in the open university and subjected to the tests of experiment and scholarship. And this complaint should be dismissed as antithetical to that goal."

He decided not to read the rest—all of the committee members had in theory read all of the statements in advance. He wasn't going to change any minds and he suspected most members were secretly with him, but could not risk voting against Unity.

The Investigative Officer, a Professor of Labor Economics who he had never met until this incident, took the mike. "We value inquiry and the free exchange of ideas on this campus. But we also value safety of students and a supportive climate free of aggression or intimidation. No student should be made to feel unwelcome or inferior because of a community member's actions, even if unwitting. Professor Wilson is reputed to be a fine teacher and a widely-admired scholar in his field. But that does not excuse the insensitivity shown to the students, who he openly suggested might be less capable of higher mathematics or less able to focus on abstractions because of their sex. And that created a climate of harassment that our policies do not allow."

Then the Title IX Coordinator took the mike. "Under Title IX, every educational institution that accepts Federal funds is required to maintain equal opportunity regardless of race, sex, and sexual or gender orientation. Equal opportunity does not exist unless an atmosphere of safety and support for all students is maintained. We can charge an institution, even one so august as this one, with a violation if we feel their disciplinary policies are not maintaining a safe space for all. We take no position on any particular case, but we do observe patterns and practices, and if they have a disparate impact on some classes of students and the environment necessary for their success, we will not hesitate to file charges and push them through the courts as necessary to get a change in institutional attitude."

An older male faculty member he didn't know took the mike next. "It seems to me that this case is going to generate more bad publicity in some circles, since Prof. Wilson became a cause célèbre for some of the opposition types ten years ago. I suspect all of that—and this school's embarrassing retreat when they became a laughingstock—will get dredged up again and make this look like more of the same. I understand we need to demonstrate our resolve against sexism, but we're in a bad position."

A woman from the Women's and Gender Studies department was up next. "Prof. Wilson has many friends in my department. I'm sure I speak for others when I say I don't believe he meant to intimidate the students, but they were clearly offended and made to feel demeaned and unwanted by some of the things he said. I believe we should have zero tolerance for sexism, racism, and any kind of genetic determinism, and I hope that if a censure is decided on, he will take it as an opportunity to educate himself on how to explain his ideas without creating a climate hostile to women."

The Chair read a short statement written by a Tyler Sheppard representing the Students for Equality and signed by four hundred students. "We commend the Board of Discipline for demonstrating to all students that faculty must speak responsibly. Hate speech no matter how disguised as scholarly speculation has no place in a safe community for students from every background. Students should be able to enjoy any campus activity without fear they will be attacked or oppressed by the privileged. There is no room for hate on this campus...."

There were a few more speakers, but everyone seemed to know there was no point in real discussion. The Chair announced the question on the floor: should Prof. Wilson be censured? The roll call was mostly against him, with some contrarian sorts holding out—but in the end, he was guilty, 15-6. The Chair spoke again: "The ruling of the Disciplinary Committee is that Prof. Wilson shall be censured and that its formal disapproval of his behavior will be entered into his record. The official document of the decision will be sent to Prof. Wilson, and he has fourteen days after receipt to appeal to the Chancellor or accept the penalty. This meeting is adjourned."

Students for Liberty

Thursday dinner; Justin picked up a tray with roast chicken and broccoli in the Student Union cafeteria and found the elevators out-of-order again, so he walked up three flights to the top floor where student activities were located. He passed the Science Fiction Society library and noted a smell of something—mold, decaying paper?—and a few students talking in their lounge. He stopped to look inside. The walls were plastered with posters and notices many layers deep, fit for an archaeologist's study; it looked like there was something from every pop-culture science fiction production since the building opened in the 1970s. A prominent *Star Wars* poster was front and center and apparently was respected enough to remain uncovered by later postings. *Starspark* appeared in several places but had not been so respected; on one poster, Captain Raley sported a mustache and beard added in black marker, so he looked like his evil mirror-universe twin from the episode "Doppelgängers."

He heard voices coming from the last open door in the hall, and entered to find six people eating and talking around a table covered with books and flyers. Samantha was there, and he recognized Ben Ramirez. The blond, bearded, wiry guy snuggled up with Sam on the loveseat was presumably the Dylan she was seeing. *Handsome but a douche*, he thought, but he would try to give him a chance. The other students kept talking while Sam gestured him over to a seat on her other side. "Glad you could make it. Everybody, this is a grad student I'm trying to recruit—Justin, uh, Smith is it?" He nodded. "He's intrigued enough to show up. Let's not bore him to death like we did the last one."

"That's what he looked like after we got done with him," said a pink-cheeked girl with blond ringlets, pointing at a cardboard Halloween skeleton tacked to the wall. "I'm Amy."

Introductions continued, and Ben Ramirez spoke last: "Thanks for checking us out. We know we're not popular and you take a risk of being labelled antisocial if you are seen with us. So we don't expect our members to be public about it."

"I don't have much to lose and I don't worry too much about what people think of me anyway. It's not like we can stop any of what's going on. But I did want to see what you guys are about."

"An open mind is all we ask. There aren't many left who have one. Thinking for yourself is dangerous; talking about it can get you expelled." His eyes were probing.

"I have already figured out how to watch what I say to avoid trouble. I spent a summer in Youth Corps—I can manage to say something that isn't false but doesn't set them off. It's a useful skill to have anyway, used to use it on my parents."

"Good. Those who remember the whole Bill of Rights and freedom of speech as it used to be are mostly older. But a lot of young people are like us—we know something is horribly wrong but we hide it to get along. No sense being mobbed for speaking up; someday we'll get a chance to speak and restore some of what we used to have."

"So what's the point of Students for Liberty, if you can't speak up?"

"Publicly? We stick to the safe topics and point out only the most glaring excesses that few would defend. Like that show trial where they stuck it to Prof. Wilson for speaking forbidden thoughts. The administration tolerates our continuing existence as part of the colorful tapestry of diversity that is student life. I doubt if they would let us start a chapter today, but we were here before the OfA, before the State of Emergency, and before Unity took over the two parties. So long as we don't appear to be effective, they won't come after us.

And in the meantime, we can continue to think for ourselves."

"Seems like... a waste of time."

"For every student who shows up at a meeting, there are ten who read our leaflets and posts, and a hundred who know we exist and what we represent, even if they make fun of us to their friends."

"A beacon of liberty in a lost world? But what can you do that actually changes things?"

"Wait and educate and talk to people. Wait for the time when action makes sense. Next year, or the year after that. Elections don't offer much hope since they control the ballots and the counting, but in the past fascist regimes have always run their economies into the ground and been overthrown, in war or revolution. We peacefully wait, and talk."

Dylan spoke up: "And at least here we can speak freely. No one's going to bother placing bugs or having an informant attend meetings. So you can let off steam safely."

Sam added, "Besides, we like being rebels. The social justice warriors thought they were cool and special because only they knew all of the right answers. Now that they are in charge, they're not special, not cool, and starting to look like the oppressors they hated. There aren't many of us, but we're the people who have the answers now. And we would never abuse our power, because what we want isn't power, it's *freedom.*"

Justin raised his eyebrows at that: "All revolutions end badly. Guillotines and jails. Gulags and warlords. How do you know overthrowing this crowd won't just let worse people rule?"

Samantha looked thoughtful. "We don't. We just do our best. At the moment it's a moot point—but you should read *Systems of Survival*, Jane Jacobs' book. We need her Guardian Class on our side. We need the military and police to disobey orders that are unconstitutional. We need a population that stands up for its rights. We need a free press and an end to unlimited surveillance. We need a governing class that respects freedom and limits its interference in daily life and commerce."

"All very theoretical." He wanted to agree, but he thought they were just another debating society, useless and a waste of energies that might actually change something.

Discussion continued. He finished his meal and stayed a half hour longer, but then excused himself. Ben Ramirez followed him out and said, "I hope we didn't scare you off. You may not want to be a public member, but can I put you on our interest list?"

"Sure. I'm interested, I just don't think I have the time to participate much."

"Listen, I wasn't going to say anything in front of the others, but I actually do have some connections with the opposition. There are rebels in the mountains and the Grey Tribe, which really exists. There's a chance we could be called on to do something that matters when the time comes."

"Let me know when that happens."

"You realize that if I knew anything, I couldn't be telling you about it, not yet—despite what I said, I wouldn't be surprised if an informant visited us to report anything subversive. Tell me why I should trust you, and we'll talk."

"Fair enough. Ask anybody, I have no connections at all. And I'm pissed off with what they're doing to Prof. Wilson. I hope to stay in touch with Samantha—I admit she's really why I came to your meeting."

"Ah, well, she does that to guys. If you want to get involved, do it because you care about freedom, not because you're after her. But I can understand wanting both."

Professor Wilson

Prof. Wilson's office was small, but had a glorious full-width window overlooking the Quad, and in the distance, the blue of the ocean. When it was as clear as it was today, he could also see the coastal mountains to the east with bright green patches where recent rains had filled in old fire scars with luxurious new growth. A scattering of deciduous trees from back east planted in the Quad before they had gone out of fashion lent autumn colors to the view.

Rasna Kapoor sat in the guest chair in front of his desk while they went over her research plans. She pulled out one last document. "Did you get a chance to look over the statistical summaries from the last few months? Number of new species way up. More complex neural structures. Evidence of learned behaviors. The beginnings of chemical communication… alarm signals and more."

"I skimmed it. I appreciate all the work you've done; the charts alone must have taken you weeks. I think we can get several papers out of the various learned behaviors and population dynamics in predator-prey cycles. Not to mention bulking up your thesis quite a bit."

"It took a lot of work to make the graphs both pretty and understand-able, to the point I couldn't tell any longer if they were clear. So I ran them by Justin, who's usually much more interested in the program-ming. But he was a good beta reader."

"Another thing to sex up your thesis and some of our papers—use the model renderer to make some 'portraits' of successful species. Like a gallery in a museum, from various angles, in various life-stages. In battle!"

"That would be nice to do. I'll try one to see how much time it would take; when we are doing PR for the papers those would be great for the media reports. But I may not have time. In theory I will be done by June… right?"

Wilson smiled. "Certainly. But you know how adding that little extra PR zest brings in more attention for your work, which makes DARPA happy, which brings more funding, which keeps us going. Maybe I can get Justin interested in doing the gallery. In any case, carry on and we'll have our next formal meeting in two weeks."

"Okay, Professor." Calling him "Professor" was a hard habit to break, and while other profs might encourage going to first names after a research team had been active for awhile, Wilson did not. He did not especially like his old-fashioned first name, Walter, or its short form Walt, so he let students keep the formalities.

Rasna left. It was late afternoon and the sun was low in the sky, with that golden color from traveling through so much Pacific atmosphere. The sun made the pictures on his desk glow—his long-dead partner Bill in front of their San Francisco Victorian; a shot of them together riding in a gondola in Venice, with the gondolier smiling back at the camera; a family portrait from his childhood in St. Louis, he in his little suit and skinny tie for church, his sister in a dress, his mom and dad formally dressed as well. His sister was still living on a co-op farm in Vermont, but they rarely spoke, and she no longer wore dresses. Neither of them had had children, so he had no nieces or nephews.

He remembered his college days. He had known he was gay since he was 12, and furtively read everything he could find about it; the *Encyclopedia Britannica* articles were grim, presenting a picture of mental disease and resistance to treatment. But in his voracious reading he had often stumbled upon less conventional portraits of gay men, and by the time he was in high school, the counterculture on the coasts included out gay people. He vividly remembered the first

time a newsmagazine put an out gay man on its cover; he remembered Joe Haldeman's *Forever War,* with its time-dilated interstellar
soldier reaching a future where nearly everyone was gay; and like
other gay men of his era, he thirsted after any appearance of gay
people as admirable characters in fiction or film.

He had fallen for a boy in high school who was smart and had a
precociously thick mustache. In the Midwest, in that era, coming out
could have gone very badly for him, but his teachers and fellow
students were sympathetic. He talked it out with the object of his
affection, Joe, who wasn't especially interested but was a close enough
friend to listen to his wild ideas of how one day they could get mar-
ried. They had both gone off to MIT but rarely saw each other there,
and Joe had ended up going to medical school in San Francisco,
where his residency at San Francisco General eventually had him
tending to thousands of gay men with AIDS.

Walter Wilson had stayed on in Cambridge. He had come out gradually while at MIT, calling the "gay hotline" from his lab late one night
when everyone else was gone. It was hard to imagine now, but then
most gay people were tortured by conflict and the years of hiding
their true feelings, and the hotline often dealt with students who were
suicidal or too afraid to ever tell the truth to anyone they knew. On
that first call, he had stumbled through his story and managed to
speak to the nice guy on the line, who turned out to be a post-doc in
his department, and in a week had gathered enough courage to meet
him at the Gay Student Association's office in a repurposed squash
court.

He'd quickly realized that these were his people—he could be himself,
a tad too precise, insisting on his full name, and fascinated by mus-
taches, and these people still liked him. Their wit was sparklier, their
dress more daring, their politics more varied than any group he had
ever been with. Soon he found himself painting banners for Boston's

Gay Pride Parade and marched with the group. Word got around, and back at his dorm no one seemed especially surprised; only one boy he thought of as a friend turned his back on him.

He wondered how the dream of the mid-1970s—of freedom to be yourself, say what you thought, marry who you wanted, be the best *you* you could be—ended up in this sour conformity of thought and repression of free speech. He had supported gay civil rights all along, and the victories started to mount up—decriminalization, first, then increasing civil rights and employment benefits, and eventually gay marriage. But at the same time, the humanities departments of most universities were taken over by post-modern, left-wing faculty who thought of their role as promoting social justice—promoting change in society to remedy the oppression suffered by gays, minorities and non-Western cultures. In turn, these academics wrote the textbooks and trained the new crop of bureaucrats, as well as the reporting staff and editors of most publications and media, in this glorious new idea of reordering society into a perfectly egalitarian and cruelty-free new world where everyone would have enough without competition or hardship.

He was busy having a life—he had gone on to grad school at Harvard, where he met his partner Bill, and they had moved west to San Francisco like many others, when houses were still cheap. They had put a lot of effort into redoing their old Victorian in the Castro neighborhood of San Francisco while Bill started a career in investment banking and Walter taught. He remembered occasional fights and the usual problems with other men and money and the increasingly sexualized street life of the Castro; down the hill a block, a school playground served as trysting place for hundreds of men every night. Buena Vista Park, up the hill, had its vegetation so eroded by cruising sex addicts that the original sand of the hill was showing through.

His memories of that time were mostly good. Until, very suddenly it seemed, everyone was talking about the mystery cancer that was killing people in months. The hospitals were filling with desperately sick men, and most of them died in weeks. Neither of them had been involved in the sex scene much, but friends who also had been cautious took ill and died. And then Bill had a blue spot, and then three, then he was covered with them, and there was pneumonia, and too many visits to the hospital, and then he was gone. Nothing of *him* left, just a husk of skin and bones.

He was numb and on autopilot for a few years after that; he took a tenure-track job at the more prestigious university down the coast and put San Francisco and what remained of his old friends—not many—behind him. His routine saved him from too much ruminating. And when he also tested positive for the virus, it seemed like an anticlimax. He stayed healthy, and when his t-cells began to drop a few years later, he started taking the antiretrovirals that were at last becoming available. So he had never had to shuffle down the street with a cane, a shadow of his former self, hoping no one he knew saw him as a frail old man…

But still he had to take his daily wonder pill, many generations improved from the early days, and he felt he was aging faster somehow even though the antiretrovirals kept the virus level undetectable. He had known men in the same situation who had suddenly had HIV encephalitis or had all their joints crumble, the result of mysterious side-effects of the years of the medications or the sneaky way the virus hid behind the blood-brain barrier. So he felt lucky to have had his relatively healthy life, even if alone. *Predator-prey*, he thought. *Parasite-host. HIV-human.*

And there had been other men in his life. Mostly, friendly affairs with guys not leading to any change in their settled lives—though one drama student had moved in with him, then rather dramatically moved out a few years later. He missed having someone beside him on the couch for an after-dinner movie. He used to love to massage Bill's feet and enjoy the sounds of appreciation he made as they snuggled.

He decided he wasn't in any mood to do more work and got ready to leave, when the phone buzzed. Hardly anyone made voice calls any more, and it was almost six; he answered it. "Walter Wilson."

"Professor Wilson. This is Andrew Gao. I'm an investigator with the local field office of Homeland Security. One of our investigations has brought up your name, and we'd like to drop by to ask you some questions. At a time of your convenience, but tomorrow around 10 AM works for us."

"What's this about?" He checked his calendar. "I have to teach until 10:30 and I'll be back in my office by 10:45. If you'd like to come then, I will be here. Do you know my office?"

"We do, thanks. And it's about one of your former students, Michael McCulloch, who I'm sure you know has been on our radar for some years now. We don't expect you to do a document search or anything —we searched the university's servers for evidence years ago. But we want to ask you about him personally, just your memories."

"Okay. I remember him well, he was my best student while he was here. I was shocked when he went outlaw."

"I'm sure you were, Professor. Everyone always is. Okay, we'll be there tomorrow at 10:45. Shouldn't take too long."

"Thank you for giving me some warning." Which they really didn't have to; since the State of Emergency was still in place all these years later, authorities could in practice question or search anyone at any time, as well as monitor their phone calls and Internet use. Warrants were automatically generated and approved in the millions by rule-based AI judges, and they were never turned down unless someone forgot to check a box on the app.

And still he wondered, where had it all gone wrong? And was Home-Sec coming after him because they knew he had communicated with Michael last week? He hoped it was only coincidence.

Chapter Three: Justin and Samantha

ALife Simulation, Model 3: Organism 13901

She had lived a long time and had many children—fortunately by this time children did not eat their parents, even when they were hungry. Her species was complex and long-lived, and no longer did every generation start fresh in a new world; the old parents and the old world remained as it was, the children were born into it after an evolved gestation in an evolved uterine organ, and born incomplete. The predators were fewer but more clever; they had learned to hide and stalk their prey, but luckily for her species there were several successful but dumb alternate prey species which the predators found easy to catch. And so her species thrived and evolved to have fewer but better-cared-for children, who would live long enough to learn much more than their genetically-coded instincts at birth.

She was tired and worn but happy to go on helping with her grand-children until the day she died. Her people salvaged her materials, of course.

Justin and Samantha

Puritanism: The haunting fear that someone, somewhere, may be happy. —H. L. Mencken, 1949

Justin had texted Samantha and asked her to dinner, but Sam would not agree to any dates while she was still seeing Dylan—who was the jealous type, and was working on campus that evening. They agreed to meet in town by the old train station to walk along University Drive and talk. Not quite a date, and by seeing each other off-campus it almost seemed like they were hiding something. Which they were.

They passed a stretch of empty storefronts. Sam said, "I remember coming here as a kid. So many expensive stores and shiny objects. Books, jewelry, furniture and art from around the world. Guess no one has the money for luxuries."

"Those luxuries were just signs of inequality. 'Everything is awesome' now that we have made sure there aren't any obscenely rich people to make anyone else feel bad."

"I do miss the beauty."

"Still a lot of beautiful things around. Like you."

Sam rolled her eyes. "I won't be objectified in that manner."

"In what manner would you prefer to be objectified?"

"Less obviously." She laughed. "And you do quite well on the looks scale yourself, mister."

"Thank you. You see, *I* am secure enough to take an honest compliment."

"You don't seem to lack for security. Good family back home? Where is home?"

Justin explained he had grown up in an inland suburb, had two brothers, and his dad had been an auto mechanic. His mother had been a schoolteacher, then a full-time mom for awhile, homeschooling the children until high school age. "And that's why I'm so independent. She let me study what I wanted so long as I could pass the state tests on the core subjects. I read everything I could get my hands on. I didn't realize how limited the regular schools' reading was until I went to public high school. Where they put me into the honors classes, but it was still behind what I already knew."

Samantha turned toward him and said, "My parents had me in private schools in West LA. Advanced but sometimes a little loopy. And then a fancy liberal arts college in Pomona. It was all very pleasant but I can't say I picked up any street-smarts."

They slowed as the street dead-ended at the railroad tracks, and Justin said, "Public high school taught me to keep my head down and not speak up. Which came in handy when I went off to my Youth Corps summer in New York. You learn to get along with less mannered folks."

"My Youth Corps summer was spent at a public clinic trying to digitize their old paper records. Not hard, not interesting, not really necessary, I think. Make-work. Daddy made a few calls and made sure my assignment would be close enough to let me stay at home."

They came to a bench and sat down.

Justin said, "The streetlights are newer LEDs, but they still don't work. Copper thieves, maybe."

"I enjoy the darkness. The surveillance cams have less light to work with." She pointed at the nearest camera pointing down at them from a lightpole.

"Maybe they're infrared. They can still ID us. So no funny stuff."

And then he leaned in and kissed her.

Homeland Security

Delayed a bit by post-class questioners, Prof. Wilson got back to his office with just ten minutes before the scheduled arrival of the Home-Sec investigators. He had already done a quick check of the books and papers around the office, hiding anything that might trigger unnecessary questions. He minimized the windows showing on his computer's screen, leaving the background photo of Andromeda galaxy and a few icons.

He refilled his coffee mug and waited. Paranoid thoughts ran through his mind—they had cracked the encryption of his correspondence with Michael. They were going to arrest him and send him to one of those black facilities where they held people until they gave in. They —

He heard a rustling in the hall and a knock on his open door. "Come in."

"Professor Wilson. Andrew Gao." A trim Asian man in sports jacket and tie, Gao shook Wilson's hand and went on, "This is Agent Michelle Taylor, my assistant. She'll handle the recording."

Wilson shook Taylor's hand and gestured to the chairs. "Can I get you anything?"

"No, thanks," said Gao. "We got coffee on the way." Michelle Taylor was a stocky black woman, 30-something, in a subdued khaki outfit. She set up a multi recorder on Wilson's desk; its 360-degree lens and microphones would capture and upload every detail. "Okay, it's going," she said.

"So I've been going over my memories of Michael McCulloch. What would you like to know about?"

"We assume you know that he is a designated Person of Interest to Homeland Security, and you are required by law to report any contact with him or information about his whereabouts. It is a felony to endanger national security by aiding anyone affiliated with a listed terrorist organization."

"I know that. He stayed around for a year of post-doc work in 2013, but then went to work at some startup in the Bay Area. That was the last I heard from him—we didn't keep in touch. Startups are intense, he probably didn't have time to do anything else."

"You have seen the stories about the group he's running—Grey Tribe. A few years ago he was indicted in absentia for assisting terrorist organizations in circumventing surveillance measures. His organization was added to the list of terrorist organizations last year. It is now a crime to knowingly assist him. Are you sure you have told us about every communication from him?"

"I'm sure. I would have remembered—we were friends, I thought, and I was hurt when he stopped responding to email. I chalked it up to busy-ness. I did hear his stealth startup did well, but then stories about it stopped and I have no idea what became of it, or him."

"What can you tell us about his family and friends?"

"Not very much. He came from North Carolina, parents worked at the university there. He visited them at Christmas once but otherwise didn't mention them. A brother somewhere, he dropped by the lab once. I remember he had a girlfriend for awhile, but I don't remember her name. Redhead, quiet. She came to a few beer Fridays when we still had those, but nothing stands out."

"Why would you think he would betray his government and aid the enemy?"

Prof. Wilson pondered his view of the *Starspark* poster just above Gao's head while he considered his answer. I AIM TO DISOBEY. He thought, *betray his government and restore his country's freedoms.* "He talked a lot about the NSA and the Snowden revelations. He said the NSA's capture of everyone's communications was mindless mission creep by people who just wanted bigger and bigger budgets. Nothing out of the ordinary at the time."

"But no hints of taking action? When do you think he became a cryptography expert?"

I'm not sure he ever did. What looks like wizardry to the government can be pretty basic stuff. "He seemed interested in the topic. Our work here involves encoding, similar to genetic coding in life forms, but nothing cryptography-related. He knew what every computer science person knows about it. His later work might have involved that—the startup was doing something about an app for secure communications over untrustworthy networks."

Gao scribbled on his notepad and said, "Did he receive any unusual visitors or talk about knowing people in Anonymous or Wikileaks?"

"No, I would have remembered. He seemed most impressed by Snowden and thought he should be given a medal and then maybe pardoned before being strung up, but he was no activist at the time. Just brilliant at programming simulations and understanding the system."

"Any personal memories or impressions? We're just trying to understand what makes him tick."

And I'm quite sure I don't want to help you. "He had been into *World of Warcraft* and became some sort of general leading hundreds of people there. He had a very responsible attitude—a sense of humor but serious about doing the right thing. Conscientious, honest, dependable. I can't imagine him doing anything to hurt people."

"But he has. The organizations he's helped have provided information about our agents to enemy forces. I can't tell you how many agents we have lost as a result, but he has worked against our national interest."

I wonder how much of that is true. Maybe a little. "I can only tell you what he was like when I knew him. He's methodical and patient. It doesn't surprise me that you can't catch him."

"Well, thank you, Professor. We will be in touch if we have any further questions. You are hereby warned that this conversation and our contact with you is a protected secret under the law and any disclosure of it to others is a felony. If any of your statements proves to be untrue, you have lied to Federal officers, also a felony. If you have communication with or receive new information about Michael McCulloch or the Grey Tribe and fail to report it immediately—"

"It's a felony! I think I see the pattern."

Agent Taylor spoke for the first time. "We need to know everything we can that can help us stop him. Help us find him. It's getting serious and he won't be treated well if one of the other powers catches him first. Your government doesn't murder and poison people."

True. They just disappear and come back slightly different. If they come back. "I'll keep that in mind and be sure to let you know if I hear anything. But it's been years, so I think that unlikely."

The investigators left. Prof. Wilson closed his office door and thought about the answer he had received from Michael, encoded in a picture of two Abyssinian kittens: "We are building a secure network for communications, and an 'underground railroad' to get people to safe locations when they're in trouble. If you ever need help or a way out, let me know."

✷ ✷ ✷ ✷ ✷

Back in his office downtown, Andrew Gao read his email. One memo from DC had come in:

```
To: Field Investigator Andrew Gao
From: DirSpecOps James McDonald
Re: Neutral Armor

Have reviewed your recorded interview with
Wilson. His interaction with Pictagram sus-
picious. Analyst now says probability of
contact with subject over 90% based on lack
of previous activity there.

You will need to break him down without
causing him to go public. He's marked as
too hot to handle because of previous noto-
riety, story is irresistible for media
overseas. I have put our IT team to work
checking his files for anything we can go
after him on. Somewhere on his computers we
will find an image of someone who looks
under 18, which is enough for a child porn
charge. When we are sure we have something,
I'll let you know and you can introduce him
to our 'Citizen Watch' program.
```

Good work. Expect to contact him again in a week or two. Full arrest team not warranted but be ready to detain and medicate if necessary. Best to leave him in place if he'll cooperate.

Chapter Four: Quantum Computing Lab

ALife Simulation, Model 4: Organism 330671

When he was born, others of his kind helped him survive, because he was small and could not move far on his own. His mother gave him food and held him, and others of the band also came to hold and feed him. He grew and learned, and eventually learned to find food himself, with his mother by his side. He learned to fashion tools and weapons out of plant material and rocks; he only had to see another make a tool to be able to make it himself, for his brain was unusually large and well-organized.

One day one of the pack hooted of danger, panicking the foragers, but no one could see what the danger was, and soon they went back to foraging. And it was then the predator attacked, killing him with one blow of its claws. But his clever sisters and brothers lived on and had many children.

Quantum Lab

DARPA had funded advanced computer research for many years, with additional secret support from the NSA, since every new development that could keep them ahead in breaking codes was important. One of their latest programs was the Quantum Intelligence Project, or QIP, which was funding development of larger quantum computers. Development had been slow, and at first it was hard to demonstrate any useful speedups in quantum computers, but recent spectacular successes in rapid factoring and simulated annealing had led to an increase in funding for the university's Quantum Computing Lab.

The lab's Director, Prof. Ray Bubna, was doing a walkthrough of the computer room. At one end, flanked by Dewar flasks holding liquid nitrogen for cooling the superconducting magnetic coils of the device, stood the new and larger quantum computer: "Vortex-5," as it was labelled for PR photos. It was a featureless black cabinet about as tall and wide as a person. Prof. Bubna conferred with lab staff around a workbench: "We have a lot of groups also funded by DARPA interested in getting their complex software up on the new machine to demonstrate that it's not just for simple factoring and traveling-salesman demos."

Steve Duong, the postdoc who had actually done the design work for the Vortex-class processors, said, "It's a bit early. We've just finished testing and are running the old benchmarks. Finishing that will take another week or two."

"I've heard from Prof. Wilson that they would be interested in porting their simulation," said Prof. Friedman, Steve Duong's boss in theory but mostly tasked with keeping the funding rolling in and managing the politics. "It's big but not too big, and the locality of their calculations matches what we can do easily. They will do all the software work."

Steve was unhappy. "This comes on top of Ft. Meade's idea of taking two weeks for themselves to mess around without letting us see what they are doing."

Friedman nodded. "It's not unreasonable, since they are thinking of building one for themselves. They paid, they get to use. We put it together, but for the 'user community.' We don't get to hoard the time for ourselves."

Emerson Wilding, the post-doc staff member who actually built and maintained the hardware, broke in: "We do need to hold back enough time for maintenance, testing, and tinkering. Preferably mornings. Like two hours a day, with overrides when there is trouble."

Steve nodded. "At least. And the software needs a lot of refinement before it's ready for outsiders to use. I still haven't rewritten the manual."

Friedman had the last word; "Just slap something together. They know it's experimental, and we'll be here to lead them through the toy examples and get them up and running. They're used to unfinished systems."

Steve Duong

Steve Duong went back to his office—really a cubicle with a window overlooking the lab floor—and considered what to do about what he had already discovered about the new machine. Like the Vortex-4, the Vortex-5 was a topological quantum computer based on braided anyons: two-dimensional quasiparticles created out of the quantum states of an electron gas kept at a temperature near absolute zero while held between two etched gallium arsenide plates. Exterior superconducting coils created a strong magnetic field that induced fractional quantum Hall effects in the gas, and the chilled electrons formed a two-dimensional array of braided non-abelian anyons. These were the more stable substitutes for the quantum particles used in other quantum computers, and the manufacture of the large gallium arsenide plates was much simpler than the dense microcircuitry of conventional computer chips.

But the new machine had eight times as many rows and columns as its predecessor, so its array of anyons held sixty-four times as many quantum elements, or qubits. It was physically much larger as well, with each plate over two meters long and wide. And from preliminary results, there were things going on during computations that had never been seen with smaller devices.

He didn't really like the idea of other people coming in to run complex software on it before he had had time to chase down some of the hints of anomalous behavior he had already seen, but there was no resisting it. The simple tests had gone well and the funding agencies would want to see different types of users experimenting as quickly as possible. The NSA would be slow to send out its team from Ft. Meade, so they would probably end up pushed back to January. Perhaps helping Prof. Wilson's team port their system to the Vortex-5 would be a safe way to both assist and do some research pushing the limits of the device.

He thought back to his childhood in the village, and how his father had told him someday he would go where no one had ever gone and see what no one had ever seen, because his grandmother (who had died before he was born) had said she knew it would be so. His father had bought him a tablet computer, and after school every day he was expected to sit outside studying at the only café that had wifi. And so he did—he found the whole world waiting to be read, and soon everyone in the village either made fun of him or supported him.

He had discovered MIT's online courses in math and computer science, and then enrolled in Athena University where he absorbed course after course, passing the tests easily and moving faster through them than anyone had before. He went home tired every night and after dinner worked from stored files late into the evening. He brought up a programming system on his tablet and started to write programs. Before long, Athena had featured him as a star student, and reporters emailed him wanting to write his story.

One of the professors whose lectures he had most enjoyed, Prof. Friedman, contacted him and told him his university had arranged admission and a graduate fellowship if he would be willing to move to California and study at their university. He was seen as a rising star, and had finished enough undergraduate coursework for a degree—and he was still only fifteen.

So he had arrived at the university still a little weak on spoken English, but otherwise more prepared than most. Prof. Friedman had helped him get settled and invited him over to his house for dinner several times a week, and being around the professor's family helped a little when he was missing his own. He had tried to stay in touch with his family by phone and online, but his messages often went unanswered, and he started to forget. Aside from the annual trip back home, he thought of them less and less.

Socially he had little in common with his much older fellow grad students. He mostly stayed to himself, and more than once had overheard someone whisper "Aspergers" when they though he couldn't hear. But then they even more often whispered "genius." He did not mind racing ahead on one track while others plodded on many.

He got to work on his computer and began by loading the array with the initial states to perform a complex optimization problem. The loading and reading of the state of each quantum element was itself a quantum process: a quasiparticle created in the gallium arsenide circuit elements was created and flipped; the state it ended up in determined the state of its corresponding anyon quasiparticle out in the electron cloud, thus indirectly setting it as desired. Later the anyon state was read by collapsing its reader quasiparticle and noting the voltage pulse. Normally the initial state was set up and the quasi-logic gates programmed, then the computation ran freely until a check of the results flag indicated completion; then the "answer" was read by reading the states of the array in the part of it programmed to hold the results of computation. He decided it would be interesting to read the entire array after each step of computation, which could be done by altering the program to halt after each state change of a toggle qubit. It would be very slow (it took many orders of magnitude longer to read and store the state of the array than to run it one step) but the results of intermediate states might shed light on the mysterious extra data showing up in the non-answer parts of the array. It didn't seem to have anything to do with what the logic gates were producing; it should have been whatever was left when processing settled in that area. But it wasn't.

Justin Meets Steve

Prof. Wilson and Justin met with Prof. Friedman to discuss the proposal to port their A-Life simulator to the Vortex-5, and then write a joint experience paper which would serve as advertising for both groups' research as well as their mutual sponsors. The meeting had gone well, and as they were leaving, Friedman suggested they drop in on the lab to discuss the project with Steve Duong, who would be working with them to get the system rewritten as needed to run on the new machine.

Down a floor at the other end of the building, they found the Quantum Computing Lab, and were directed to Steve's office. Steve was staring at his screen and seemed to take a moment before noticing their knock on the doorframe. He looked up at them blankly before saying, "Yes? What is it?"

Prof. Wilson took the lead and introduced them. "So," he continued, "We're to start working on porting our simulation to your machine as soon as possible. Justin here knows our software inside out. Friedman says you'll be our resource person in learning your interface and understanding how to cut up the problem."

"Oh, yes. I was told to expect you." Steve looked around and picked up a ring-bound manual from a stack. "This is the obsolete manual for the Vortex-4, but much is the same so it will get you started—sorry we haven't had time to document the upgraded programming interface. And here's a collection of theory papers so you'll have an idea of what's actually happening. It's quite different from a Von Neumann[3] machine in some ways, and the best algorithms for simulation use it more like a programmable gate array. It's all wrapped in a conventional programming environment with special commands for loading and reading results; the tricky part is setting up the initial state data and gate logic."

Justin took the stack of manuals. "This should keep me busy tonight. Is there a desk I could use when I come in?"

Steve pointed down the row of cubicles. "Sure. That office is empty for the moment and it's already set up. I'll let our lab manager know you'll be using it. Two weeks?"

Prof. Wilson and Justin exchanged glances, and Wilson spoke. "Prof. Friedman didn't set a definite time limit."

"There's a lot of demand for time on the new machine. You are the first users we've had, but we expect to have too many requests. Don't be surprised if others start to muscle into your time after a few weeks, some of them from remote locations. And we still have to take it down and do checks fairly frequently. There's a persistent problem in the electron cooling pump which we haven't been able to diagnose yet."

Justin said, "I won't be on the machine itself for some time, I expect. Just wrapping my head around the different way of thinking and rewriting the critical sections to use your commands will take a week."

Good, Steve thought. "I'll be here running tests and tuning algorithms full time, so you can use me as needed to help get started."

Chancellor's Memo

It was the evening before Halloween, and already a few students on the streets were in costume in the early darkness, headed to parties or events. Prof. Wilson was in his office looking through email when a new one came in: from the Chancellor's Office.

His appeal of the Disciplinary Committee's decision to censure him was denied. The letter graciously went on to say that while his appeal had made a good case for open inquiry, the Committee had been correct to find that he had unnecessarily intimidated members of the community in violation of Title IX obligations, and in the interest of a campus which felt safe for everyone, censure was justified. The Chancellor hoped he would see this as an opportunity to improve his understanding of the importance of tailoring his discourse so that all members of the community would feel welcome and valued.

"Just a Little Anomaly"

Steve Duong looked over the screens full of charts and data analysis from the last test of the Vortex-5. He had set a "deep learning" program loose on the enormous amount of data produced by saving the state of the two-dimensional qubit array at every step of the computation; if there was an interesting pattern inherent in the data, the deep learning program might puzzle it out without any human help. It did find patterns, but most of those were directly related to the computation. But a few seemed to originate from parts of the array not involved in the programmed logic. And those patterns, examined separately, formed a pattern of their own. What did this *mean?*

Several ideas connected in his head. The concept of a quasiparticle, broadly extended. The apparently dead-end work on the fabric of space as a quantum cellular automaton. The phenomenon of eerie action-at-a-distance of entangled particles, which could be separated by large distances yet still be in some sense *aware* of each other's state. But no hidden variables, and the many-worlds hypothesis... The mathematics churned in his imagination and led him to the brink—and over. What if—?

Chapter Five: Blackmail

ALife Simulation, Model 5: Organism 6810711

She had nurtured her children carefully, and watched them closely as they played. The village had been fenced many generations ago and predators no longer came near, but the children still played games where one would pretend to be the monster and the others would run screaming to hide behind bushes, or gather to defend themselves as a group with sticks from the forest floor. Her mate was often away hunting with the other males of the band, but they returned with heavy loads of meat and salvaged materials. She often spent time gathering plants and berries—and destroying the non-edible ones so that others would be safe. Sometimes at the end of the day there was time to sit around the fire and swap stories of the hunt or who had been seen with who before going to bed, and sometimes the band living on the lands toward sunrise was talked about—when would they attack again? Should they be attacked first?

HomeSec Threat

Prof. Wilson had not allowed the Chancellor's decision to bother him. *Forget it, Jake. It's Chinatown.* The kabuki theater of academic discipline was required to bow to commands from the Feds, but was not as yet truly punitive, and would have no effect on him for the time being.

The project to port their A-Life simulation to the Vortex-5 was underway; Justin had spent the last three days going over his changes to the code with Steve Duong, who pronounced them likely to work, but only experience would tell if further fine-tuning would be needed. It was time to start loading and testing on the real machine, which they planned to do tomorrow.

Justin sat in his guest chair and talked about some of the work. "Steve talked about the many-worlds hypothesis—that perhaps many universes containing this same computer have different patterns of data and all of them are running simultaneously and somehow communicating. Or perhaps the quantum states of the machine are creating one vast quasiparticle which is reaching out to the fabric of the universe to farm out some of the possibilities of the computation. I asked him if they really understood what the machine was doing, and he said 'Not entirely!'"

"That seems par for the course with quantum devices. Yet they get answers and speed up some problems more than can be explained without something more going on." Wilson tapped on the stack of papers. "I haven't had time to do more than scan these, but there's some fascinating stuff. I haven't been following recent work in quantum computing. There are some otherworldly ideas here."

"This is why I didn't go into physics. Heavy-duty math and conceptual mazes, when you leave the normal scale of Newtonian existence.

But I don't really need to understand it, if it can simulate a hundred times faster than our hardware."

"If you don't understand it, why would you trust the results?"

"I'll try it on simple runs we've already done and check if the output matches. Which reminds me, he said there are interesting further speedups possible if you give up on 'right' answers—accept 'pretty close' answers and it can leap ahead faster. And our environmental simulation could be a little fuzzy without affecting the validity of the results."

"Something to consider later, maybe. For now just duplicate what we have done, then do some runs way beyond what we have done. Store all the results and if we can't get machine time, we'll have lots to analyze while we wait for more."

"Okay, I'll—" Justin was interrupted by Prof. Wilson's phone buzzing. Wilson raised his eyebrows and motioned for Justin to stay.

"Walter Wilson."

"Prof. Wilson, it's Andrew Gao with Homeland Security. I hope you have been well."

Wilson quietly put the phone on speaker and gestured to Justin to keep silent. He hadn't fully thought it through, but he had been intending to talk to Justin about the messages he had exchanged with the outlaw Michael McCulloch. This might be the time to start sharing his problem with a collaborator who was more than likely sympathetic. And he might need a witness. "Yes, I have, thank you. I haven't heard from Michael."

"We found a pattern of encrypted message exchanges through a

Pictagram photo stream featuring cats, on a server outside our juris-diction. You started this exchange after receiving an untraceable email suggesting you do so. While we can't break the encryption, our analyst tells us you have communicated with him. I don't think there is much point in denying it."

"Well, I am denying it. I like cats. I stumble on sites I enjoy from time to time."

"We are going to operate under the assumption that you have a link to Michael McCulloch. There being sufficient evidence to show you have aided a terrorist organization, we have examined your work and personal files and gone through several years of metadata."

"That must have taken a lot of time and been really boring."

"Mostly automated now—the AIs can figure out what something is very quickly and filter out most of it—but I digress. We discovered nine photos of what appear to us to be underaged males in sexually suggestive poses. While we could probably successfully charge you with aiding a terrorist organization, the evidence for a child porn conviction is much more solid. And so that's what we'll do."

"That's outrageous. I've never been interested in children."

"The 'child' can appear to be 16 or 17, Professor. In any case, you will be convicted. I should point out that tenure will not protect you—the California legislature made sexual felonies by educators a special class, so you can be stripped of both your job and your pension rights. And forced to register your every move with the state from now on. And not be allowed contact with children, or a residence within a mile of a school or park."

Prof. Wilson almost enjoyed the stunned expression on Justin's face.

But he had seen this movie on the Classic Movies Channel, and knew what was coming. "So this terrible thing you would do to me. You won't do it if I do what you want."

"Very good, Professor. My superiors knew you would understand immediately. Our goal is not to hurt you, but to locate and neutralize Michael McCulloch. He is a danger to our country's security and we can compel your cooperation if necessary. Which it appears to be."

"What exactly would I have to do? And for how long?"

"Show us the means and keys you use to exchange messages. Cooperate by sending the messages we ask you. We will coach you on what to say—you will include personal information necessary to insure he believes they come from you. Our goal will be to get him to reveal some key details that our computers can use to locate him."

"And when you have found him?"

"We release you with a letter of service. We keep our word—you'll be free to go about your life, so long as you avoid contact with terrorists."

"How long do I have to think this over?"

"Not long. We didn't arrest you as a courtesy—my boss thinks you will do the right thing. But we can at any time, which would be bad for your reputation. Why don't I call you tomorrow to get your answer."

"Very well. I'll think about it. And Mr. Gao—I have to say I'm ashamed that our government could stoop so low as to blackmail innocent people to force them to do things."

"You weren't innocent as soon as you failed to report the contact. You know the law."

As soon as Gao hung up, Justin spoke. "What! In Hell!"

"That was my reaction. I was going to tell you soon that I had heard from my infamous former student, now head of the mysterious Grey Tribe. I thought it was safe enough to talk via encrypted public channels, but apparently not. These HomeSec guys showed up a week later asking about him."

"So what are you going to do? You could run—leave the country, go to a neutral place like Sweden."

"Michael offered to get me out via some 'underground railroad' if I was in danger. But then I'd still lose my job and my life here, which I enjoy. I'm inclined to stand my ground. Fighting them legally is almost impossible now since they've found so many ways to punish lawyers and judges who stand up to the government. But if I appear to cooperate but slip in false 'personal' comments to clue Michael in that I've been compromised, he might escape and they might give up on using me."

Justin looked intently at Prof Wilson. "You know that I will help out any way I can. We will help out—I've been talking to some people in Students for Liberty. I can ask for their help."

"Don't do that, at least now. There's nothing they can do—they would only create more trouble. If I'm lucky, this will all blow over when Michael realizes I've been compromised and stops replying. No, for now, just keep quiet."

Wendy and Justin

Justin made his way over to the Student Union for the dinner meeting of the Students for Liberty. He and Samantha had been texting each other since their non-date, and it was getting harder to pretend they weren't interested in really seeing each other. He picked up his dinner tray and went back to the elevators; Wendy Fields was waiting there, dressed in a retro-60s red flight attendant's outfit.

"You're always so stylish. Where did you find that?" Justin nodded toward the dress.

"This was actually my aunt's. She had a closet full of things that fit me when she died."

"Oh, I'm sorry to hear that."

"Don't be. She had a fabulous life and even though she was much less petite when she got older, she saved all her career clothes to remind her how much fun she had. She was one of those ladies who never had anything nice as a child and got a real charge out of having great clothes; they made her feel special. We had that in common."

"I wonder where you're going that that would be appropriate for...."

"FinCom. Finance Committee meeting, for civilians. Don't look so surprised; I'm a designer, but minoring in business and accounting, and the group needs a bit of style to spice it up." She emphasized that with a toss of her now-flaxen hair. "We know who's paying for what and why some groups get their funding cut."

"I'm headed to Students for Liberty. I've kind of got a thing for Samantha West...."

"Watch yourself. Those guys are always on the list to get squeezed. Last time we were discussing cutting down their space. And as for Samantha—she is very sharp. Don't get cut. And that boyfriend of hers—Dylan—is trouble."

"I have no beef with him. Samantha sounds like she's ready to break up with him anyway."

"But is he ready to break up with her? Rumor has it his last girlfriend had to file a restraining order."

"She told me about that. Much overblown by gossips. He seems a little controlling, but she wouldn't put up with abuse. She's probably better at defending herself than I am!"

"Could be true, Justin. But don't provoke him. Dylan is slick, but for guys like that, it's all about the image. Make him look bad and he'll blow up."

"Yes, Mother." He checked his phone. "I should go. I need to alert people to what Prof. Wilson's going through. More than just the censure, real threats from the government." He pushed the up button again.

"You won't help him by getting the toothless rebels involved."

"And I was thinking of asking the Redshirts, too."

"That's great. Reactionaries and geeks." The elevator doors opened and they went in. "Everyone's tired of the State of Emergency and the power-tripping politicals, but you can't do anything but hurt yourself by opposing them in public." The doors opened, but she kept talking as they walked. "I am not the joining kind. I make a statement just by being myself. I do wish you luck—one of these days someone will put a stop to all the messing with people's lives they do. But be sure it's the right moment. And be sure you have a way out. I'd hate to see you disappeared."

Students for Liberty: the Ask

The meeting had already started when he got to the Students for Liberty office. The seating arrangement was the same as before, with the same people, and only one new face. He pulled up a chair next to Sam, with Dylan's raised eyebrow the only notice anyone seemed to take of his arrival.

Ben Ramirez was speaking: "...and we have some alum support. Which is more than we get from student government now." He looked over toward Justin. "And I see we have a return of Justin, who we hope is considering joining us."

Justin cleared his throat and started into his speech, not really knowing what he planned to say. "I'm still thinking about that. But actually I came tonight because I wanted to ask all of you for help. At some future time when I have some idea what you might be able to help with. It's Prof. Wilson—not only did the censure go through, but he's being threatened by the government. Because he knew the leader of the Grey Tribe."

Several people tried to speak at once; Dylan won: "The Grey Tribe is real? I thought they were just wishful thinking."

Ben looked serious. "I know they exist and coordinate the resistance, such as it is. It's mostly about technical support, the geek crypto community making it safe to talk to each other when HomeSec and the NSA listen to everything now."

"They exist." Justin wondered how much to tell them. "Their leader was Prof. Wilson's best student ten years ago, Michael McCulloch. Homeland Security thinks Prof. Wilson can help them find him. I'm trying to round up support in case he needs it."

"I don't think we can do anything useful," Ben said. "This is a talk and education group. As much as we'd like to help somehow, our skills are limited to leafletting and panel discussions. We can't—as a student organization—go up against the law or do anything that would make the school look bad."

"Well, I'm asking for your personal help. Be ready to support the Professor."

"You've made your plea and all of us are free to consider it, unofficially. As an organization we may be able to write a letter or appear at a meeting, so if that's the level of action, we can do that."

Samantha spoke up. "I move we resolve to support the Professor in fighting for his Constitutional rights."

"Seconded." Dylan held his hand up.

Ben looked around. "Any debate? No? Ayes and nays?" One feeble nay, amidst all the ayes. "Ayes have it. There, Justin, you have our moral support."

Ben and Justin

After the meeting broke up, Justin picked up his tray and went out into the hall, where several people were still talking. Ben motioned him over to an alcove. "Sorry I had to cut you off in there. What you are talking about is way too 'hot'—too dangerous to speak of in a room full of people. Did you notice the new girl? First appearance tonight, claims to be an undergrad but not one of us knows her. It could be you are already under surveillance—the state and country are bankrupt, but there is always more money for security. That's exactly what a plant looks like. And we might be bugged, too. Cameras the size of pinheads sending everything back via spread-spectrum radio."

"Paranoid? I guess sometimes they really are out to get you."

"Probably she's what she says she is and nobody's watching us. But be careful; this is the kind of stuff that gets you targeted. And as for your problem, I told you I know more than I can let on to the general membership. Samantha and Dylan and I are the 'Central Committee'—I tell them more about what's really going on than the others. I became a Grey Tribe leaf node last year. I'll talk to a few people online who may be able to really help you guys out, but it takes awhile for messages to get passed along to the leaders. Like the McCulloch guy, Grey Leader. We can get him backchannel messages."

"Let me talk to Prof. Wilson about it. That might be a real help. But only if there's no way HomeSec ever finds out."

"No guarantees, but they won't hear it from me." Ben turned to leave. "This is kind of exciting. I've been reading about the American revolution since I was a kid, and I've always wanted to crusade for Constitutional rights. My father was a history buff and wished he had been there, and I caught the bug. But it's as dangerous now as it was in 1773 when they threw all that tea into Boston Harbor. The bad guys can send you to the 'Velvet Gulag' if you embarrass them. Don't get caught."

Samantha and Dylan

Downstairs he ran into Samantha and Dylan coming back from leaving their trays in the cafeteria. "Sorry," Samantha said. "I know you were looking for more support. I hope Ben explained the problem."

"He did. And besides, who knows? A strongly-worded letter may get HomeSec to back off…."

Dylan grinned. "We can write a ripping good letter. If logic and reason work, they'll surely see the light."

"Hah, yes." Justin moved to walk on. "Well, I have more people to talk to. I think the Redshirts will still remember the Prof's role in that *Starspark* poster debacle."

Samantha grabbed his arm. "They do—Prof. Wilson is still their honorary advisor. Just don't tell them as much as you told us. It's dangerous to even hear it."

The Red Queen's Race

Alice never could quite make out, in thinking it over after-wards, how it was that they began: all she remembers is, that they were running hand in hand, and the Queen went so fast that it was all she could do to keep up with her: and still the Queen kept crying 'Faster! Faster!' but Alice felt she COULD NOT go faster, though she had not breath left to say so.

The most curious part of the thing was, that the trees and the other things round them never changed their places at all: however fast they went, they never seemed to pass anything. 'I wonder if all the things move along with us?' thought poor puzzled Alice. And the Queen seemed to guess her thoughts, for she cried, 'Faster! Don't try to talk!'

Not that Alice had any idea of doing THAT. She felt as if she would never be able to talk again, she was getting so much out of breath: and still the Queen cried 'Faster! Faster!' and dragged her along. 'Are we nearly there?' Alice managed to pant out at last.

'Nearly there!' the Queen repeated. 'Why, we passed it ten minutes ago! Faster!' And they ran on for a time in silence, with the wind whistling in Alice's ears, and almost blowing her hair off her head, she fancied.

'Now! Now!' cried the Queen. 'Faster! Faster!' And they went so fast that at last they seemed to skim through the air, hardly touching the ground with their feet, till suddenly, just as Alice was getting quite exhausted, they stopped, and she found herself sitting on the ground, breathless and giddy.

The Queen propped her up against a tree, and said kindly, 'You may rest a little now.'

Alice looked round her in great surprise. 'Why, I do believe we've been under this tree the whole time! Everything's just as it was!'

'Of course it is,' said the Queen, 'what would you have it?'

'Well, in OUR country,' said Alice, still panting a little, 'you'd generally get to somewhere else—if you ran very fast for a long time, as we've been doing.'

'A slow sort of country!' said the Queen. 'Now, HERE, you see, it takes all the running YOU can do, to keep in the same place. If you want to get somewhere else, you must run at least twice as fast as that!'

—Lewis Carroll, *Through the Looking-Glass*

Part Two: The Arms Race

Chapter Six: Campaigning

Redshirts: Zach

Justin sought out the leader of the Redshirts, Zach Lee Donner (he was insistent about his middle name, and that had made him memorable—both for the name and his insistence.) Justin emailed and texted him, and set up a meeting at the statue in the quad; they'd never talked, but Justin knew his face from public events.

"So what's this about? Prof. Wilson needs help?" Zach was a short, wide, muscular man built for stability and strength; his crew cut would have fit in on the first season of *Starspark*.

"He's in trouble and he doesn't want people to know about it because he only thinks it will cause more trouble. The government is after him to help them find his former student, Michael McCulloch, who's now leader of the Grey Tribe. They're making threats."

"The Prof is our honorary faculty advisor, ever since that incident with the poster where he showed he was one of us. He hasn't really been involved in years but he comes to the occasional party. Of course we'd help him if there's anything we can do. The bad guys are a lot tougher now, though."

"I realize we have to be careful and quiet. I've been rounding up allies who can be counted on in case a moment does come when we can do something useful." Justin paused to look Zach in the eyes and decided to trust him. "He doesn't know I'm doing this—he'd hate to think of anyone else getting hurt to help him. But I figured it can't hurt to be prepared. He may not understand how bad things could get for him."

"So what do you think we might be able to do?"

"There might be a chance to shame the government with publicity. The Internet made him famous over the poster incident; the hook to the new story can remind people of how much worse things are now. We'd be taking a risk, but they can't go after hundreds of students who demonstrate on his behalf."

"Or can they? Remember what happened to the group at Harvard distributing copies of the Constitution last year. Gone, disbanded, expelled, blackballed."

"So we'd all be taking a risk. But that was a few students. We can get half the campus on our side if we try."

"I can't give you much encouragement, but I'll quietly test some people out and see what their reaction is. We mostly live in a fantasy world of heroics and courageous action—real action is a much tougher sell. Fans of the show have the heart, but do they really have the guts? Let's wait and see what happens and in the meantime I'll be making a list of the willing. I know some of us will be."

HomeSec Memo

To: Field Investigator Andrew Gao
From: DirSpecOps James McDonald
Re: Neutral Armor

Field report on student meetings reviewed.
Approved all suggested targets for intercepts: Justin Smith, Ben Ramirez, Samantha
West, Dylan Foster. Note no action to be
taken unless concrete evidence of contact
with Grey Tribe or planning activity for
unlawful actions.

Tyler Sheppard

Justin was crossing the street between the quad and the Student Union when he spotted Tyler Sheppard waiting for him on the other side. Tyler hailed him: "Justin, hey! I've been meaning to talk to you…."

Justin joined him on the sidewalk. "What about?"

"I'm sorry I picked on you the other day at the Fair. In my performance mode, entertaining the audience. I know you're an okay guy, and I really do feel bad about what happened to Wilson. Everyone knows he's just old-fashioned and didn't mean any harm."

"If 'everyone knows' that, how come everyone let him be railroaded?"

"As my dad says, don't be the nail that sticks up and you won't get hammered. My dad learned how to get along with Unity when he was a venture capitalist, funding renewable energy companies. The only way to get approvals and start projects was to cooperate with them on publicity and give them credit. When he didn't, nothing went right; when he did, permits appeared on time and things got done."

"That seems unfair to the little guys who didn't have your dad's pull. Won't they stop trying, or start working harder on getting friends in government instead of doing better work?"

"Probably. But Unity is doing a lot to bring the oppressed into the system and giving them a boost. Competing with the Chinese means we need everyone involved, all the time, and pulling the same direction. Unity is making that happen. My dad's solar projects are powering this campus right now."

"So as long as it works," Justin said, "ignore the woman behind the curtain?"

"Who got us through the emergency. And got the two parties together to get things done."

"They say she's going to go for a third term. No one opposes her. Things are going so well we don't have time to change horses."

"Who else could hold everyone together the way she has? Anyway, I just wanted to say it wasn't personal."

"I appreciate that," Justin said. "I have to disagree with your politics, but then maybe I'm old-fashioned myself."

"I'll be running for the Unity regional board next year. I hope you'll support me—you will when you see my opponent. I can make things better if I have your support."

Justin smiled at that. "I will be paying attention when the time comes, certainly."

Back Channels

Justin stopped in to see Prof. Wilson. He explained Ben's offer to convey a message to Michael McCulloch. "—And so I wanted to check with you to see what you thought about sending him a warning to play along without revealing anything."

"How do we know such a message won't be intercepted? How do we know HomeSec doesn't have spies in the Grey Tribe?"

"We don't. But McCulloch is free now, so they haven't been able to get him if they are somehow reading some of the Grey Tribe's message traffic. Our message can't help them locate him, though they might use it to come after you. Which I guess means it ought to appear not to come from us."

"It's been two weeks since I agreed to cooperate and gave them control of my phone and the code keys. I've heard nothing and it makes me nervous. Maybe they are sending him messages and he's not answering, so I don't need to do anything. Maybe it is taking them this long to think up what to say—they haven't asked me for personalizing material, which is what they said they needed my help with. If they don't get material from me, I can't spin something clever to warn him. He may fall for whatever they have in mind to get him to reveal too much."

"So spin a message I can have Zach deliver that will do the same thing —something only he would understand means you are compromised and he should stop answering."

"Let me see what I can come up with. I'll let you know when I have something."

Justin left, and Prof. Wilson thought of what Michael would know that he could refer to without tipping off the source or the meaning to anyone else. *Worlds of Warcraft* came to mind—Prof. Wilson had tried it briefly at Michael's urging. He might recognize his old character's name…

＊ ＊ ＊ ＊ ＊

```
Forward to: Grey Leader
From: Astaroth's Ghost

Warden has won this round. I am out for
now, return to game delayed. Trolls active.
Do not accept substitutes.
```

＊ ＊ ＊ ＊ ＊

Ben's transmission of the warning message up the tree to Michael McCulloch did not get any reply, but that did not surprise him. There would be no way to tell if it had done any good.

Chapter Seven: Breakthrough

ALife Simulation, Model 6: Organism 230019738

In the flat plain along the river, one of the first cities grew. Gorak in one of the nearby villages had learned to plant grain as a boy and now that he had children to help him, it was not impossible to plant a large area in a few days using the plow. The children would follow behind and plant the seeds while he worked hard pulling the plow through the soil. The plow was at least better than a hoe, but he was sure it would go faster and the plants would grow more quickly if he could somehow strap the plow to an ox to pull it through the dirt, instead of painstakingly trying to pull it through the soil by hand. The furrows he made were never all that deep or extensive enough to keep down the weeds. He tried a different harness every year and at last got one furrow plowed using his least-reluctant ox, then a whole field, before the harness broke and planting season ended. Most of his neighbors thought it was not worth the trouble, but they stopped teasing him when the field he had plowed with the ox yielded far more grain at harvest time. The chief's tax collector came by and took more of his grain than usual, but he still came out ahead, and meanwhile word of his plow and ox harness had spread up and down the valley....

Quantum Lab: Breakthrough

Justin had been busy for that week rewriting critical parts of his A-Life simulation code to use the Vortex-5's programming model. He'd bring a piece of the problem to Steve Duong for his opinion, and his answer was usually some form of *that won't work,* and then Steve would sketch out for him how to go about it. The whiteboard in Justin's temporary office was covered with boxes, arrows, and arrays. So far he had succeeded in getting the environmental simulation to run without any life forms: objects moved, heat and scents flowed, and light rays propagated as they were supposed to.

Steve had been hard at work on what Justin assumed were tests of the machine. There was a lot of muttering and drawing on his whiteboard. He was beginning to understand that Steve was "special" in the sense people used when there was something not quite right about a person; he would stop in the middle of a conversation and stare off for a moment before resuming. But he was clearly brilliant and focused. He ate ramen noodles at his desk and did not appear to ever leave—at least Justin always left before he did. His grooming was bad even for a physics guy—shaggy hair, patchy stubble, sometimes an odd smell. But Justin wasn't dating him, and he had run into worse —guys you couldn't stand to be near because they smelled so bad.

It was getting late, but before Justin left he knocked on the doorjamb of Steve's office. "Got a quick question for you."

Steve was unusually absorbed in his screens. "Come here—look at this," and he pointed to a window showing an exotic forest scene.

"That's beautiful. Where is it?"

"A planet orbiting 61 Pegasi. Real-time. See the fronds moving?"

Justin tried to process the statement. "Real-time? Don't you mean simulation?"

"No. We're looking *through* the Vortex-5's braided array. I've been working on some discoveries. Some breakthroughs, actually. And I need to tell someone, because it's beginning to scare me."

Justin pulled up a chair. "So you have somehow captured a view of it —how far is it?"

"Fifty light-years."

"How is that possible? No telescope could have that resolution. We can barely detect planets at that range."

"The photons are captured there, not here. It's a closeup view."

"So this view is what's happening there 50 years ago?"

"No, it's what's happening *right now*. No time delay. The photons cross a defined plane in midair on the planet and come out of a defined plane just outside the front plate of the electron gas chamber. Instantaneously."

Justin was fascinated and at the same time wondered what could possibly have gone wrong in Steve's head. Yet on the screen there was a convincing picture of familiar yet alien life, moving gently in the wind wherever it was. "So you have a cam looking through this 'window'? Show me the window."

"I have stayed away from the machine in case something went wrong. But let's go look." Steve led them to the machine, where he undid a loose screw on the front access plate and moved it aside. "See?"

Justin did see. In 3-D and high resolution, now that his two eyes were receiving streams of photons directly from a planet around another star, as if looking through a window.

Whiteboard

Steve told him about the anomalous data appearing in the unused parts of the array during computations, and the logical leaps he had made to explain it. The sun had set, but Steve's whiteboard began to fill up as Steve talked and drew.

Steve drew a checkerboard grid with dots in some of the squares. "A cellular automaton[4] is a regular grid of cells which can have a small number of states. The next state of each cell is set by a rule that looks at the current state of the cell and its adjoining neighbors. Surprisingly complex behavior can result from simple rules and very few states. John Horton Conway's game of Life[5] was the popular example."

"I've played with it. It had self-reproducing patterns, and so got the name 'Life.'"

"Theories of a cellular automaton basis for the universe run into several problems. Mapping the cellular grid to location in space would seem to introduce nonuniform directionality: objects could travel at the "speed of light" only in special directions. Disturbances in Life can only travel at full speed aligned with the grid, or at lesser speeds in any other direction. And if cells can only change state in response to cells they are directly connected with, how does something like quantum entanglement occur?"

Justin just raised his eyebrows. "I remember Life had gliders, right? Moving on diagonals. Cyclical patterns that move."

"Yes. A lot of people tried to map that onto a quantum physics that operated deterministically on a cellular scale so small it could reproduce quantum phenomena. Like string-theory-eleventh-dimension small. Where particles were traveling patterns."

"And so what became of those ideas?"

"There was a brief flurry of interest. Some Italians developed a cellular automaton that seemed to reproduce Schrödinger's equations in
one dimension. Like a lot of the string theories, though, it was hard to
find testable consequences; these theories were tailored to exactly
reproduce the standard model's behavior in all the conditions we can
normally test. And getting to scales below that experimentally where
there might be differences proved difficult." He went back to drawing
on the board. "I had a another idea. Suppose that the connectedness
of the cellular automata grid is not mapped to spatial location; in fact,
location is some sort of emergent property of long-lived patterns
formed by the operation of the automaton, so that a particle is just a
pattern whose location is determined by its ability to interact with
other particles—which will tend to be 'near' in space, but not always.
Suppose, for example, each cell of the cellular grid is connected to *all*
other cells, anywhere in the universe, and the computation of its next
state is a function of its current state plus the states of every cell it
addresses."

Justin thought about this for a bit. "Doesn't that mean each particle
would have to know the coordinates of every particle it interacts
with? Wouldn't that be an enormous number of bits? Where is all this
data stored?"

"That's the elegant part. It's the connections between particles that
determine the fabric of space itself. You have to stop thinking of it as
a physical array of cells in space. They are all connected to each other,
all the time; it's not a computer. The patterns determine the particles;
the particles only talk to particles they interact with. But they could
potentially talk to any other particle. They simply don't, as the automaton normally operates. Unless I tell them to."

"'Tell them to?' How exactly do you do that?"

"We're creating quasiparticles in the electron gas between the plates. Those quasiparticles, in turn, form an array which acts as one giant quasiparticle. Which I can program from my console. And that quasiparticle can recruit any and all particles in this and nearby universes into its computations, and ask them to change states as directed. It turns out the quantum computations we were doing only scratch the surface of what is possible—infinite storage, infinite computation—"

"You *ask* the particles? You're the particle whisperer?"

"Well, I set up the array to do certain things, and it asks the particles, but yes."

"I can't see it."

"Of course you can't. You were evolved in a Newtonian world of 'normal' space and time and physical objects. There is no analogue in your brain."

"Well, I see some problems. What about relativity? Everything we know tells us nothing can travel faster than light—not even information. If something could, we would have seen evidence of it."

"This phenomenon would not happen in nature. The braided array that creates the quasi-particle could not occur without intelligent assistance. The organized array, the cold, the magnetic fields, and especially the external control and programming are required. So it turns out there are exceptions to some of the basic laws of physics, but they never occur naturally; only high technology and unlikely organization can create conditions where exceptions occur. The normal laws of physics are emergent properties of a much rougher underlying process, and can be subverted by 'addressing the substrate.' We have found a way to route around the operation of the laws of the universe we know."

Travelling Without Moving

The evening became night, and still they talked. Steve pulled out extra ramen and they ate that for dinner, still talking and drawing. Justin pointed at the scene still displayed on Steve's screen, which was going dark as apparently that place approached its own night. "How does this viewing window work, exactly?"

"You ask the device to scan particles near a plane in space bounded by a rectangle. If a particle is approaching the plane, its connections to local particles on the other side of the plane are replaced by connections with particles on our side of our plane. It's set now to allow through only photons, and only one-way on one side. If you were on the planet, the backside of the window would appear to be a perfectly black square hanging in the air."

"So what stops other particles from going through?"

"I'm only asking for photons. If I asked for other particles, they could come through also."

"So if you asked nicely, you could set up a door we could walk through, and end up there?"

"That is on my list of experiments. Send a camera in one-way. Then live animals."

Justin was again wondering if Steve was sane. Not because this wasn't obviously a breakthrough, but that he'd done it in secret, in a few weeks, and already he planned to test *animals*. Some hazards seemed obvious. "What makes you think this planet isn't teeming with microbes, or dangerous life forms, or aliens, even? Isn't it just a little premature to risk something coming through to our side, or deadly germs? How do you know the atmosphere supports life as we know it?"

"That took weeks of work. It turns out one of the limitations on using the device is the difficulty of programming it—I could give it relative coordinates and ask it about particles within a radius of that spot, but my first experiments returned little data since I was unsure of the coordinate system. I finally found some smarter ways to locate things, by asking it to find a pattern of local particles that matched criteria I set—that also took a lot of experimenting, and I had to add a tailored query language. Using selected criteria, I detected the Sun and then had some idea of how the relative coordinates worked—good thing I had the viewing turned off for that. I have it down now so I can give it any Earth surface coordinate and open the window within a few feet of it. I added on this joystick to give me fine control over positioning and the directionality—the problem is similar to controlling a remote camera."

Steve used the joystick to move the scene closer, then panned left, where one large "tree" blocked the view. "So I can clumsily control position from the console, and get fine control from the joystick. And I found this planet using a very complicated query: give me a gas with such-and-such range of composition, temperature, and pressure, with solid surface below, water vapor, carbon dioxide, sunlight near Sol spectrum, and so forth. This is the nearest. Looked around the area, nothing but plants so far. And we send animals first to be sure. It's unlikely any microbes would be danger to us—they haven't evolved to be parasites to our kind of life. It's possible there's something poisonous in the air or plants, but that's a testable question. Thus the animals. We don't let anything come the other way until we know a lot more."

"Okay, another basic this-is-impossible question. Isn't that planet hurtling through space at some enormous relative speed to ours? How is it this is rock steady?"

"The whole thing is based on local particles. The local particle frame of reference is steady. The device is addressing particles, not locations or speeds."

"What about conservation of energy? How can it be that we move objects instantly without using a lot of energy?"

"The objects don't accelerate; their idea of what they are near changes. No energy required."

"Okay, suppose I set up your window to open high above us and start pouring water through it. I can run a generator using the falling water and extract energy as it returns to this gravitational potential. Where does that energy come from?"

"The universe. Everywhere. Nowhere. The quantum foam. Yes, you can use the device to generate as much energy as you want. You could open a port to the inside of the Sun. When the gateway is open, the universe just deals with it."

The Rebel Alliance

The sky to the east was beginning to glow when Justin decided it was time to get some sleep. "We need to go home. I have to ask you—you're keeping this secret because you think it's too dangerous, and I agree. So why are you telling me?"

"I had to tell someone. You're here, you're smart, and I think you can be trusted to help me with it. I want to explore the device and use it as a tool to understand the universe and give us backup in case this planet ever becomes uninhabitable."

"But in the wrong hands, it could destroy us all—"

"Yes. The ultimate surveillance tool, bomb delivery system, and assassination weapon. Allowing easy murder, theft, and cheap energy production. Anyone after power would do anything to get it, and use it to commit crimes and control people, limited only by their imagination. I can see that, and you can see that. And if I can discover it, someone else using the same kind of hardware eventually will, so even if I erased my work and forgot it all, the knowledge will eventually get loose. And so it is my responsibility to try to use it for good and to keep it from those who would use it to hurt people."

"Who could be trusted with that kind of power? Us?"

"If not us, who?—My dad told stories from his childhood about the American soldiers and the Viet Cong. There were cruel Americans, but on the whole they were good people. The Communists—and our own soldiers—were not so good. Those days were long ago, and the government there now is not so different from the government here. But you are the kind of decent American he remembered, and I have heard of what your Prof. Wilson has been going through, and what you are trying to do."

"So far we've done nothing to help him."

"But you are willing to talk about it and take the chance of being singled out and destroyed. We know how those things work. It is foolish and noble to stand up for what is right when bad people rule. It will be foolish and noble to take responsibility for the device when more than likely they'll come after it and try to destroy us."

Chapter Eight: Desaparecidos

Rebel Meeting

Justin had texted the people he thought he could trust as the nucleus of what he was beginning to think of as The Rebel Alliance: his lab partner Rasna Kapoor, Ben Ramirez and Samantha of the Students for Liberty, and Zach of the Redshirts, calling for a meeting at an off-campus cafe. He didn't want Steve Duong to be known as a conspirator just yet, and Prof. Wilson was as much as possible to be kept out of it until the threat to him was over.

Samantha and Dylan were late. Ben started it off: "First, I have some bad news. One of our less careful members started handing out leaflets, nothing unusual, just describing us and where we meet. Fifty feet outside the Free Speech Zone, and she was arrested by the campus cops and expelled yesterday. I spoke to her and her mother—they hustled her home to Fresno last night. They've pulled her financial aid and as much as told her she's blackballed anywhere she might go."

"That's an escalation, isn't it?" Justin said. "They've only warned people before, right?"

"That's right, unless someone has refused to move when asked. This is the first time they didn't ask."

Justin addressed everyone around the table. "Well, that fits a pattern. As I told you all earlier, Homeland Security is leaning on Prof. Wilson, and it's a lot more serious than I let on. We have to expect pressure will be put on the administration to keep us from doing anything. They're likely to have us under surveillance soon, if not already. That's why I had you come here."

Samantha and Dylan came through the cafe door, looking unhappy, and Sam said, "Sorry we're late. Still trying to find out more about Amy's arrest. No one seems to know anything."

Ben was angry. "That was a warning to the rest of us. Shut up or lose your career."

"Things will get worse before they get better," Justin said. "I guess I should tell you all that Prof. Wilson has been in touch with Michael McCulloch, the leader of the Grey Tribe, and they caught him at it. They've threatened him with arrest and prosecution. We need to have some plan of action in case that happens. And we have some tools they don't know about that might help us beat them. But I have to warn you all, it's very, very dangerous—we could lose everything and end up in the Gulag ourselves."

"'Our lives, our fortunes, and our sacred honor.' Isn't that the price of freedom?" Ben went on: "I couldn't respect myself if I did nothing. But anyone not committed should leave now. We'll be talking about plans and it's better you not know what they are if you don't want to take the risk. So leave now if you want out. We will understand." He looked at each of them around the table.

No one moved.

"Even this meeting is risky," Justin said. "I studied up on the clandestine cell system—I got the idea from *The Moon is a Harsh Mistress*, but it's something every secret organization has used to limit the damage spies and defectors can do. The basic idea is each member is in a cell of three or four, and communicates only as needed with the leader of the cell. Each cell member, in turn, can lead another cell, and so on down the levels to more and more members. But capture of one means only a few are compromised, and information is only available to the few who require it."

"I can address that," Ben said. "I've heard that the Grey Tribe communication system is organized that way. Messages are passed up and down the tree without any central location where they can be intercepted, and even Grey Leader has no idea who or where the members are."

"Compartmentalization, it's called." Justin "Since we're meeting, we all know too much, but from now on new members will come via recruitment by a single cell leader. And we have to assume all of our calls, texts, and email are being scanned. It's not safe to talk by any means but face-to-face."

HomeSec Memo

To: Field Investigator Andrew Gao
From: DirSpecOps James McDonald
Re: Neutral Armor

The analysts have reviewed the recording of
the student meeting. Quick thinking on setting up the bugs in the cafe on very short
notice.

The situation is getting out of control.
While the students have no specifically
illegal plans, this sort of talk comes
close to requiring us to act. We are not
getting any useful responses from McCulloch
and suggest you have Wilson quietly arrested and medicated for further debriefing.
Team should pick him up early in the morning at home. Track and monitor all communications by students Ben Ramirez and Justin
Smith very closely until further notice. If
you see any evidence Ben Ramirez is sending
covert messages to the Grey Tribe network,
arrest him as well.

Love Triangle

It was mid-November, with warm but short days and cool nights. Samantha had texted Justin that she was free to go out since Dylan was busy, and so they met at the bus stop and hopped the shuttle into town.

They got off and walked to a cheap Thai place. They ordered and the soups came. The aroma of coconut milk and cilantro rose from Justin's soup and the pepper started to clear his sinuses. "I love this soup. When it's cold especially."

Sam used her spoon to try it. "Almost too rich. But tasty."

"Watch out for the pieces of galanga. You can't actually eat them."

"I realized that when I tried to chew one."

Justin looked around—no one was close enough to hear them talking over the buzz of background noise. "We're making progress on the cell system. You're in my cell, so I get to tell you what you need to hear."

"If you know what's good for you, you'll tell me everything."

"You know what I mean—about the project. Security! In theory I'm not supposed to tell you who my other two members are, but that probably doesn't matter until the organization has grown a lot."

"I have recruited two people from Students for Liberty and one from the Redshirts. If I told you who, I'd have to kill you." She looked pleased with the idea.

"If we are only recruiting from people we already know, we're not

going to reach other students very quickly. Have your recruits recruited?"

"One has her three. The others are slow, and I'm not sure they are
serious. Time excuses, social lives…"

"The revolution does not make time for fun." He imagined himself
with Lenin's glasses.

"I think most of us were brought up to be passive. Parents and
schools planned everything for us, scheduled us up, watched us every
second to make sure we weren't kidnapped or raped. When you're in
the habit of doing what everyone else wants you to do, it's hard to
strike out and do something different, in secret."

"So it's part of your job as cell leader to support them. And nag them,
and be another voice telling them what to do. But this time for the
cause of freedom. So they can do what they want to, eventually."

"If we make it. And if they don't get sacrificed in the process."

"Independence requires taking graduated risks and learning what is
and isn't a good bet. This is a good bet. I can't even tell you why yet,
but I can tell you I know we can make a difference. I know we have a
good chance to win."

"And I trust you enough to follow you. Not blindly, but because I can
see what kind of person you are. And that gives me confidence."

A feeling of warmth spread through him, and it was more than just
the effects of the spicy soup.

* * * * *

Outside the restaurant, Dylan Foster observed them through the window. He had started checking Samantha's text messages and emails after she had told him her phone's passcode a few months ago when he needed to borrow it for a call. On reading the texts planning this dinner, he decided to blow off his night class to check it out. He knew Justin was dangerously interested, and while he couldn't tell for sure what was going on from the bland texts between them, they were meeting more and more often. They seemed to be smiling at each other far too much.

Justin and Steve: Prof. Wilson Gone

Prof. Wilson did not come in for several days. His administration calendar showed sick time; emails to him got an out-of-office reply. Justin went by his house and rang the bell; no answer. Justin noticed a car cruising slowly down the block while he waited at the front door. He decided he should pretend to be unconcerned and go about his business, if they had taken the professor in for questioning. Appearing to be disturbed would only keep them on his tail, if that was a tail.

More days passed, then weeks. A woman from Human Resources came by the A-Life lab and explained to Rasna that Prof. Wilson was very ill and would be out on disability for some time longer; it would be wise to make alternate arrangements for faculty advising. Notices went out in email.

In his visits to the Quantum Lab, Justin quietly stopped working on the simulation code and helped Steve develop better software for controlling the device. The user interface for searching for locations meeting specific conditions improved, the coordinate database grew as they discovered more locations, and the joystick turned into a 3-D control that offered knobs to control the size and transparency of the window. Additional refinements allowed the local window to be anywhere, not just a fixed distance from the plates, and they explored the vast storage and computational power which could be summoned up.

"Is there a chance we could get this to find a certain strand of DNA? Like, a missing person's?" Justin asked.

"It's theoretically possible, but how would you describe the terms of the search? It's not like you can give it a nail clipping and let it find the similar molecules. We have no way—yet—to scan or describe that level of chemical complexity. We're pushing our limits finding certain isotopes in certain combinations and concentrations."

"Just wondering what's become of Prof. Wilson."

"We could spy on the local office of Homeland Security. Listen in on conversations."

"Is there a way we can detect sound on the other side of the window without actually poking a microphone through?"

As it turned out, there was. The position of air molecules just on the other side of the gateway could be directly queried and pressure waves detected; the sound generated from that data was as clear as from a microphone. This took days to code up; the result was sound from the console's speakers and sound files which might prove to be useful. They looked for and found Andrew Gao's office downtown and set up a tiny gateway a few inches from the ceiling to record video and sound near his desk.

Meanwhile, they discussed how to test the gateway further when the lab was often visited by Professors Bubna and Friedman, as well as parties of VIPs from funding agencies. They decided to confine active gateway experiments to nighttime, and to close off that end of the lab with a portable divider, blocking the view from the hall windows. These changes went unremarked on, and their experiments continued.

"So why can't we bring Friedman and Bubna in on this?" Justin asked.

"I owe Prof. Friedman a great debt—he has been like family to me— but he is looking for grant money and a name for himself. And I could not endanger him and his family by involving them in this. It is better that they not know. As for Bubna, perhaps, later. He is a good man, and single. But for now we are better off telling no one else."

"How about Sam?" Justin was seeing more and more of her, as Dylan's thesis work became obsessive and he stopped monitoring her every move. In a way they got to know each other better without the experience of sex, which Sam had ruled out until she had broken up with Dylan—who she thought would take it badly, and so she held off while he was so hard at work. Justin thought this possibly unnecessary but a sign of her integrity, and simmered quietly as they met like some courting couple from the last century.

"If you trust Sam with the most dangerous secret in history, then, sure, show her what we're doing."

"When you put it like that, it seems unwise. Maybe I can bring her by and show her what I'm doing without really telling her everything. I am her cell leader, so it's not breaking discipline."

"'See, Sam, here's another planet viewed in realtime!' I think that would be too much."

"Well, she's asked how things are going and why I spend so much time here at night. Giving her a look might keep her from being more curious."

"That sounds better. Try not to tell her we plan to steal the machine and abscond with it to another planet. Meanwhile picking up hundreds of outlaws and stealing gold from government vaults. Then launch a rebellion to take down the worst governments from our safe position off-world."

"Shh! Don't even talk about those things." They had worked out a plan weeks ago; when the technical development allowed, they would bring in some of the others and try to contact the Grey Tribe to get Michael McCulloch on board as well. Through him, they could recruit those hundreds with little to lose and a willingness to risk a lot. "I know I'm being watched. They could be using a laser on the windows to listen in."

"That would be funny, when our eavesdropping is so much better. I don't think they have bothered with anything that elaborate. As far as they know, you just grind away at research here."

"Which reminds me again to point out the irony of our stealing a government-funded machine to undermine the government. DARPA will not be happy."

"Our next grant request will be tough."

"I guess bridges are made to be burned. Which reminds me, how is the plan to order up more parts for a duplicate device going?"

"I've spoken to Bubna, asking innocently how we'd go about that if we got funding. It turns out the NSA and an even-more-secret-agency have ordered up several more. You'd think they would wait until they had run more of their own tests, but they didn't like the lead time of six months—so what if it turns out to be wasted money."

"So if we find those parts in the fab, we can steal them."

"If they are done in time. More work for us, trying to spy on the fabs to find out their schedules and where they store the work-in-progress."

"This is why we need more people and more devices to execute even the basics of the plan."

"That is true. But for now it is all up to us." Steve went back to slurping on his ramen and tweaking some stubborn code.

* * * * *

The next night, Justin brought proper food for dinner. They ate at the console desk and Justin said, "I've had a deep thought."

"Forty-two! No, I mean, what?"

"If, as you say, the device can tap into unlimited storage and computation on the substrate by marshaling as many particles as it needs to assist, what would stop us from uploading an AI—or ourselves, suitably encoded—to it? Has it occurred to you that the reason why we haven't seen any evidence of advanced alien civilizations might be that they develop to the point of finding a similarly-capable quantum computer, then upload themselves? Could they be happily living vast, simulated lives far faster than we can imagine? Leaving the universe apparently empty?"

"Yes, that occurred to me about day two. Some of the 'noise' I found in the unused areas of the array during computation may have been the result of organized activity of that sort."

"If so, what if we somehow disturb them or damage their computations by mucking with the particles they are using? Wouldn't they be like gods, able to see and do anything, anywhere as the mood strikes them?"

"My guess would be that such collisions are very rare and the density of computations directed by intelligence is very low compared to that used by natural activity. And as for gods, there is no reason why an intelligence running on the substrate wouldn't be able to observe and meddle with matter at will, though why they would bother when they have a rich internal society to deal with, I don't know."

"Maybe they once did—like the Greek gods!—but some authority rides herd on the substrate civilizations and makes them keep hands-off."

"I don't know—all of these questions would be excellent advanced research topics. For now, we have no way to digitize people's brain states, and our AIs are too feeble to use more capacity than we provide with conventional machines—they are more like glorified search engines with associative memories and crude reasoning. True self-aware AIs are still far away. But this would give them the power that they would need to leave us far behind. And if alien civilizations have done that, then they are already there. We see no evidence of interference."

"Maybe it would be wise to upload ourselves first, before enabling Skynet."

"No one knows if the human brain could be expanded somehow by adding more and faster connections. It seems evolved and organized to handle only the senses it has. It may be very difficult to take an adult human and turn him into a super-human directed by the personality and memories that make him who he is."

"Sounds like a challenge."

"Probably a challenge for the next generation. We have yet to save ourselves from murderous bureaucracies. And planetary destruction."

✳ ✳ ✳ ✳ ✳

It was Steve who brought up deeper topics the next day. "This is not right."

"What is not right?" Everything on screen looked normal to Justin.

"The universe we know is regular and predictable, with laws of physics we have found reliable down to the quantum level. This is not supposed to be possible; it's like there was a mistake in the universe that allows this escape hatch. This flaw. As if it were a simulation and we have found a bug in its software."

"That's what you told me the first night. Science is what *is*—we observe things that don't fit what we know, we have to come up with new laws that do. Even if something *shouldn't* be true, we have to work with what *is*. If it gets messy and irregular, that usually means some simpler system we can't see is behind it. As with chemistry, which sorted the zillion wildly different chemical compounds into regular structures made of a limited number of atoms by fairly simple rules. And those atoms turned out to be made of even simpler and fewer parts. And so on."

"Yes, but. Suppose this universe is itself a simulation run on the substrate we're addressing. What we are doing is escaping the simulation—like one of your simulated organisms discovering how to trigger a program exception and get itself promoted to local godhood, able to smite predators at will. We are accessing the substrate directly, against the rules. If there is a Simulator running this simulation, won't it be noticed? By opening gateways to other planets, could it be like sending up a flare that even a sleeping God would see?"

"If so, too late."

"Perhaps that is an answer to your question about alien civilizations. Maybe a giant foot comes out of the sky and squashes any civilization that dares to meddle with the substrate."

* * * * *

The next day, Justin reviewed all of the files recorded since they had set up the recording window above Andrew Gao's desk. He skipped through them as quickly as he could; intriguing bits and pieces, but nothing about Prof. Wilson or the Grey Tribe. Frustrated, he started to think of other places they could listen, but without understanding Homeland Security's inner workings, it would be hard to identify likely spots, and he didn't have time or a safe way to search for information that they wouldn't be monitoring. He vowed to do more if something didn't turn up on the recordings in the next few days.

But as they days went by, he forgot more and more to set up the listening window after they had run other experiments, and when he did, nothing interesting turned up in the recordings.

Prof. Wilson: Secure Facility

Walter Wilson had lost track of the days that he had been in this place. He had been rousted out of his sleep before dawn one day by men—and one woman—who had somehow entered his house without making a sound. They were outfitted like a SWAT team and had their pistols drawn, but the closest was pointing a taser at him. Groggily he packed a bag with a few clothes and critical medications and did what they asked. Then one of them injected his arm with something, and everything went away in seconds.

When he woke up a little, he was in the back of a van strapped into a seat. He could see a little out the front window, but they were on a highway he didn't recognize. One of the men noticed him moving and said, "Hey, Prof. You back with us a little?" He gestured to someone behind him, and the needle stuck him again. Blackness.

Much later, he came to on a bed in a small white room. He was restrained—straps held him down. He went in and out of consciousness for some hours before someone came to feed and bathe him.

For the first few days, the routine was always the same: someone woke him and brought him breakfast. He was given a few minutes to eat, then taken to a room where a handsome young man, impeccably dressed, asked him questions and got him to tell stories about Michael McCulloch. As the days wore on he ran out of memories about Michael. The young man asked about other people—past students, current students and faculty. He wondered why he was being so cooperative, but it just seemed easier to make the young man happy by giving him what he wanted. He felt bad that he had run out of things to say.

Gradually the sessions shortened, and other people asked him the same questions. He tried to make his answers interesting by varying the wording. Finally they stopped asking him questions, and he only saw the young man one other time, when an important visitor was shown to the questioning room. He was a serious older man, and seemed unhappy with him.

Then the days began to pass more quickly, as he was left alone except for people bringing food and cleaning the room. A burly male nurse gave him pills and encouraged him to exercise on the stationary bike next to the bed, and the TV showed scenery he might have been passing through had he been biking in various national parks. He thought that was a nice gesture. But still his head was so cloudy....

Chapter Nine: Demo Days

Quantum Lab: Demo

Justin got to the quantum lab to find Steve in one of the storage rooms staring into a cage holding three mice. Steve noticed him, and said, "I got these from the bio supply. She wanted our account number and I made up a number one up from the lab's real number. Told her it was a new project."

"We could have just caught some squirrels in the quad." Justin eyed the mice. "These guys are kinda cute."

"I've also got a camera on a pole and some rocks to toss through."

"Sounds like we're ready for real science. And this is the time to start bringing in other people who need to know about this if we're ever going to get all the work done. Sam, Rasna, and Prof. Bubna, at least. Ben Ramirez—without him we have no connection to the Grey Tribe. Those four we absolutely need."

"I'm ready to try matter transfers tonight. We'd need some time to round up those people, and I'd rather not wait until tomorrow."

"I can get Sam over here in an hour—we were thinking of getting together for dinner anyway."

"Then I guess have her observe. I would explain what's going to happen in advance so she isn't surprised."

"I'll do that." He had already been dropping hints and talking about remote viewing capabilities; Sam seemed politely interested but apparently missed the full significance of that phrase.

Justin texted Sam and asked, "Can you meet me at Student Union in an hour? We'll get food."

She responded quickly: "Sure. Thesis Man is going to be at his office until late."

*＊＊＊＊

Samantha arrived at the door of the cafeteria a few minutes late. Justin said, "Let's just get some water and sit for a minute. We're supposed to pick up food here then go to the quantum lab for a demo." They got water and sat at a table by the doors.

"Sorry," she said, "grading final projects for the course I'm TA-ing. End-of-term crunch coming next week, then the holiday break."

"Wouldn't the break be the ideal time to break up? With you-know-who? He can mope while he's on vacation."

She looked thoughtful. "You may be right. His deadline is next week, and if I tell him after that, he can recover at his parent's place in St. Barts. I was invited, but made up a reason I couldn't go. The Caribbean at Christmas! His parents are really great people, but no."

"It would be nice if you were free to publicly display affection." He touched her little finger with his.

"Not to mention privately. I know you want to, and so do I."

"So it's a plan. —And there's another plan I need to tell you about. Steve and I have been working on that remote viewing I was telling you about. I haven't told you very much because—"

"Security, I know."

"More than just that. Steve has made a discovery. Not just any break-through, but *the* breakthrough. Of the century, or even the millenni-um."

"Okay, I get it—it's big! Get on with it." She tapped her glass impa-tiently.

"To start out, 'remote' is light-years away. And by 'viewing,' I mean a window you can look through in real-time. And tonight we are going to test using it as a gateway—sending objects to a planet 50 light-years away."

Her head tilted and she looked at him for some time. "What? That's… hard to believe. Steve runs a computer lab. What does that have to do with—?"

"The quantum computer is the key to it all. It lets us do incredible things—see anywhere, go anywhere, compute anything. The main limit is our ability to program it. It will change the world, and let us leave it. Steve made a breakthrough in physics—I guess we will call it substrate physics, now, not quantum physics—and worked out how to get the machine to do just about anything he asks."

"I am suddenly getting scared. Who else knows about this?"

"Nobody, just me and Steve. Steve did not want to bring in Prof. Friedman yet—I think he doesn't trust him to handle it right. And Prof. Wilson is who-knows-where in the Gulag. We're going to bring in Ben Ramirez and Prof. Bubna soon—we'll need them. We have a plan."

"A cunning plan. Where have I heard that before? Do I get to hear it?"

"World—no, Galactic!—conquest. Freedom and dignity for all. Cookies."

"I may have a few quibbles with your plan, but not with the cookies part."

They talked for a few more minutes, then made their way out and walked across the street towards the quantum lab.

* * * * *

Justin and Sam ate dinner in Justin's office while Steve stood in the doorway and talked. "You realize you can't tell anyone about any of this, right?"

Sam looked annoyed. "I do understand how dangerous it is to try to keep this a secret. You know if they find out, you'll be taken away and never seen again. Slave scientists. National security orders."

"And what's our alternative?" Justin said. "Make it public? Have every country lobbing bombs through gateways and spying on everything?"

"They do that well enough now." Sam crossed her arms.

Justin grabbed her hand. "But this would be far more effective, and deniable. The perfect weapon for sneak attacks and assassinations. At least now the surveillance is mostly electronic, and you can work around it with some effort. This would be much worse. And if we reveal it only to a responsible US agency—let's say DARPA—we give them a hot potato and they will end up handing it over to the scum running Homeland Security. Same consequences but enabling one country to roll over the others. Despite it being our country, I don't feel at this time that that would be a good outcome for anyone."

"I'm not liking it, but I'm finding it hard to disagree."

"The logic compels us to hide it and use it for good. Very, very carefully. And keep anyone from following us in finding it."

* * * * *

For the demo, they opened the Vortex-5's front panel and watched from behind the console. Steve keyed in a command line, and the machine disappeared behind a perfect mirror reflecting a view of them watching. "Just a cool trick—world's most high-tech mirror. Photons reflected from our side."

"What would happen if I stuck my hand in?" Sam said.

"Nothing—only photons get reflected back. Might have some odd physiological effects, so I wouldn't try it…. Next, some geography…" The gateway changed to show a view from high up of a sinuous wall on a hilly landscape. "Great Wall of China. Before noon tomorrow there—no, it's not a time machine, it's just across the International Date Line."

"So I could toss a bomb through and create an incident?"

"No, it's set to let only photons through, and only one-way. Next: a test of the search engine; I've set it to find a dense concentration of Au, gold that is, over 100 kilograms…." The gateway showed a wall of stacked gold bars. "Backing up a little." The wall of gold fell away until they could see the walls of vault it was sitting in. "A bank in New York."

Sam looked thoughtful. "I'm surprised it's not Ft. Knox, but who knows if there's actually any gold there anymore. It may all be in China."

Steve continued to click and type. "Some stored locations. The Oval Office." The gateway was pitch black. "Whoops, that's inside the closet next to it." He used the fine control and the view slid to show a view from above of a dark room and a cleared desk. "Keeping the gateway size small there and it's dark anyway."

Justin added, "We should start recording there, and get the chief of staff's desk as well. Might come in handy."

Steve moved along. "We'll get to that, but we have more to show. What we've christened as New Earth." The view changed to the landscape of alien trees and ferns. The light there was gray and looked like it might be raining. "If I changed the setting, we could step through right now."

Justin looked around. "Were we going to try sending the camera in?"

"We could do that now. I wish we had a robot so we could direct it from a distance. I've never changed the settings to allow matter across, and it would be wise to take precautions."

"I'll do it wearing safety glasses," Justin said, "and use the extender pole from behind the console. If it's a big explosion it won't matter, but you two could go out into the hall and wait until I give the okay." Justin went to get the pole and screwed the camera to one end while Steve typed in new settings. Air began to move toward the gateway as the unequal pressure forced a breeze into it.

Safety glasses and apron on, Justin shooed them out.

It was anticlimactic. He kept as much of himself behind the desk as he could, and extended the camera on the end of the pole toward the gateway. The camera was displaying what it saw on the console, and the view didn't change as it slid through the gateway plane without resistance—the same landscape, but viewed directly. He pulled it back. "All clear. Nothing happened. I guess it must have gone through and come back without a problem." And the camera still functioned as if it had not been sent 50 light-years away and back in a few seconds. The only difference was that it came back *wet*.

"Oops," Steve said. "That was unexpected. First transfer of alien water full of microorganisms back to us. I hope it's safe."

It was late, and they decided to postpone the animal test until tomorrow, when they would have had a chance to round up Ben Ramirez and Prof. Bubna. Steve was assigned to break the news to Bubna, while Sam and Justin would talk to Ben.

Prof. Wilson

Jim McDonald, Director of the Homeland Security's Advanced Threat Assessment Task Force, sometimes wondered how he had ended up with the job. After two tours in Iraq and an uneventful career state-side, his early retirement plans had been disrupted by the bombing of New York and the State of Emergency. They had made him an offer too good to refuse, and friends looked out for him. He was getting the highest salary of his life, plus his military pension, plus another pension which would kick in when he finally retired from this job. He did enjoy most of it, but there were times when he had to do things that left a bad taste in his mouth.

As now. He was again visiting the secure facility in Maryland where the highest-value detainees were held and questioned. The facility had grown in size every year, and it outgrew the former military hospital building that had been repurposed for its use. Prof. Wilson was held in the new wing, as white and clean as the old hospital had been worn and dirty.

He spoke to the officer in charge as they viewed Wilson through the one-way glass panel inset in his room's door. "He looks malnourished."

The officer, a clean-cut young man in hospital scrubs, looked down at the pad in his hands. "Weight 74 kilos this morning, just a bit less than when we got him. He's eating and exercising."

"I would imagine being constantly on the drugs has an effect."

The officer nodded. "They affect neural control and mood. Safe in the short-term, but long-term there is a chance of permanent damage. If no one is questioning him further, we'd recommend taking him off them."

"Do that. I'll deal with Immerman." Immerman was McDonald's liaison with the White House; what used to be called a political officer or commissar, in authoritarian regimes. There was an Immerman in every important security office, reporting and relaying orders from on high on matters that came to the White House's attention. "And get him a pad computer with some books. We want him alert and writing. We didn't get very much that was useful from him under drugs—might as well see if he starts revealing more when he's fully functioning. Send anything interesting to my office."

The officer made a note. "I've added the order at your direction."

There was a rumble of conversation from down the hall as a group of doctors approached. They were lead by a small Asian woman in a tailored lab coat. "Mr. McDonald," she said. "I've been looking forward to meeting you."

"And you must be Dr. Zhang. I've read your file—very impressive work."

"Call me Grace. This is rounds, so we can't stop long. But Ms. Immerman has told me she believes it is appropriate for this detainee to receive our implant."

"She has discussed it with me. I am concerned that the implant is still experimental, and we have a lot invested in this subject—we need to reinsert him and get more intelligence. I'm not sure I trust your implant just yet. And I find it hard to believe he won't know we've planted a device in his head."

"It doesn't interfere with functioning. It reports the compressed signals of critical sensory nerves passively—in only one case out of over fifty was the patient aware of anything unusual, and that was because of incorrect sensor placement. And the control functions are very subtle, stimulating pleasure and pain imperceptibly. Reinforcement can be provided at a level below conscious thought. Fear can be induced while the patient rationalizes a reason for it."

"So what good is that to us? How is he going to know to do as we say if he's not even aware of what the consequences are?"

"The monitoring software will gently nudge him in the right direction. When we are in contact with him, oppositional thoughts will be recognized and discouraged. Cooperative thoughts will make him feel better. It doesn't take long for the conditioning to take effect."

"I'm more in the threaten and cajole school, myself. But those are my orders." He motioned to the officer in charge. "The doctor is authorized to operate on this patient as soon as possible. I want a report every day on his condition."

Telling Ben

Justin rode his bike to Ben's office in the engineering building, thinking to intercept him there rather than risk a text. He found him there, but he shared the office with two other grad students, so Justin pulled him out to the hall, where they found a safe alcove.

"Any word on Prof. Wilson?" Ben asked.

"I think we can be sure he's been arrested—I've been by his house a few times and there's always some signs of surveillance. We started recruiting people to make a public stink to stop them from coming after him, but now we can't do much because they're covering it up with the illness story. Not sure how they did it, but the administration thinks he's on sick leave, and we're supposed to look for alternate advising, which means he's not expected back soon. So tell your people he's in trouble but for now just wait for instructions."

"Will do. I have fifteen people in my tree, and it's still growing slowly."

"Good. We'll let them know when there's something they can do to help," Justin said. "And I've been meaning to suggest we ask your Grey Tribe contacts for some help with more secure communication. Like throwaway phones using their apps. I'm pretty sure HomeSec intercepts all our phone communications."

"I'll ask. You have to be invited—so we'd need those cheap cellphones even to start the setup protocol. I have stopped using the Grey Tribe messaging app on mine, so I'll have to send the encoded photos from a library computer or something. I'd need to send a message asking for restoration to a different device, but I have to have the device data and email address."

"Another project for me, then—buy a lot of cheap phones at a discount store and make up identities to activate them. Fun."

"Just keep track of what fake identity goes with what phone, and set up email accounts accordingly. Give me the list and I'll forward it to my contact." Ben checked the time on his phone. "Are we done here? I have to teach a class soon."

"No, there's more. Steve Duong and I have been keeping a secret, and it's a big secret. Steve has made a breakthrough—a beyond-Nobel breakthrough, if it ever gets recognized. His quantum computer can do a lot more than compute…." Justin went on, sketching the possibilities: instant interstellar travel, ultimate surveillance, use as a weapon, and free energy. "An end to shortages, the beginning of human expansion off Earth. But the end of human freedom, in the wrong hands."

Ben listened in silence, then broke in: "I knew you guys were up to something, but I had no idea. This isn't some kind of joke? You're sure about this?"

Justin explained how Steve had stumbled on anomalies and made the breakthrough. "We're having a demo tonight and running our first test with a live animal. After dinner, around 7. Sam and Prof. Bubna will also be there."

"Bubna? Is he safe?"

"We don't know yet. But we need his help to get hold of more parts for more devices, so Steve is supposed to get his cooperation."

"Steve is not the ideal salesman."

"But he knows Bubna, and he thinks he will be good. We don't have much choice, we need his expertise."

"I'm going to be late, but who cares." Ben paused. "This is the most dangerous idea I've ever heard of. But I've wondered if I would ever get a chance to make a real difference. I was thinking of going to law school, but then I realized no one is allowed to be a crusading civil liberties lawyer under this regime. So I still think you may be crazy, but I'm in. 'Let justice be done though the heavens fall!'"

They talked for a few more minutes. Ben tapped his head and said, "I've got a million questions and ideas, but time's up. I probably won't make any sense at all in class, but I need to go. Nobody to sub for me," and left.

Animal Test

As they were preparing for the evening test, Justin asked Steve, "How'd it go with Prof. Bubna?"

"I caught him in his office and laid out the story. He was angry at first —not consulted, not asked! But I told him what has really happened to Wilson, and he calmed down. He's very interested in seeing for himself. He agrees that Prof. Friedman would feel like he had to ask his contacts what to do, and that would mean disaster. He tried to sell me on destroying the data and forgetting about it, as the safest thing for us. But he agreed it is only a matter of time, and having the secret-agency people discover it would be much worse for everyone. I was right about him...."

"So do you think he's safe to handle it?"

"Can't be sure, but I think so."

✳ ✳ ✳ ✳ ✳

The conspirators gathered in the quantum lab again after dinner for the animal test. Prof. Bubna looked around warily, apparently feeling odd that his lab had been taken over by outlaw grad students and used for unapproved experiments. Justin introduced him, and he seemed to relax a bit with Samantha. Justin thought, *she's soothing if she likes you, at least.* Rasna struck up a conversation with Steve; Justin recalled something about their dating briefly.

Ben came in last. Steve opened the front panel and set up the console. For the newcomers' benefit, he quickly went through his favorite Earth locations. Then he set it for the planet at 61 Pegasi.

"We've taken to calling it New Earth," he said. The view was again sunny and lush. "Almost a perfect duplicate of Earth, perhaps a little younger. And with two smaller moons instead of one large one."

Bubna spoke up. "How extensive a survey have you done?"

"Not very," Steve responded. "We've looked around this area mostly. Some slow-moving small animals but no obvious dangers. We can map the planet using the device, but haven't had time yet—we need more people to do all these things! And we're about to see if it's even safe to cross the gateway, using our little friend here." He held up a mouse wriggling in a mesh bag.

"I guess it would be wise to be sure it is safe for an animal before planning to use it ourselves," Bubna said.

Steve typed at the console. "I'm resetting the parameters to allow solid objects to cross the gateway plane. The air pressure there is slightly lower, so expect a slight breeze from here to there." He hit the return key, and something changed—not visibly, but in the quality of sound in the room. The air did seem to move a bit toward the machine. "I haven't figured out yet how to set the parameters to keep a pressure difference from pushing air through. Not a huge problem for this site, but it will be, even on Earth itself, like at higher elevations."

Samantha said, "Can you hear that? A kind of rustling?" They listened. There was a faint sound, not leaves but something like them, rustling in the light breeze they could see through the gateway.

"Well, time for our friend here to try it out," Justin said, taking the bagged mouse from Steve and fastening the bag to the end of the pole with a metal tie. He again stood behind the console and slowly pushed the end of the pole through the gateway as they all watched the mouse.

Closer and closer, and moving even more slowly. As the mouse crossed the plane, a high-pitched squeal filled the room; the mouse convulsed and then went still, and silent.

"That didn't sound good," Steve said.

Justin brought the pole slowly back into the room. The limp body of the mouse accused them; no one needed to check that it was dead.

* * * * *

The mood was grim. While the rest spoke quietly with each other, Steve and Justin went to the back of the lab to discuss the problem. Justin said, "It didn't die from the atmosphere or being on the planet. It died crossing the gateway plane."

"That's what it looked like. Even a poison in the atmosphere would have taken longer to affect it."

"The camera came through without a problem. What's different about an animal?"

"Maybe neurons are especially sensitive to transition issues. Wires, solid objects, no problem, but neurons transferred through might have their firings interrupted or something. If you think in particle terms, all sorts of local fields are being mediated by short-lived particles, to a level we don't understand yet. I have the transit plane tolerance set to about the size of a nucleon; maybe it should be much finer, so detachment and attachment occur much more quickly. Let me fiddle with it…"

Justin watched him review and change some of the parameters to the transition program. Thinking it would take awhile, he went back to break it to the others. Samantha and Rasna looked unhappy, talking to Bubna, while Ben stood silently listening. "Listen," Justin said, "Steve thinks neural transmissions might be disrupted by crossing, but he thinks he can adjust the program to keep them more continuous…"

"And… done!" Steve said, turning to them. "I had already thought of this but forgot to change the parameters. I bet that fixes it." He looked over to the dead mouse on the table. "Sorry, little guy. Or girl."

Steve loaded the new program to the device and reopened the gateway. They tried again with another mouse. This time, the mouse kept wriggling, didn't squeak, and came back as apparently alive as ever. Justin suggested a longer-term test, so they put the mouse back in the cage with the others, then used the pole to lower the cage and its inhabitants to the ground of New Earth. They left the mice there with the camera recording it all, and shut down the lab for the night.

The next day, Steve and Justin were relieved to see the mice had made it through the planet's night, uneaten and healthy. The recordings showed them moving about, then sleeping, then waking, with no appearances by local animals. Justin retrieved them and added new food to the cage before returning them to the back storage room. Steve commented, "It is probably a bad idea for any complex nervous system to transit the gateway at a high rate of speed which could overload the program. I should put that in the notes…."

Chapter Ten: Holiday Break

Breakup

Christmas decorations made the restaurant Samantha had chosen for Dylan's celebration dinner more festive than was appropriate, she thought. Fake holly and mistletoe did not quite set the mood she had been looking for. It was normally a sober, wood-panelled sort of traditional steakhouse, but now it seemed like the the better class of English pub, merry and bright, with two gas fireplaces going. She was tempted to order a Guinness.

Dylan came in at the front, and she caught his eye. He joined her at the table and said, "We came here for your birthday last year."

"Right. And it's one of the few reliable places left. I remember you loved the steak. So I thought this would be a good place to celebrate the end of your thesis pain."

"It's not quite over—still have defense and who knows what to go. But it's uploaded and locked. The tearing-my-hair-out phase is over. I was so sick of seeing Grant, and he was sick of me."

"Now you can rejoin us meat puppets in the land of the social beings."

"I'm sorry, babe. I know I have not been around for you much…."

"That's really okay. I understood you had to focus. What's the advance word on how they're going to receive it?"

"Good, mostly. 'An important contribution,' and that from Prof. Ito.

She rarely has anything nice to say about anyone, so that was praise. Edwards didn't reply at all, but I suspect he's unhappy that I have stepped on one of 'his' ideas. Too bad! But at least he didn't try to trash my work."

She paused to consider again whether to rip the bandage off fast or wait until they'd had time to mellow. She decided to wait. "What's the outlook on the post-doc? I suppose a tenure-track position is out of the question...."

"None of the old buggers in the field will retire. There might be two hundred professorships in the whole English-speaking world worth trying for. Maybe ten will open up this year, with a hundred applicants for each one. You have to have an in. And they won't hire me here."

"And the post-doc...?"

"Grant is asking around. He probably can't find the money in his budget this year, until one of his other post-docs leaves. Things are still tight. There are a few positions in private research labs. But just too many graduates looking."

"Guess you can worry about that later, about-to-be-Dr. Foster." The waiter came by to ask if they wanted drinks. Samantha asked, "How about a bottle of Champagne?" The waiter pointed to the wine list, and they looked through it. Prices for imported Champagnes were startling.

Dylan looked down toward the bottom of the list. "Any Proseccos you'd recommend?"

The waiter shook his head slightly. "If you're having steak and you want something bubbly, I can recommend the sparkling Pinot Noir from California. Crisp, a hint of pomegranate, enough body to stand up to a steak."

Dylan checked the price. "That sounds good. Bring us a bottle."

As they talked and the meal arrived in stages, Sam began to feel the stress of not saying what she needed to say. Every time she had tried to talk about what was going wrong between them, he had shut her down and changed the subject. It was actually part of the problem— he would not talk about how he felt, or have the patience to at least pretend he cared what she felt.

They had nearly finished the food, and the alcohol was adding to the effect—she felt sleepy and relaxed enough to forge ahead. "It's been a month since we've slept together."

Dylan put his fork down. "I know, I'm sorry. Stressed and obsessed. I'll make it up to you."

"I have to tell you something I didn't want to tell you while you were so stressed. I think it's time we took a break from each other."

Dylan looked down at his plate. His face turned red. "A break?" His voice was rising. "You're breaking up with me?… It's Justin, right?"

"I'm getting to know Justin, but I've doubted you and I had a future together for months. He has nothing to do with it. I just don't feel… much for you now. You didn't seem to hear me, or want to know about me, other than to have me around for your convenience." *Ouch*, she thought. *I could have softened that a bit.*

"I listen to everything you say! It's just that there's so much *blather*…" He stood up, throwing his napkin down on the table.

"That's what I mean. Disrespect. You're the only important person in your life, and you think of me as a just a player in your play. That's not what I want to be for someone."

Dylan pulled out some bills and threw them on the table. "That should cover it. If you think you can come back to me, ever, you can't. You fucking cunt." He turned and walked out.

She sat there for a minute, stunned. She realized she was crying. People at other tables were staring. Why had she decided to do this in a public place again? *Oh, that's right—in case he got violent. Mission accomplished.*

Holiday Rush

The last few days before the holiday break were always hectic; everyone had deadlines, tests, and travel plans. Sam and Justin met up for lunch at the cafeteria.

"It was bad, but it could have been worse," Sam said. "He was an asshole, but I knew he would be. And it was over fast. No trying to reason with me or pleading to give us another chance."

"Like a normal guy would."

"I'm glad it was in public place. He tried to hurt me with words. It might have been a fist if there hadn't been people watching."

Justin cocked his head and looked at her. "You didn't tell me you expected anything like that. I might have wanted to be there to punch him out."

"He's lashed out at me before when I didn't meet his expectations. He would punish me verbally if he thought I was taking too much of an interest in anyone else. Like I was being disloyal if I didn't stay by his side and admire him constantly."

"He's a handsome guy. Maybe a little spoiled because of that?"

"Worse than just spoiled. I've known lots of thoughtful handsome guys. Like you, for example. No giant ego, and you care about people's feelings."

"You're just after my body."

"Well, now I am!"

"I don't have to work late every night, you know. The fate of the planet can wait—tonight I can be free for dinner. Come over to my place? I make wicked spaghetti and meatballs."

"Sounds good. At last I get to see the den you live in."

"I have some cleaning to do first. Come about seven."

* * * * *

Sam made her way up to the third floor of the graduate dorm Justin lived in. The stairs had bikes chained to the railings most of the way up, but there was enough room to get by as long as one was careful to watch for protruding handlebars. She went right, as she had been directed, and found Justin's door open near the end of the hall.

"What ho," she said. "I bring wine." She went in and looked around; an efficiency, slightly larger than an undergrad dorm room, but not by much. There was a tiny kitchen with a hotplate and a microwave, a table just large enough for two, a loveseat which was presumably a foldout bed, a bathroom off to the side, and that was all.

Justin came out of the bathroom. "Just finishing up. Had to wipe out the advanced civilization that had grown up in my toilet. They had progressed to manipulating symbols—I think they were trying to spell out 'WHY?' in the scrubbing bubbles in their last moments."

"We'll never know all that they might have accomplished if you'd allowed them to evolve."

"They would just recapitulate everything we've done. A micro-Shake-speare writing micro-plays about tiny little kings and lovers."

"I hope whoever's watching us evolve is more sympathetic." Sam started to unscrew the cap on the wine bottle.

"'Intellects vast and cool and unsympathetic, regarded this earth with envious eyes....' I see no reason why they would want to interfere, if there are such watchers. We mean nothing to them. I doubt if we're infecting their metaphorical toilets. Or have resources they would want."

"So where are your wine glasses?"

"Wine glasses? They're of a unique modern design. They look like tumblers." He opened the cabinet and took out two glasses. "Sorry, that's all I have."

They made spaghetti together. It was clumsy, and they laughed a lot. They ate, and the spaghetti was good, even with bottled sauce. Justin washed the dishes and put them away. "Shall we sit by the fire and talk? Let me refill your wine glass...."

The love seat was comfortable. Samantha relaxed into his arms. "Now this is quite nice." She pointed at the taped-up picture of flaming logs on the wall. "The fire isn't as warm as I would have expected, though."

"I bet I can warm you up." He made an effort. "You're coming with me to my family's Christmas dinner, right?"

"I'll go with you—you're driving, right? My parents are on holiday in Mexico. Daddy is hot for diving lately."

He went back to work on the kissing and exploring. The long wait made it all the more sweet to finally do more than steal a kiss.

"It's like you've done this before," she said.

"I can see the future. We will do it often."

Family Christmas

Christmas Day, Justin picked Samantha up at her apartment and they took the freeway over a pass in the first coastal range to the suburban town Justin had grown up in. Because it was inland, it had never been a wealthy place like the coast—it was hot in summer and sometimes colder in winter, being cut off from the marine influence. But he had good memories, and even after years of decline, the middle-class inhabitants of all races and ethnicities shared a pride in keeping it looking tended.

He parked on the street in front of a large two-story house; there were already cars parked on the double driveway. "Dad took over part of the garage for his workshop and Mom uses the rest for storage, so they park outside. That's my sister's family's car there." He pointed at an old Toyota SUV. "And that's grandpa's." He pointed to a battered pickup.

"Nice. Very whitebread Americana."

"Next door are the Garcias. This town is only whitebread if you count tortillas."

✳ ✳ ✳ ✳

When the door opened, the smell of cooking turkey and pies wafted out. A graying blond woman greeted them first. "Justin! You're late! And you must be Samantha. So nice to meet you…" She hugged Samantha. "Jim, get over here."

Justin's father came in from the living room. He was a big man with a bit of a potbelly. "Justin, looking good, son. And you brought the prettiest guest. Welcome, Samantha. Justin has told us a lot about you."

"Now, Dad," Justin said. "Don't scare her off."

"Just making her feel welcome. She knows I don't bite. And here's Emily, Justin's sister, and Jeff, her husband. The kids are downstairs playing some game. Your grandpa is taking a nap upstairs."

Introductions went on for some time. Sam and Justin ended up in the living room sipping hot chocolates and talking to Justin's father while his mother and sister finished dinner preparations.

Justin put his cup down on a well-placed coaster. "There's something I have to tell you, Dad."

"That doesn't sound good."

"It is and it isn't. I—we—may be leaving soon. We're involved in a special project that we think is more important than school right now. We might leave at any time."

"Now, wait just a minute here. You told me your Prof. Wilson has disappeared—and I wasn't supposed to worry. Are you involved in something that might get you disappeared, too?"

"I hope not. That's what we're trying to prevent. I haven't been able to talk to you about any of it because we think our phones are tapped. They monitor our texts and emails, too."

"Why would they do that?"

"Prof. Wilson was caught contacting a former student of his, who's now leader of the Grey Tribe. We got sucked in. And then we found out some things that are dangerous to know—so I can't tell you anything about them. They may come and question you, so you shouldn't know."

Justin's father looked grim. "I raised you to stand up for what's right. Unless you can't win, anyway. Can you win? Is this worth leaving school for?"

"We think so." Justin looked toward Samantha. "Sam here will be coming with me." He squeezed her hand.

"I see. I do see. It's a shame you've almost got your degree, but if it's something you have to do, then I'm with you. Whatever it is."

"Thanks, Dad. I'll be careful, and we'll come back."

"Don't tell your mom yet. I'll explain it to her later; now is not the right time, it would upset her. Will we hear from you?"

"Eventually. It might be weeks or months before we can safely get messages to you. If we leave, the Feds will start watching you, too."

"While you're fighting the government, see if you could get our retirement accounts back. I suspect their promise of an additional payment from Social Security is as much of a lie as everything else they put out."

Justin laughed. "Not sure I can fix that, Dad. They already spent it."

✳ ✳ ✳ ✳ ✳

The family gathered around the dining room table, which Justin had helped his mom expand using two extra leaves. Justin's niece and nephew came up from the basement playroom, and the boy ended up next to Justin, with Samantha on his other side.

Justin motioned to Samantha. "You haven't met Noah and Sarah, my sister's kids. Kids, this is Samantha."

Sarah spoke up from across the table. "Good to meet you. Are you Justin's girlfriend?"

"Sarah!" Justin scowled.

"Yes, maybe, almost," Samantha said, laughing. "I thought you said they had manners?"

"Usually they do," Justin said. "Noah's twelve, so we have higher standards for him."

Noah took this as his cue. "Sarah's rude. Better than she used to be, though!"

"Your sister is not rude," Justin said. "She's just learning how to show good manners. You don't have that excuse." He gave Noah a look of disapproval.

At the other end of the table, Gramps harrumphed. "Can we get everybody sitting down? The food is getting cold!"

* * * * *

After pie, Justin's sister, Emily, got into a side discussion with Samantha. They had been speaking of schooling.

"Our mother home-schooled us until high school," Emily said. "She had been a teacher, and it just seemed natural that she'd give up the low pay and save on taxes and expenses to educate us herself. She was worried about the lack of rigor in the public school curriculum, and the political messages teachers were required to teach. She wanted us to think for ourselves."

Justin broke in. "I'm very grateful that she did. It was a shock going to public school, but I knew a lot more than those kids did, and I already knew what was bullshit in what they were teaching. I had to go there to get the credits and grades in labs and such, but I kept on learning what I wanted instead of what they taught."

"And for 'socialization.'" Emily added. "We had plenty of friends before, but they were kids like us, homeschooled. Very different from public school kids. If we had not gone to public high school, we would not have known how to handle them."

"I went to private schools in Westwood and Santa Monica," Sam said. "They weren't typical public schools either. But my friends were a spoiled bunch. Some, like me, had parents who paid attention and cared about what was happening with their kids. Others, not so much —their parents gave them toys and bought them cars, but otherwise they were on their own. I envy you having your mom's full attention that long."

"It was great. I'd like that for my kids." Justin realized he was getting into dangerous territory. "When the time comes, of course. If it's practical."

Samantha gave him a look that meant—what? He wasn't sure.

His mom joined them and said, "Your dad helped with cleanup, but then he wanted to see what the kids are up to downstairs. You're stuck with me."

Justin squeezed her shoulders and said, "We were just talking about how wonderful it was for us that you quit your teaching job to teach us."

"It was a great relief to me, too. The middle school children were getting more and more difficult to deal with, and they kept adding politicized material to the curriculum. There was less time for real learning about literature and history—and no time at all for economics. The science was less about science every year, and more about climate change, and renewable energy, and composting. We stopped learning about real scientists of the past and introduced mysticism about Mother Earth and how evil humanity was destroying the planet. Every year the legislature would pass more laws adding to what had to be taught, and the Federal government was requiring testing. There was no room left to let children think and learn for themselves."

"Well, we're glad you did it," Justin said. "I got to read Adam Smith and Jane Austen, Heinlein and Asimov, Dante and Machiavelli, Dawkins and Dennett. And college history books! And you let me follow where all that reading led. So we aced the tests."

"Of course you did. You didn't have your curiosity blunted by the committee-written textbooks they were using. You read original sources, and the deepest thinkers. I learned *with* you two. And I didn't have to fight the bad influences of the children whose parents let them run wild. There were many days in middle school where more than half of class time went to dealing with bad behavior and disruptions."

"But I thought you enjoyed teaching," Emily said.

"I did. After you two started high school, I taught younger children in the much better district on the ocean side of the mountains—it was a commute, but it was a pleasure not to have to deal with gangs and abused kids. The wealthy neighborhoods make sure their public schools are good, and leave all the bad teachers for the poor neighborhoods. It was unfair, but teaching in bad schools was burning me out. I wouldn't have gone back there."

"I owe much of my ability to think clearly and solve problems to you, Mom," Justin said. "More than most. You didn't take the easy default option."

"This family never does," she said.

＊ ＊ ＊ ＊ ＊

The sun had set and the western sky was a deepening blue-green when they left. Carrying bags of leftovers and presents back to the car, Samantha commented, "I really like your family."

"Good. You may have to put up with them."

"I liked seeing you with the kids. I can see what you'd be like, as a dad."

Chapter Eleven: Resource Limitations

Quantum Lab: Limitations

Steve and Justin continued to refine the Vortex-5's gateway software during the holiday break. Justin wondered why Steve did not visit cousins he had mentioned in LA; when he asked, Steve said, "I visited them a few times, but I stopped. Waste of time."

Meanwhile, bringing Prof. Bubna in was helping. Bubna had worked his contacts to find the production schedules for the duplicate Vortex-5s being ordered by government agencies. He also sent out the orders for the next version, the Vortex-6, which would quadruple the number of qubits available in the braided array.

Justin asked Steve why they might want a larger array—wasn't it impossible to overload this device is it could recruit computing power from particles everywhere? Steve looked at him with the pained expression he had when he was having to explain something obvious. "The complexity of the initial program we can run is limited by the size of the array. The more space we have, the more detailed the specifications can be, the larger the area of a gateway, or the more complex the program logic. You could say the extra computing power we can recruit now is dumb, in a sense. Like vector processors added on to a conventional machine. They can do the same calculations on a much larger amount of data, but they can't handle dependencies between subsets of the data. Ultimately we will figure out how to upload programs into the computational fabric of the substrate and remove that limitation, but I haven't had time to look into how that might be done."

"What could we do with a lot more program space, though?" What the machine did already seemed miraculous to him.

"One thing I'm thinking about is matter assembly. We can easily *transport* objects in all their complexity because we just transfer each particle as it goes through a plane, keeping the same momentum and internal structure. Suppose we *duplicate* instead—have the device characterize each particle, transport an equivalent particle from somewhere else and attach it to the new assembly, and keep on until the entire object is duplicated in a new location."

"Copying matter. But where would these new particles come from?"

"Insides of metal-rich Population I stars, maybe. Almost every type of atom and particle would be available in one area. Or maybe just keep a library of locations where the device has found concentrations of what it needs. That's the computational issue: having to go out and relocate so many diverse particles in so many places would overtax even the Vortex-5."

"So we could duplicate ourselves. This sounds like another idea we should not be thinking about until our current problems are taken care of."

Steve nodded, and they went back to editing code.

Quantum Lab: Bubna

Prof. Bubna dropped by to update them after hours. "To keep visitors away, I'm giving all the funding agencies a story about the machine being down for repairs to the electron pump, and I'm keeping Friedman in the dark. He's taken a real holiday, so we're not expecting to see him back until next week, but he's seeing email traffic. He was upset that the Vortex-6 orders went out before he had authorized them. I made up a story about the fabs requesting pre-orders to put them on the production calendar for summer, just placeholders which we could cancel if DARPA didn't fund it. He bought that."

Steve pulled up a calendar onscreen. "So when will those assemblies be available?"

"Weeks at least, even with a rush bonus. Turns out the government Vortex-5's are mostly finished—all the critical pieces are sitting in warehouses. The cryo components and magnets are done, too."

"So we can steal them now," Justin said. "Just a matter of looking around in warehouses for hours to find the right crates."

Bubna wrote a note on his pad. "I can put together a list of the locations and part numbers to give you a start."

Steve looked back at his screen and opened a new window. "I've hooked up the device software to the Google Maps APIs. This will let us type in addresses and zoom in on satellite views to aim at locations inside buildings. Should save a lot of time."

"The problem with that," Justin said, "is that every search you do through them is recorded. HomeSec isn't watching that now, but I bet in the long run their AIs will notice when robberies happen at locations somebody searched first."

Steve thought for a moment. "It's clear we're going to have to use the Internet somehow. Open a tiny gateway to intercept wifi from shielded sites in the neutral countries like Sweden or Switzerland. Move it often so there's no pattern of use from one location. There'd be no way to trace it back to us."

"Which leads me to more logistics questions," Bubna said. "First, why doesn't it make more sense to hide out in a base on Earth? New Earth looks pleasant enough, but there are certain to be hazards we don't know about. I accept your view that parasites and viruses and the like that might attack us won't have evolved there, but we could still be eaten. By alien tigers. Or fungi. We still don't know a thing about the chemistry of the life there."

"True, we could hide out in a cave in a neutral country and be almost as safe," Justin said. "But that's 'almost.' If they ever found our location, that would be the end. Look at what happened to those rebel preppers in Idaho—they made the mistake of broadcasting on shortwave, and got droned for their troubles. Bunker-busters took out their caves."

"And being in a neutral country makes no difference with the drones," Steve added. "They've used them wherever they could claim local authorities weren't apprehending the 'enemy combatants.'" He added, "And as for chemistry, we can be pretty sure the life on New Earth is very similar, given the trace atmospheric composition. Studying that will be a priority. If we're going to live there, we have to plan how to grow food. It would be nice if we could digest some of the native plants."

"I see much bigger problems," Bubna said. "And let me suggest you want to look for a different kind of location. We're going to need tents, generators, batteries, solar panels—so a lot of sunshine would help. And places teeming with life are also teeming with dangers. In a forest you can't see what's coming."

"Good point," Justin said. "We haven't surveyed the forest yet, much less the planet. We need more data on weather and climate. It might be wise to select our location carefully for safety and access to what we need right now, rather than beauty. Maybe a desert area near a freshwater stream and the sea, but not far from forest and fertile areas."

"And for the short term," Bubna added, "we'll be dependent on shipping everything in from Earth. We have technology for that—camping stores have freeze-dried food, water purifiers, and everything you need to live cut off from supplies."

"And for the longer term," Steve looked up in the air as he did when he was imagining the future, "we have all the problems of a colony world. Parasitic, dependent on stealing until we find something worth trading. No industrial base, no high-technology manufacturing, no ability to duplicate the devices we will depend on. And loss of contact with Earth would doom us to a Stone Age existence. Not a big enough gene pool to avoid inbreeding. I did some research on this, and it might be decades before we would truly be independent."

"But what about the matter assembly and other tricks the device might do?" Justin said. "Wouldn't that let us leapfrog some of that industrial technology problem?"

"Some, not all," Steve said. "An economic system that can duplicate but not create complex technologies will still eventually fail when the templates break or are lost, and certainly stagnate. We'll have to find a way to manufacture complex tech ourselves, maybe by assembly from specifications. That's what we do now with chips, with the plans for etching and deposition designed in CAD programs. With the device we can eventually assemble chips atom-by-atom instead of using complex fab technologies, which should actually make design easier and eliminate the need for fab equipment. But that would take a dozen top engineers years to develop."

"Another thing we can't do yet, even with magic," Justin said. "It's still a 'mere matter of programming' away."

"Ideally we win," Steve said, "and everyone on Earth gets the benefits of the device. We live in peace and harmony with our brothers and sisters forever, trading and learning and expanding into the universe. But you always plan for the worst case, not the best. And until we end tribal government and have a way to control use of the device by bad guys, we'll be outlaws."

"But back to our current task list," Bubna said, referring to his pad again. "I was consulting for a small startup on the east side of town. The company went bankrupt and the space is legally entangled, but I contacted the bank trustee and they can lease it to us on a short-term basis to get a little cash flow. I'm telling him we're doing a stealth startup, very hush-hush—true enough. I put down a cash deposit and we have the keys." He held up a large key ring. "I'm going to need Wilding to help out with the setup, but without telling him much other than to duplicate what we have here. So don't let anything slip when he's around."

Steve checked the calendar again. "What's the timeframe for getting set up there?"

"A few days. Services, moving furniture, getting new computers and duplicating all the software. When we get the components, we can have another Vortex-5 assembled in a few more days." Bubna scribbled another note on the pad, and left.

Quantum Lab: Wendy

Justin and Steve were starting to get hungry when Samantha arrived with takeout for dinner. She brought Wendy Fields with her; this time Wendy was dressed conservatively in a plain wool skirt and jacket.

"Welcome to the pirate lab, Wendy," Justin said. "I take it this means you decided to accept our offer?"

"I'll do it. The interesting part is helping you set up shell businesses and bank accounts while keeping myself totally out of it. It may surprise you to know I have an uncle who dealt in profitable but illegal merchandise."

"That only surprises me a little," Justin said. "You have a lot of accomplished relatives."

"This uncle did very well and never got caught. He knew how to set up new recruits to get arrested, and they never knew enough to trace anything back to him. Even in a security state, black markets create their own channels and there's always a way to pay for what you need."

"So how can we do apparently legitimate business transactions without ever being traced?" Steve asked.

"Shell companies inside shell companies. Two levels of anonymity to be safe, in those jurisdictions where recorded owners are never checked. Nevada is one place that allows that, which you might think odd, except the cronies of state government there have preserved it for their own purposes. And there are still a few neutral islands supporting anonymity. You start a new company and bank account for every operation, to make the detection of one less damaging. Once you have a corporate entity, you open bank accounts in its name and do all business electronically. Your passwords give you access from anywhere on the Internet. It's probably safer to hide in the flow of normal banking transactions than to try to use a cryptocurrency—those are watched and busted frequently."

"But we need local agents for some things, don't we," Justin said. "Like actually setting up companies, filing reports, and so forth?"

"That's true, but you can hire them anonymously, online. They never need to know anything, and they know not to expect to know anything about their clients except the money transfers that pay them." Wendy used one finger to move her long black hair out of her eyes. "I know where I can find some private bankers who will be eager to help if we pay them well."

Justin was amused. "I thought you were going into fashion design."

"Fashion is a business," she said. "If you don't know how to find the right partners and get the production done right and wherever in the world it's done best and cheapest, you're going to lose your shirt. Or blouse, as the case may be. This is an opportunity for me to get a quick start building capital for my business. And I'm flexible, it may end up being my business. I can design later!"

"So we have something to get you started," Justin said, opening a drawer in the console. "We can get you lots of these." He had to exert himself, but lifted a small gold bar into view. "These things are heavy."

Wendy tried to pick it up. "I've never seen one." She managed to take it from him on her second try. "Did you know these bars are manufactured to a variety of standards, and some of them are traceable? See this serial number?" She turned it to show the face that had a stamped number and manufacturing seal. "You want the kind that aren't. Fungible, anonymous, possession-is-ownership gold."

"That didn't occur to me," Justin said. "I thought a bar is a bar. I just looked for one small enough to pick up with our gripper."

"Well, run these things by me before you set off alarms and get caught," Wendy said. "You're safest stealing from private stores. Larger vaults will have inside cameras and motion detectors."

Steve typed a command into the console. The view of New Earth was replaced by the wall of gold bars they had seen before. "These are in a bank in New York. Are you saying these are off-limits?"

"Definitely too dangerous. I bet if you pan back you will see security cams on all the walls; you steal a bar from there, and they'll have a video of a gripper reaching for it out of thin air. That would blow your scheme fast. You want to steal from people who won't even realize anything's missing, which means small banks in backward countries, or small private holdings. If you want to be moral about it, from thieves and corrupt rulers. Why can't you just find nuggets in the earth and steal those?"

"Then we'd have to refine them, or sell them as is, which would bring up questions about where they came from," Justin said. "More trouble than just grabbing bars."

Wendy put the bar in her shoulder bag. "This is a one-kilogram bar, worth a few hundred thousand. That should be enough to fund your operations for a month. I may have to have it recast or sell it to someone who will give us less for it, since it's numbered, but since it's small that may not be a problem. Just don't steal central bank gold— it's tracked. I can see you guys need somebody who knows what they're doing. I'm worth every gold bar you're going to be paying me."

Dylan Eavesdrops

Dylan Foster had gone to be with his parents in St. Barts for the holidays. He fumed about Samantha and the casual way she had dumped him—for a nobody like Justin. But he pretended everything was fine and tried to meet someone interesting at the many parties, since many of the partiers were children of the billionaires that favored the island for the holidays. When his parents asked about Samantha, he told them he was thinking she might not be right for him, so he was probably moving on.

After he returned to California, he started to get angry again. *The nerve of that bitch.* He had warned her not to cross him. If she was going to dump him, he was going to make life hard for her.

Briefly he considered just letting go of it and looking for a new girl. But her betrayal was like an itch—he had to scratch it. He would follow her—weeks ago he had used his access to her phone to download a remote tracking app, so he could see where her phone was from any browser. He fired up the locator program, and found her near the quad, only a few blocks away.

He walked over and saw her in the distance, talking with a black chick—no, that was campus celebrity Wendy, not a chick but an amazingly fashion-forward re-creation. They started to walk across the street, so he followed. When they went inside a building, he held back until they had taken the elevator up. He went to the same floor a minute later and listened.

Nothing. Just the faintest of hums, machine sounds, gases moving. At the end of the hall a brightly-lit room threw light into the hallway. He made he way toward it. Cautiously he looked through the interior glass to see what was in the room. Nothing, but down at the end where the view was blocked by a partition, he saw motion and heard voices.

He could see side offices with windows looking onto the room, and it occurred to him some of those featureless doors he had just passed might lead to those offices. He made his way back to a door that in about the right place, and he carefully tried the knob—unlocked! He eased the door open and peeked through the crack. Through the dimly-lit office's interior window, he could see a glowing rectangle and a console in front of it; Steve Duong was seated at the console, and Sam and Wendy were standing nearby, talking to Justin.

He moved into the office slowly and slouched down in a chair at the desk. He had a perfect view, but the sound of their conversation was muffled. He noticed there was also a door to the room, and opened it a crack—there, now he could hear what they were saying. He sat back and listened, and watched.

Chapter Twelve: Traitors

ALife Simulation, Model 7: Organism 810552801343

The pace of change had quickened, and while she was born in a village with no running water or electricity, the city she had moved to had streetlights, indoor plumbing, and tall buildings (up to seven stories!) Her husband worked in a factory, but she quit her factory job after their marriage. Managing the household was huge job, now that there were four children, and she had worn herself out taking care of them and keeping up with the cooking, cleaning, and laundry.

She did not have time to read past the headlines in the newspaper, but one day war was rumored and the people in the market seemed worried about attacks on the border. She carried her purchases home in a basket and was crossing the street toward her house when the whistling sound began, and after a second of dread as the sound grew, her world exploded. When she came to, she was surprised to be alive. But when she looked over to where her home had been, all that remained was piles of smoking rubble.

Homeland Security

In his office in DC, Jim McDonald savored his second cup of coffee while paging through the morning's reports. He leaned back and stretched, pausing to look out the window at the glazed white world that was the city after snow. His gaze wandered to his picture wall, restrained compared to most; photos of him shaking hands with several Presidents and Congressmen, his units from Iraq, his Army retirement party, plaques and awards from his later career.

He kept his family photos on his desk—his wife in happier days, a group photo with his children.

He leaned forward to get back to the tedious job of responding to the few reports that required it. Several were ass-covering copy-to memos, a phenomenon he could not seem to stamp out even when he singled out the worst offenders. They would restrain themselves for a few weeks, then go back to broadcasting their inability to handle any decision without spreading the responsibility around by informing everyone else; if something went wrong, it had somehow become a group error.

One note had come in after DC hours, from Andrew Gao in California.

```
To: DirSpecOps James McDonald
From: Field Investigator Andrew Gao
Re: Neutral Armor

Two items:

— Justin Smith purchased 8 prepaid phones
from Walmart. The next day, we detected
```

anonymous access of known Grey Tribe stream
sources from a library computer at the university. We conclude it was likely Smith or
Ben Ramirez trying to set up a Grey Tribe
cell. Await your authorization to arrest
and question.

— Dylan Foster (see attachment) called this
afternoon. He claims to know very important
information about Prof. Wilson and his
friends and a quantum computer that could
be used as a weapon. He said he would give
us this information if we would agree to
make him lead researcher after we arrest
everyone running it. Foster appears to be a
peripheral actor but we have taken this
seriously enough to have him by for a meeting today, recordings to follow. We need
authorization to arrest him at that time if
that seems advisable.

He pondered this for a few minutes. Arresting people was unlikely to
get them any closer to locating Michael McCulloch so he could be
removed, which was the President's goal, and therefore Immerman's,
and therefore his. But these people were surely up to something, and
mention of a weapon made it impossible to ignore, so some response
from him was required—sometimes he had to do his own ass-covering. Wilson had provided nothing useful and McCulloch must have
realized that the carefully-crafted messages apparently from Wilson
were intended to get him to reveal himself. It was possible this group
had somehow warned McCulloch through a Grey Tribe connection,
which would all by itself be a crime.

But getting McCulloch was the goal. He decided he would let matters proceed for awhile longer. When Prof. Wilson was returned to his job they would have a much better chance of getting information when he and his friends thought they weren't being watched.

He began to compose his response memo, then decided to call Gao in case he was available.

"Gao."

"McDonald here. I just read your memo. Foster is trying to sell us something, but he doesn't want to get specific unless he thinks he's getting a reward. Play along. We have to take any mention of weapons seriously."

"Okay. The meeting is scheduled for one your time, and we can set it up for telepresence if you'd like to be in on it."

"I'll watch but not participate unless I see a good reason. I've got too much paperwork to do here," McDonald said.

"What should we do about Smith and Ramirez?"

"I'm inclined to wait to get more information. Do we have a way of adding those phones to our watch list?"

"Yes, but it takes some time—we have to go through the carriers requesting each look for activation of this model in a small area. They are slow to respond, and have resisted giving us direct access to their databases."

"Not for much longer, I think, given the new Congress. Send out the requests and start monitoring those phones when you can. Report back and we'll look at whether arrests make sense, when they might be telling us everything we need to know on their 'secure' phones."

Quantum Lab: Transfer

It was tedious work using the gateway to look through warehouses and workshops for the parts on the list provided by Prof. Bubna. The gallium arsenide grid plates weren't hard to spot, since they were two meters square and thin; packaging made them even larger.

Justin and Steve had been working on the smaller parts all day, and they had used the gripper arm to grab the smaller items one by one. The heavier boxes had to be grabbed by hand, but they had assembled a pile of boxes holding coils, cryopumps, circuit boards, and other parts before tackling the large and heavy grids.

"Tell me again how you planned to modify the software so the edge of the gateway doesn't slice through anything it touches," Justin said.

"That's another improvement I haven't had time to get to. It's complicated to treat the edge cases specially so it doesn't just cut through objects that intersect the edges. The result would be resistance, as if the edge were a solid. But the additional program logic would take a day or two to write and test. And we don't have that much time."

"I am willing to take risks, but it would be a sad end to my career if I was sliced in half because I stumbled trying to walk through the gateway."

"I am increasing its size to close to maximum, so you should have plenty of room for mistakes. Three meters square."

And when Justin turned to look, the gateway was taller and wider than before, showing two large boxes leaned against a concrete block wall. "I'm remembering that comment about complex nervous systems and speed of transit."

"You should be okay. If you're worried we can test it on a mouse." So they did, and the mouse seemed fine.

"Okay, I'm going. Rubber gloves on. Take one more look back to see if anyone's around."

Steve panned around, and as before, no one was visible. "No watch-men or cameras."

"I feel like I ought to have black makeup and a watch cap on. I'm going pick up the box and start it though the gateway. You pick it up on this side so we can guide it through without touching the edges."

"Okay." Steve came over to stand close to the gateway.

Justin stepped carefully over the gateway threshold, and onto the concrete floor on the other side of the continent. He looked around, looked back to make sure he could see back through the gateway into the lab, and then started to move the first box. *Uh-oh,* he thought. *This is too heavy.* "Tell me again about the software refinement for recognizing contiguous objects and moving them all at once. We need that."

"Trouble?" Steve said. "They're supposed to be twenty-four kilograms, fifty pounds. Is that too much?"

"This large and hard to grip, I think so. It needs handles. I can lift the weight but I can't hold it away from me to push it through."

"All you have to do is get it partway across where I can grab on."

"Wait a sec," Justin said. "I see a dolly down the way." He disappeared from view, and returned a few seconds later rolling a flat platform. He labored to get the box onto the dolly, holding it upright, and rolled the dolly toward the gateway until the forward edge of the box went through.

"I got it," Steve said. "Roll a little further, the wheels aren't even close to the edge yet."

Steve was able to tilt the box down to the ground on the California side, and then Justin held the box up while he pulled away the dolly from underneath. Then they were able to pull and push it into California, most of the weight taken by the floor of the lab.

"Whew," Justin said. "One down, one to go. No one told me freedom fighters had to do so much manual labor."

When they had finished retrieving the list of components from the assorted warehouses around the country, they opened the gateway to the new off-campus lab and transferred everything to a storage room there. It started to go faster as they grew more experienced with the motions.

"I've been through four times now, and I feel fine," Justin said. "Let me know if I act funny or start to drool."

They carefully uncrated the grid plates and nailed the crates back together to return them to where they had found them, hoping to delay discovery of their theft for as long as possible.

Dylan and Gao

Dylan had thought through his strategy for getting maximum advantage from what he had learned in eavesdropping at the quantum lab. While he still wanted to hurt Sam—and Justin—for their betrayal, the prospect of getting control over the technology they were using—probably invented by that loser Steve—was a lot more enticing. If he played his cards correctly, he could end up being official discoverer. The Nobel prize would be just the beginning; nothing could stop him if he controlled who got to use it and for what. But he'd have others sniffing around and jockeying for a piece of the action as soon as it became obvious how much power would come with controlling it. So he'd have to be very careful to get into the right position where he couldn't be knocked out.

He had agreed to meet with Andrew Gao at the downtown HomeSec office, and he went over his script in his head as he went up in the elevator. The receptionist gave him water and took him to a meeting room, where he waited for a minute.

Andrew Gao and a stocky black woman entered and closed the door. "Thank you for coming down to meet with us, Dylan," Gao said. "This is my associate, Michelle Taylor."

"Nice to meet you," Dylan said. "I've got very important information about a conspiracy, and a technological breakthrough."

"And we appreciate that you've chosen to come forward," Gao said. "Who is involved in this conspiracy?"

"Some of my former friends in Students for Liberty. Ben Ramirez. Samantha West. Justin Smith. Ben has some sort of contact with the Grey Tribe, so that may be part of it."

"We've had the Grey Tribe on our list for some time. Do you know anything about Prof. Wilson?"

"Justin was trying to set up a group to try to defend him from charges," Dylan said, thinking, *pin something on Justin.* "But I don't know that he's involved."

"Tell us more about this technology. You said it could be used as a weapon."

"I am going to withhold details until I have assurances from you that I will get what I want from you. In return for my help, I want a bounty for turning them in, and to be appointed chief scientist to direct the research into the new technology."

Gao doodled on his pad. "You're asking us for a deal without telling us enough to know if your information is really valuable to us. We can't do that. And why shouldn't we just arrest the lot of them, and you, and sort it out by questioning? When there are national security implications, we can hold you all indefinitely."

"You might get one of them to talk," Dylan said. "But you might not. I have to withhold what I know or you won't need me. And if you piss me off, I won't cooperate."

"All we can do is promise you immunity in exchange for your information, and if it's that important, we would of course consider your other requests."

"That doesn't meet my needs."

They went over it a few more times. Andrew Gao raised his eyebrows and looked over to where he knew the hidden camera was transmitting it all to McDonald in DC. Nothing happened.

Gao rose abruptly. "Thank you for coming, Dylan. I'll take up your conditions with my superiors. Call me if you have any further thoughts or want to change your position."

* * * * *

When Gao returned to his desk, he called McDonald in DC.

"He's a weasel," Gao said. "He may know something important, or he may be exaggerating to get himself immunity. I was sure you would want him arrested, but you said nothing."

"I think he's unstable and probably a flake. But we don't want to deal with him and end up having to give him anything, even if he's onto something important. We've got the conspirators bugged, so start planning to detain them all for questioning if we hear anything actionable. In the meantime, put a tail on Dylan and add him to the monitoring list. I want to know everyone he talks to, everything he says, and every place he goes. And as for putting him in charge of anything, if he'd sell out his friends, he'd sell out his country, too—the traitor type. String him along and keep him talking until he gets desperate and starts to tell us more."

Warehouse: Wilding and Ben

At the new warehouse lab the next day, Justin and Emerson Wilding, the chief tech for the quantum lab, worked side-by-side assembling a duplicate Vortex-5. Benches, shelves, and a console were arranged roughly as they were at the campus lab. Piles of boxes to one side showed how much equipment was left to unpack.

Rolls of teflon seals and tubing were on one side of the bench. On the other side were the grid plates. Since they didn't have a clean room environment, Emerson used blasts from a can of compressed air to remove any dust that might have contaminated the surface, which shimmered with rainbow colors from diffraction by the etched circuitry.

"So on the seals themselves, we use this silicone goop?" Justin picked up a squeeze tube.

"Yes, just a thin bead all the way around, on both sides. By the way, that stuff is basically expensive lube. Not that I've tried it for that, but it's the same silicone," Emerson said. "Also used to make hair shiny."

They picked up and cleaned the matching plate once more, then carefully lowered it onto the prepared one. A little goo came out the edges. They used rubber mallets to pound on metal edging to clamp and hold the two plates together under pressure.

"Not bad," Emerson said. "Now we run a vacuum check to be sure the seals don't leak." He hooked up some of the tubing to a vacuum pump and started it.

They both looked at the side door when it opened, and Ben Ramirez walked in and said, "Lots of progress here, I see."

"Some," Justin said. "Emerson has done a great job getting things set up. Steve is supposed to be along shortly to set up the computers and get the software installed."

"We should get away from the noise," Ben said. "Need to talk to you."

"Be back in a bit," Justin said; Emerson nodded and kept watching the gauges.

Justin and Ben went into the glass-enclosed office and closed the door. "My understanding is Emerson doesn't know much other than that we're cloning the lab for some purpose of Bubna's," Ben said.

"That's right. Bubna thinks he might be a good recruit, but he didn't need to know anything to get the job done, so he doesn't. We can always talk to him about it when we're about to leave."

'But he knows this location. If he isn't with us, they might question him and he could give us away."

"Bubna was careful to cover his tracks," Justin said. "The rent will come out of an anonymous account, when we have that. And the lease is in the name of an anonymous holding company, scrawled signatures of made-up people. We do have to worry about Emerson giving us away if they get rough with everyone left behind, but if he comes along, not a problem. If he doesn't, then we'll see what we have to do. One thing I don't think Bubna thought through—if we try to sell him on coming, he will definitely know too much. Then we'd have to kidnap him for his own and our good."

"This is morally questionable." Ben looked worried. "We should tell him. Or at least test the waters."

"He seems apolitical. Interested in machines, physics, and occasionally weed."

"Ah, I thought I detected a bit of the stoner in him."

"He's not a big user, or so he says, "Justin said. "Just an occasional weekend excursion. I guess what I should do is tell him what's really happened to Prof. Wilson, and see how he reacts to that. If he's on our side and volunteers to help, I'll take him to the second level and talk about joining up with the Grey Tribe. If he makes positive sounds about that, I can tell him about the machine and our plans."

"But wait until we are about to leave for that last," Ben said, "leaving the morally questionable option open." Ben opened the box he had carried in and pulled out a phone. "This one's for you. I made a good case for us and they got approval from McCulloch himself to give us direct contact between him and all of us. I've disabled the GPS, and it would probably be a good idea to avoid using it from here or any other location you want to keep secret, because they can still figure out where you are using cell towers. The app installed on this has a little drop down menu of who you can call or text, and we have our own private communications network, with McCulloch on tap."

"You must have been convincing."

"I told them what had happened to Prof. Wilson and that we are about to go outlaw in a major way," Ben said. "McCulloch okayed it himself. So now that we have his attention, what do we tell him?"

"Like, do we want him to know about the gateway, and New Earth, and our plan to bring down the fascist states? We might want to wait until we are actually safe before going into details."

"And he will know things we don't. We don't actually have a plan for after we're safe yet, do we? Just some ideas and a collection of nifty tools that all require Steve to program them." Ben looked thoughtful. "We haven't had time to think through what we could do. Terrible things, or great things."

"We're going to need some kind of government to make important decisions and control use of the gateways," Justin said.

"Eventually," Ben said. "But for now, New Earth will have a Communist command economy based on theft, and a gentle dictatorship of you and me, with Steve as our android technical advisor. We have plenty of models to examine, all with problems—the US constitutional system was great, aside from that problem with slavery. With wars and depressions the government grew to deal with each crisis, and when the central government started to control what was taught in schools to favor increasing its own size as the solution to every problem, it grew even more into a bureaucratic blob with no restraints on its powers. The positive feedback loop which left us bankrupt and governed by Puritan thugs. Which is why we are here defying it."

"'Free your mind, the rest will follow,'" Justin said. "We teach a new generation the truth about history, economics, and science. We teach them to seek out the truth for themselves."

"That would be a start, because a limited-government republic relies on the intelligence and self-reliance of its citizens," Ben said. "Long term, government structure is something we will have to think about carefully. Government always starts with parasites and thieves— warriors and brigands who loot and pillage. Then they settle in and protect their territory. The territories compete, and the best governments learn to respect the rights and property of the citizens, making the country strong and prosperous. Then it's more like symbiosis, with enlightened government providing essential protection without destroying its host. But in a democracy, demagogues will rise and erode those rights so they can give their voters things they haven't earned. When the politicians start to mold their voters by controlling news and education, game over. The citizens lose the will to find their own way—they've been trained to think there's no point in doing anything for themselves because some other group is keeping them down, and they're owed a fair share. The demagogues then kill the golden goose by setting their clients against the remaining productive citizens."

"And some other strong man running an authoritarian state comes along and destroys the democracy," Justin added. "The barbarians take over. The cycle repeats. But now the weapons are terrifying, and the last war could really be the last. Nukes were bad enough, but the gateway is an order of magnitude more dangerous."

"The gateway is a complex technology which for now can easily be kept under control, but Steve tells me he thinks the same effects could be achieved with much more compact and easier to build quantum computers, someday," Ben said. "He thinks even if we destroy all of his work before it falls into the Feds' hands, someone else will discover it—a year from now, a hundred years from now, but more likely sooner. Especially if they discover it exists—knowing something is possible by example makes it much more likely to be rediscovered."

"For now, I know I can trust you, and me, and Steve, and Sam. Bubna seems good. Rasna, too. But beyond that, even the people we've recruited aren't carefully vetted. If we start to grow, we'll have the usual tribes and power grabs starting up on New Earth. And if someone smart with a thirst for power gets control of the gateway technology, the result would be almost as bad as if we gave it to the Feds right now."

"That's years away," Ben said. "You save the galaxy now, and worry about tomorrow later. We can't return to the days of yeoman farmers and militia as defense, when every two-bit terrorist group can get its hands on a nuke."

"It may be we'll have to invent an all-seeing AI to keep watch over us and prevent bad people from hurting others, or so Steve thinks." Justin said. "But liberty—aside from those limitations necessary to prevent harm to others—is what encourages us to try to create great things, knowing some busy-body won't stop us or steal our work. And being allowed to fail in our own way is what makes us learn and grow. If we can find a way to help the people of Earth throw off their commissars and committees and start growing again, Earth can use this technology to solve all its problems. And we'll find a solution to controlling it."

"As I recall," Ben said, "the Roman Empire took centuries to collapse, leaving decadent remnants that took centuries more to recover. And the real blossoming of creativity had to wait a millennium longer. Let's hope we do better this time."

The Red Queen Effect

The Red Queen hypothesis, also referred to as Red Queen's, Red Queen's race or The Red Queen Effect, is an evolutionary hypothesis which proposes that organisms must constantly adapt, evolve, and proliferate not merely to gain reproductive advantage, but also simply to survive while pitted against ever-evolving opposing organisms in an ever-changing environment....

Such examples of arms races can also be applied to human conflict and can be seen as a prominent cause of conflict.... [T]he Red Queen effect is established when two competing groups find themselves in a security dilemma. The security dilemma, resulting from defensive measures taken to improve one's security which possess inherent offensive capabilities, triggers a military arms race. This arms race... causes each side to consume ever increasing amounts of resources in order to outpace the other and gain an advantage. If an advantage is gained, the arms race is over and the group with more resources has won. However, typically both sides continue to match each other stride for stride, thus triggering the Red Queen effect as no matter how many resources each side invests, neither is able to gain an advantage. The situation is somewhat similar to the prisoner's dilemma. Each side cannot stop the arms race because of mutual suspicion and fears that the other group will gain a significant tactical advantage. Because of this, the Red Queen effect is a common outcome of inter-human competition and conflict.[6] — "Red Queen hypothesis," Wikipedia.

Wonderful and admirable as most instincts are, yet they cannot be considered as absolutely perfect: there is a constant struggle going on throughout nature between the instinct of the one to escape its enemy and of the other to secure its prey. —Charles Darwin

Chapter Thirteen: Escape Plan Alpha

First Steps

With the new machine and its software up and running and Emerson Wilding gone back to his campus duties, Steve and Justin began working from the warehouse and quietly bringing backpacks of necessary items over from the campus. As the bookshelves filled up with manuals and the ramen wrappers built up in the trash of the kitchenette they had set up, it began to feel more like the old lab.

Steve had been busy refining the gateway software in the last few days. "I've got the edge effect routines down and tested. Now you won't get cut in half if you run into the edge—but you might get bruised as it refuses to cut the edge bonds of the object that runs into it."

"Like any doorway, then," Justin said. "You could add a cushioning effect."

"Too complicated. Not really possible without changing the location of the edge to 'give' when you bump into it. So people will just have to be careful. I was also able to solve the air pressure differential problem, up to a point—gases crossing are adjusted in speed to form a kind of air curtain which holds back flow. People crossing should be careful to have their lungs and airways open."

"What about inner gases? Like upcoming farts and bubbles in the bloodstream?"

"Those will be dragged through with slight additional resistance.

Again, living things should transit the gateway slowly to avoid problems." Steve opened up a new window on his screen. "And I've made progress on the mapping routine. Open a gateway on a new planet, and it can automatically open a series of gateway windows pointing straight down over every part of its surface. The camera snaps a photo for each spot and adds it to the database. These photos are combined into a model of the surface by some nifty open source software, so you can then ask for a detailed photo of any spot."

"Show me how to use it. We need to find that better camp site—near fresh water and ocean, drier, lots of sun for solar power...."

"Which may not be necessary. I have some ideas for directly generating electricity from the device."

"But again we'll need power now, not when you have had time to think that one out."

"True. But it's a top priority if we want to avoid moving hundreds of solar panels through the gateway. Or barrels of gasoline for the generators."

Justin spent several hours searching for a good site by scanning the planet database. He was looking near the original viewing site, assuming a site near the same latitude was likely to provide suitable temperatures. "How do we know this planet doesn't have extreme seasons?" he asked Steve.

"Can't be certain, but the axial tilt is much less than Earth's, and there's little evidence of seasonality in the landscape or the lifeforms, so my assumption is that seasons are less extreme there. I'm sure there are still storms, so the local equivalent of hurricanes and tornadoes might be problem. Be sure the location is elevated above sea level enough, avoid lees of continental masses. Not much more we can do without long-term weather records."

Finally Justin had settled on a likely-looking spot, near a river flowing into the sea, but on a rise overlooking the inlet. Forests began further inland, rising to a weathered mountain range beyond. "Look s nice and quiet," he commented to Steve. "I should look all around the area before we send anything over." He used the controls to check every spot within walking distance. "Some unexplained dark spots, maybe animals or rocks. But nothing moving that I can see." He zoomed in on a spot. "It's a rock." In the view, some local equivalent of beach grass crossed with moss spread over the rock and seed stalks waved in the breeze. "It reminds me of Del Mar."

Steve came over to look. "It's amazing that the details of the plants are different but the effect is much the same—very familiar-looking."

"Parallel evolution. Most forms will end up looking similar to perform similar functions. But we shouldn't let that lull us into complacency; the differences might be dangerous. So we need some biologists and botanists to investigate the life here."

"But our schedule doesn't allow time to do that first," Steve said. "If we are to be moving people and equipment over in the next few days."

"We just have to hope our luck holds and any surprises will be survivable."

＊＊＊＊＊

Finally the moment arrived when Justin was sick of looking at screens showing the base camp area and decided to go through himself to check it out. They had brought the remaining mice over from the campus lab, and once more their cage was left on the ground to see if any predators or poisons would effect them. When they came in the next day, the mice were fine and the time-lapse video showed nothing unusual.

"Looks safer than Earth," Justin said. "Time to go look around myself."

"I'll hold the fort and keep an eye on you. Don't leave the view of the gateway."

Justin put on hiking boots and tucked his pants into the tops. "Just in case there are hidden varmints in the grass. I'd hate to be brought down by alien ticks." He went over to the shelves and dug into a box, pulling out a rifle. "And I'm taking this, just in case," he said, "because you never know when you're going to run into an id creature. No silver bullets, so I'm out of luck if there are werewolves."

"That seems unlikely. Your most likely hazards are not so obvious—poisonous plants, insects, quicksand. Take it very slowly and look around beneath you before stepping. Don't touch anything."

"I was planning to run ahead blindly and trip over an alien boojum, but now that you've reminded me, I will be more cautious." Justin stood before the gateway for a moment. He remembered to push the rifle's safety button off and held it ready.

Then he stepped carefully over the threshold.

Looking back, he caught Steve's eye—Steve waved. Looking around, nothing seemed dangerous. The air smelled fresh and somehow different, but not enough to give the smell a name. There was a slight breeze coming from the ocean side. Looking down at his feet, he was stepping on a small-leafed plant in sandy soil. All was quiet.

He scanned the horizon and could see the edges of the forest. In front of him was a bare spot that looked safe, so he took a step forward. Pausing to look around again and check the area around where the gateway had blocked his view. Nothing; a rock outcropping to the left, a clump of bushes to the right. It was early morning, and the sun was still climbing in the eastern sky; above him a small, silvery half-moon was just visible against the blue of the sky.

And another step, then another. Looking back at Steve, the gateway was now a small, dark door silhouetted against the horizon. Justin shouted, "Looks good. Not seeing anything unexpected."

Steve replied, just loudly enough to hear, "I'm getting bored watching. Does it seem like the ground will work for tents?"

*   *   *   *   *

Justin came back through the gateway after a slow walk around the area, finding no obvious hazards. There was a large flat area of sandy soil that would be suitable for base camp. He had left red surveyor's flags at the corners to mark the spot.

After some discussion with Bubna and Wendy, they had decided to open online retail accounts in the name of the dummy company on the warehouse lease. Connected to one of the new bank accounts, they had begun to order the masses of supplies and equipment needed for the camp. After their initial efforts at stealing supplies, they had realized it was far faster and maybe less likely to clue in authorities if they used the gateway only to steal highly valuable and compact items from places that were not closely watched and where the items taken would not be missed for some time. As Justin explained to Steve, "It's faster to order from Amazon than to steal most stuff. We need to use the gateway only when necessary, and try to keep evidence of its use from accumulating."

Delivery trucks started arriving the next day. They opened the boxes and stacked the tents, freeze-dried food, and supplies near the gateway. "At some point," Justin mused, "it will make sense to have one of those roller-covered sloped conveyers for sending boxes across using their own weight."

Steve thought about that for a second. "Maybe. Getting one set up is more trouble than lugging things through for the time being. And we'd end up with boxes everywhere on the other side, and no recycling truck to take them away."

"We could throw our trash through a gateway opened to a spot in the other side of the planet."

"Thus restarting the time-honored human technology for dealing with waste, on a brand-new planet—spoil some other spot by dumping your trash there."

* * * * *

At their side-by-side consoles, Steve nudged Justin. "I've changed the security for accessing the gateway program. Before, anyone with a login password in our lab group could use the program. Just to be safe, I have added an in-program password as a final barrier."

"What is it?"

"It's set to 'xyzzy.' You can only change it in the source code, where it's disguised by an addition cypher so it doesn't stand out in a program dump."

Justin laughed—he still remembered the text adventure game which had magic commands to move between rooms. The magic word "xyzzy" was still well-known in the gamer community.[7] "I'm surprised you knew about that, being so young. Easy for us to remember, hard for non-geeks."

"I would propagate these improvements back to the original codebase," Steve said, "but since we're planning on destroying that soon, I don't see much point."

＊ ＊ ＊ ＊ ＊

Steve came back from a bathroom break. "So how did it go when you talked with Emerson?"

"He expressed his support of our efforts to help Prof. Wilson, so now I've been leading him toward saying something more definitive. He was very interested in talking about the Grey Tribe, which everyone has heard of but is afraid to talk about openly. I told him about the Prof's contact with them and why that led to his disappearance. He sounds willing to be on our side, if maybe not willing to join the expedition. No way to ask about his feelings about that without telling him too much."

"So we have him come here the day we start leaving and give him the pitch. If he says no, then what?"

"We beg him to leave town for a few months," Justin said. "Or more likely, we make an executive decision to bring him along anyway, which he'll understand once we explain it."

"You'd be surprised how touchy people can be about choosing their own destiny."

"And speaking of the Grey Tribe," Justin said. "Ben has been exchanging messages with them. Michael McCulloch has been brought in and completely understands the plan, though it took some time to persuade him we weren't making it all up. He's sent word out to all the rebel groups that there's a big opportunity coming up for action at an unnamed new base camp, and that we especially need biologists and other scientists, programmers, and pioneers willing to cut themselves off from life for awhile to contribute to the effort. We don't tell them anything more until they're assembled and waiting to go at the various assembly locations, then we give them a chance to back out when we tell them it's on another planet. Reactions should be interesting."

"If you can arrange to keep them from communicating until the ones who are leaving have left."

"That's doable by collecting all phones and searching everybody before they're allowed in. Then they aren't allowed to leave until the gateway is closed there."

"Best laid plans. If there are a dozen collection points, there are many opportunities for failure."

"As usual, we don't have a choice…. And meanwhile, I'm more worried about our campus cells, and how to get some of those people involved without giving away the game. We're asking cell leaders to recruit by asking if their unit members would be willing to travel to join a real rebel group. The word back is mostly a negative response."

"They were committed to part-time secret work, but not willing to give up their comfortable student lives to go anywhere."

"Mostly. But there's a motivated minority, maybe one in four, that say yes. We'll pull the same assemble-in-a-locked-room trick on them. We might collect twenty or so recruits that way, judging from the fuzzy numbers that trickle back up."

"The crazy ones. It would be nice if we knew more about them."

"We'll find out about them on the other side. Not likely anyone too erratic will have been recruited, but we have no way to be sure. At some point we'll have to figure out how to handle our own criminals and dissenters, but I hope not soon."

Dylan Goes Rogue

Dylan Foster was brooding. Since the meeting with Gao had ended without any promises, he had been in touch by phone several times, only once reaching Gao himself. He had tried several times to suggest he knew of plots to steal gold from central banks and that he suspected the conspirators of planning much more direct actions against the government—after all, he knew Ben would approve and he was one of them. But nothing seemed to happen—they said they would let him know but nothing changed. It had been almost two weeks and most likely they were stringing him along until he cracked and told them what they wanted to know without getting anything in return.

So he had started watching the quantum computing lab, and on this Sunday night there were no lights on. He entered the building and tiptoed down the corridor toward the lab windows. No one was there, so he tried the knobs of the side office doors that had been unlocked before; no luck this time. But he had brought his kit with him, which included a pry bar which he used to jimmy open one of the doors. *That was easy,* he had thought, *and it doesn't look damaged, even.*

He surveyed all of the offices and the main room, and tried the computers—all were logged off. He turned on a desk lamp and used its light to take photos of all the notes scribbled near the computers, some of which looked like they might be password crib sheets, but he would sort through the photos later and check each possible password by remote login. He photographed the list of personnel and email addresses he found on one desk, and stole some pads full of notes from Steve Duong's office. Not being able to log in meant not being able to get at the files and programs they were using to operate the machine, but he exited with a stack of manuals and enough data to have a chance at finding a way.

Back in his apartment, he read until sleep hit him, and the next morning blew off all his regular duties to try logging in from his home machine. The notes he had photographed were mostly meaningless, but the few likely passwords—which conformed to the university's requirements of upper and lower case letters, at least one numeral, and more than seven characters—stood out. He thanked the security people for making them so easy to pick out of the scattered jottings. He had four likely passwords and twelve lab personnel login names, so he methodically went through each password trying it with each name, then waiting a bit after failing to try a different name. On the next-to-last password, he was in, as Prof. Bubna, with full access to project files, and he methodically copied everything he could find to a memory stick.

He sifted through program code for hours looking for command structures and learning from the cryptic program comments. He wrote down a list of commands and parameters, and the outline of what the program did and how you told it to do it became clearer. Steve's scribbled notes had more meaning read in light of what he now knew the Vortex-5 could do, and the crude drawings of boxes and arrows between dots going through a line were another clue.

Dylan stayed home all day and read. He thought he knew enough to try running the machine, and his first target would be those stacks of gold bars he had seen. There was a stored location file in ASCII format giving labeled locations, one of which was GOLD, which seemed a likely place to look. So after dinner he made his way back to the lab—again dark, which was puzzling because they were almost always there on weeknights. But he went ahead and broke in through the same (now weakened) door.

He turned on the desk lamp at the console in front of the Vortex-5. He logged in as Bubna, and started the control program. Referring to the list he had made of program options, he set flags for viewing only and selected GOLD from the pulldown list of stored locations. A dimly-lit scene of the side of a stack of gold bars appeared in front of the machine. Since he was not too concerned about being detected, he set the option for passing all matter through the gateway, then got the gripper arm, put the gripping end into the gateway, and tried to pick one bar off the stack. It seemed far too heavy to budge with the limited force of the gripper. *What the hell,* he thought, and reached through with his two hands.

He was able to lift and move the bar toward himself, with some effort. When the edge of the bar came off its supporting stack, the weight pulled him forward, and his left shoulder went into the edge of the gateway. He felt a shock and then pain as blood begin to drip down his arm, and he quickly pulled back and got the bar into the lab with him. But his shoulder was cut deeply, and he held the wound closed with his other hand for a minute while he pondered his options.

I need bandages and probably stitches, the sensible side of him thought. *Or I'll go into shock and lose too much blood.* On the other hand, his strategic side said, *I won't have this chance again, probably,*

So he rummaged through desk drawers for scissors and tape, and finding those, made his way to the bathroom down the hall, leaving a trail of blood droplets. Once there, he fashioned a bandage from his shirt sleeve, cut into pieces, and added paper towels and tape to hold it tightly in place. That seemed to reduce the pain and the bleeding, and so he went back to work, telling himself, *If I start to feel weak and like I might black out, I go outside and flag down someone to take me to the emergency room. But for now I can keep working.*

Dylan wasn't thinking very clearly, but he obviously wasn't going to be able to get another gold bar through without use of both hands, unless he stepped across to do it. So he did, through the short and narrow opening, moving very slowly to make sure he avoided the edges this time. He found himself up against the stack of gold, and he had to contort himself to grab one bar off the top and drop it through the gateway. He did this a few more times, then realized it was a bad idea to continue, since most likely his presence was being viewed by the security cams he could see at the corners of the vault, now that he had stepped into it. Anyway, it was enough, since each bar was worth several million dollars. He carefully stepped back through and went to the console to close the gateway,

He later wondered why, even in his hazy state of mind, he chose to click on the location drop down menu and let it go randomly on another selection. This did not close the gateway, but opened it to a new place.

An explosion of blinding brightness and hot gases threw him back across the room and blew out all of the windows of the lab. When he came to, the glowing gateway was gone, the console had been turned over, and the other computers in the room were dark. The Vortex-5 itself looked undamaged, but his face had been badly burned and he could barely see out of one eye. His bandage had come undone and he was losing blood again.

He managed to stand up and found his backpack. He put the gold bars into it, but realized he couldn't carry that many in his weakened state. So he began dragging the backpack across the floor toward the door, then down the hall to the elevator.

Also injured by flying glass, but observing from the other end of the hall, was a shadowy figure in black clothing. He pulled out a phone to report to his superiors what he had seen.

Lockdown

The next morning, Justin woke up and checked his email as usual, and found a memo from Prof. Bubna explaining that a gas explosion of some sort had damaged the quantum lab, blowing out all the windows and damaging some of the computers. While the Vortex-5 itself showed no signs of damage, some of the auxiliary equipment appeared to be unusable. And the university had locked down the lab pending investigation by insurance and fire department investigators, so no personnel were to report until further notice.

He called Bubna using the secure new phone. "Gas explosion?"

"The gateway must have opened to a high-pressure gas or plasma location," Bubna said, out of breath. "Everything was scorched or melted directly foreword from the Vortex-5, but the machine itself is untouched. Someone opened it last night."

"Are we allowed in?"

"No, I was only allowed a quick walkthrough. The lockdown is real, and they are posting a guard."

"How long?"

"No way to tell," Bubna said. "They said we could go in and get things after tomorrow when the investigators have recorded everything."

"We need to get everything we need out of there now, before the investigators notice the damage pattern and conclude it came from the Vortex-5."

"We can't go back to the lab now. So I'll let everyone know to go to the other place so we can decide what to do."

"Sounds good. I'll be there in an hour." Which gave Justin time to chug down more coffee and a protein drink and get showered. He could barely think until he'd had more time to wake up anyway.

Chapter Fourteen: Homeland Security

Arrested

> To: DirSpecOps James McDonald
> From: Field Investigator Andrew Gao
> Re: Neutral Armor
>
> Explosion in the quantum computing lab
> Justin Smith was working in part-time, uni-
> versity has it secured. Phone intercepts
> indicate the conspiracy has been using that
> lab. Propose we send in a team to secure
> the facility and arrest the conspirators.
>
> Our tail on Dylan Foster had him at the lab
> for hours before the explosion. Tail did
> not see him leave the building. Working
> assumption: he went rogue and decided to
> take action on his own since we didn't give
> him what he wanted.
>
> Call at your convenience. I'm getting a
> team together.

* * * * *

Jim McDonald ate lunch at his desk and considered the possibility he
had made a mistake in not subjecting Dylan Foster to the full interro-
gation that might have averted this forcing of his hands. But there was

no stopping an aggressive reaction now.

He picked up the phone and called Gao. "Just saw your memo. Looks like I called this one wrong—pick them all up, and send in a team to secure that lab. I'll send out an expert on quantum computing to check out what they were doing."

"Do we have anyone?" Gao said. "Not the kind of thing we usually do."

"I have contacts over at the NSA. They will know who's good, preferably somebody already on the west coast. We need to understand more before we sound more alerts, so it looks like we have handle on it when we go upstairs. And another thing in the morning report that may have a bearing on this—we have reports from inside China's security apparat that something big is focusing their attention on that university. I can't discount the possibility that Foster tried to shop his story to them and they have bought it. So now we have the Chinese sniffing around, meaning we bring in the big guns and make this a much bigger project. We'll need a new codeword."

"Great. How about 'Awesome Clusterfuck?'"

"Probably won't pass the test, but a good description."

Next he called his hunting buddy Alan at the NSA—only a few miles from his office. "Alan, we have a problem on the west coast." He described the explosion at the quantum computing lab and the Grey Tribe connection.

"That's an interesting coincidence," Alan said. "Our advanced computing group is working with that lab on a new machine. Let me talk to those people and I'll get back to you."

McDonald read more reports while he waited. The phone intercepts from Gao were intriguing and implied a more organized conspiracy than he had suspected. The kids were playing at spycraft, not realizing their phones were bugged but still being careful not to say too much. But what they did say still convicted them.

The phone buzzed; it was Alan. "So here's the story. NSA has chipped in on a new machine at that lab, big quantum computer which has been scaled up. They have some of their own on order now because they're very excited about getting a jump on the other side's codes. Prof. Friedman is the man to talk to there, running the project."

"That name has not turned up so far on the list. Any experts they know of out there who are known good?"

"Tony Perreti at Berkeley. He's on retainer to consult on their quantum computing projects, so he'd be one to ask. I hope your budget has room for consulting fees."

"We'll manage. Thanks for the assist."

"De nada. They were quite surprised to hear about the incident, but they're holding off contacting Prof. Friedman in case you need to surprise him."

"That was smart. He gets added to the list, and we'll sort out his actual involvement later. Talking to him should be useful."

McDonald set an assistant to compiling a dossier on Prof. Friedman and his research group, and went back to finishing lunch. His coffee was cold.

* * * * *

Wendy Fields was walking to the library when she noticed a lot of unmarked black SUVs and a larger Hummer-style vehicle with official markings pulling into the side alley near the engineering buildings. She paused under a tree to watch as agents swarmed the side entrance, with the door opened from inside by a campus cop. What looked like a SWAT team took up positions and held military-style rifles ready. Students passing by were told to move on, and the area was rapidly cleared.

A few minutes later, Wendy saw the agents leaving by the same door, with Prof. Friedman handcuffed and looking dazed. They shoved him into one of the vans and left. The SWAT team stayed and appeared to be settling in.

Wendy decided she should really get further away. And she knew she would find the others at the warehouse lab, so she turned back to find a cab.

At the Warehouse

At the warehouse, Justin and Steve filled in the others who had arrived over the past few minutes. Some of them had just heard the news of the explosion and lockdown when Wendy arrived and took the floor. "Guys," she said, "I saw a SWAT team take over your old lab, and they arrested Prof. Friedman and hustled him away. Looks like we're in trouble."

"Why Friedman?" Bubna said. "He doesn't know anything."

"They may not know that," Justin said. "He's officially running the Vortex-5 project. That probably means they are after all of us. So if we go back, they might arrest us. We're not really ready, but looks like we have no choice—time to go."

"I wonder if they've staked out our apartments," Steve said. "I have to get some of my stuff and my computer."

"If you're not high on their list," Justin said, "you might be able to sneak back in by a side door and get some stuff out. I doubt if they have a team after each one of us. And, everyone—stop using your phones unless it's critical, you are somewhere anonymous and public, and you send all messages through the Grey Tribe app. I have a feeling they are intercepting texts and phone calls. For now, turn it off, take out the battery, and pick it up only when you are leaving, Put the battery in to use it and take it out right after."

"I'd like a chance to talk to my family," Samantha said. "I have been dropping hints, but if I'm going to disappear, I want them to know I'm okay and working on something important."

"We can do that," Justin replied. "Safest to call them from on the road. Or just go visit them, it's not too far."

Wendy looked thoughtful. "This is different—before they were just looking for Grey Tribe contacts through Prof. Wilson. Now they will use every tool. You have to realize nothing is safe—they know your credit cards, they know your license plates. You buy something using a credit card, they'll know; you drive through any of the camera checkpoints, your license can be read and they'll know where you are and where you're heading. The only wiggle room we have is using cash and they've tried to stop that."

"So you mean," Justin said, "that if I take my car to drive out to Sam's parents' house, they'll identify the license plate along the highway and come after us."

"Yes, they have set a system up to report all their sources to a central database, which spits out notifications to interested law enforcement," Wendy said. "Homeland Security is slow, but I would bet they have all of you on their list. Maybe not me, yet, because I've been very careful. But I should lay low, too—visit my cousins in Atlanta, maybe."

"And use cash. Do we have cash?"

Wendy walked over to the office. "There's a safe in here. I've been filling it up." She came back with bundles of hundred-dollar bills. "Everybody take a few. If there's one thing we are, it's well-financed, with mail drops and corporate shells in four countries, and twice as many bank accounts."

"I'm impressed," Justin said. "But I am starting to think there is nowhere safe, except through the gateway."

"You might be right," Wendy said. "I need to get back to my usual habits since I'm pretty sure they have no idea I'm with you guys, and there's a lot to be done."

✳ ✳ ✳ ✳ ✳

When Emerson Wilding came in, Justin took him into the office and closed the door.

"There's something we haven't been telling you until now, when we have to," Justin said.

Emerson looked puzzled. "I was wondering. Why are all these people here?"

"I've told you about Prof. Wilson and the Grey Tribe. Steve has come up with a use of the Vortex-5 that gives us a shot at helping them fight the government, and we've decided to go for it."

"Why didn't you tell me? I'm all for that. And what kind of use?"

"We'll show you. And we didn't tell you because you didn't need to know. And now we have to, because Homeland Security has arrested Prof. Friedman and would probably arrest and interrogate all of us if they could find us. We can't go back."

"But I don't know anything."

"You know where this lab is, and we can't build another one right now. If they have you, they use drugs to make you talk. So we have to take you with us."

Steve was watching them through the office windows. Justin motioned to him to go to the console. "Steve will show you. He found a way to make the Vortex-5 set up a gateway to anywhere else, and we are building a camp on a near-Earth planet."

Emerson stopped chewing his gum. "What?" Steve tapped a key, and the gateway showing the sandy site overlooking the ocean of 61 Pegasi appeared, glowing brightly as the sun of another world sent a beam into the room. "I'm going to need a longer explanation for this."

"Well, it works. That's what I've been helping him with these past few weeks."

"Okay. But—I have work to do. I have a cat! What will my mom think? Can't I just tell them I know nothing?"

"They won't let you do that," Justin said. "And your job is gone, since they've arrested your lab head and taken over the lab. The university won't just keep paying you to show up. You will be disappeared and your mom may never hear from you again. Your cat will go unfed anyway. We didn't mean to do this to you. But your old life is over anyway."

Emerson took a moment but then brightened. "On the other hand, this is very cool. Another planet. I can leave Alfred with a neighbor. And call my mom."

"You can call your mom later. We can start talking to people directly through little gateways, which can't be tapped. Soon we'll be out of their reach and it no longer matters if they pressure relatives."

As they left the office, Steve made the okay sign behind Emerson's head. Steve and Bubna relaxed. No need for the takedown they had feared.

Samantha pulled Justin aside. "Where's Ben?"

"No one has heard from him," Justin said. "Bubna sent him the message to meet up at the safe house—here, in other words. But he either didn't get it or maybe they've arrested him."

"It feels odd not to be able to just call or text someone to ask. We can't go there and we can't call from here."

"Well, here's what might be safe. Take your phone with you and drive a few miles before putting the battery back in. Check your email and text messages and the Grey Tribe app. We can't afford to give them any clues about our location, but that will put them off the trail if they are tapping our phones. If nothing comes in, call his office and speak to his officemates."

"Okay. I'll be careful." They hugged, and held it longer than usual. "I'll be back." And she left.

Half an hour later, Samantha returned with the bad news. No messages from Ben, but his office mates reported he had been taken away by armed men. They had whispered, as if someone might hear them.

＊ ＊ ＊ ＊ ＊

They waited until later in the evening to proceed on the plan they had come up with weeks earlier. Darkness and an empty building were critical.

"We need to retrieve the original Vortex-5, or destroy it. We need as many as we can get, so we're going to try retrieval. We've checked out the lab by gateway viewing, and no guards are actually posted in the room. So we can probably get in and out in a minute or two without problems."

"Or get shot by a sniper," Sam added. "For all we know."

"There is that chance, but from viewing how they're positioned, they are focused on someone coming from outside their perimeter, not someone appearing inside. So none of them appear to be aimed at watching the lab itself."

"I've made the gateway as big as it's safe to make it," Steve said. "And the threshold is set exactly at floor level. So just unhook the tubes and cables and unlock the casters on the machine, and you can roll it through the gateway in a few seconds. Should be easy."

"Emerson," Justin said, "you know the machine. Is it easy to unhook it?"

"Not too bad. Two big plugs from the magnetic coils to the transformer. Insulated tubing for the liquid nitrogen. There's a twist lock and some clamps that need to be unscrewed, so maybe I should do it. Hard to explain the tricks."

"You willing to help me? It's a risk, as Sam has pointed out."

"Sure. I can do it faster than anyone, and I can bring the screwdriver I need for the clamps. Not too worried."

When they stepped through the gateway, all was quiet. Justin went around one end of the Vortex-5, and Emerson the other. There was little light but they couldn't risk a flashlight, so Emerson felt as much as saw the parts he was unhooking. "There's one clamp," he said, "and now the twist lock. Unscrewing the other.... And it's free."

Justin had spotted the electrical connectors and was working them loose. Emerson helped him pull and one came off, then the other. "Unlock the casters." They each freed up two of them. "Okay, let's roll," Justin said, and they worked together to push the machine forward toward the glowing room beyond the gateway.

The casters stuck on the edge and they had to push hard to get them over, but then they were through and back to the warehouse. They heard a shout from the room they were leaving, but as soon as they'd cleared the gateway, Steve closed it.

"That was close," Steve observed.

* * * * *

Steve was at the console. For once he had a larger audience watching him work, so he made it seem like a demo. "I have tested out this new option on a few cinderblocks. The gateway works by detaching bonds between particles at the gateway plane and reattaching them to particles on the other side. This option simply detaches the bonds of particles near the plane, so any object intersecting it is sliced. I've set the gateway plane at a steep angle for this application, and pro-grammed in a series of locations to slice, one after the other."

"What locations?" Rasna asked.

"The executive committee—that's Justin and I, since Ben's not here—have decided the only way to keep the technology secret a few years longer is to destroy the lab and the software."

"'Destroy?' What about the people there?"

"We've waited long enough and the guards are out of the building," Steve said. "No better time than now. Someone might get hurt stand-ing nearby but they should be okay. We don't have a choice."

Justin nodded, and Steve hit the return key. "My program targets the cross-section of the beams carrying the load in that end of the build-ing. It's already over—each one has been sliced on a diagonal, which I'm guessing will result in structural failure in a few seconds at most as the ends of the beams slide past each other and the top floors of the building collapse onto lower floors, until they all end up in the sub-basement."

Steve typed in another command and hit enter. "And that does the same to the IT annex where the servers live, along with the backups. Unfortunately that will mess up a lot of people's work, but it can't be helped. We have no idea which storage units have our program files, so I'm slicing across all of them in a fine grid. And we still can't be sure they haven't contracted with some cloud storage place for backup-backups, but knowing them, they prefer old ways of doing things."

Since they could see no evidence of anything happening, Steve opened a camera window high over the central IT building. It was dark below, but a fire had started at one end, and the crumpled roof was evidence that he had succeeded.

"That definitely puts us on the wrong side of the law," Justin said, looking around at the stunned faces. "Is everyone here okay with that? 'We mean to disobey'—and we have, and we will. The worst thing that could happen for everyone in the world is for those people to get the gateway and use it to increase their power to control and hurt people... so a little property damage is nothing. And almost everyone on campus has local copies of what they're working on. We couldn't afford to have Homeland Security picking through the lab and our files. There was no choice."

* * * * *

It was good that you could still buy pizza with cash; Rasna had gone out to get them some, and they ate while watching the local TV news on the office TV. Every channel showed helicopter views of the building collapses and fires on campus. One person was said to be injured, condition good. Students and police were interviewed, students awed by the destruction and police not revealing anything except that an investigation was underway, and Federal investigators were considering it terrorist activity. A large contingent from Homeland Security and the FBI were to arrive tomorrow. Everything was under control. "And," the police spokesman said, "If you see something, say something."

"So far," Bubna said, "they haven't put up our pictures and asked people to be on the lookout for us. So that's good."

"Give them a day," Justin said. "They'll have a story manufactured and we'll be dangerous terrorists as soon as they realize they can't find us."

* * * * *

Everyone was getting tired and realized there was only one cramped bathroom and shower for all of them. "We can't risk going home to sleep," Justin said. "We can survey our apartments tomorrow, and we may be able to gateway into them once to pick up our things, but we can't risk appearing where they might expect us to be."

They were surrounded by boxes full of camping gear, so they started unpacking the sleeping bags and finding spots to settle into. Justin and Sam set up their sleeping bags on a pad of folded boxes and tried to sleep. The snoring from the other end of the warehouse seemed to be Prof. Bubna's doing. Justin held Sam's hand and said, "I think New Earth will have better accommodations than this." But soon after that, they slept.

Chapter Fifteen: Nothing Left to Lose

Visit to Grandpa

Samantha woke as the morning light filtered through the skylights overhead. It took her a few minutes to remember where she was—in a sleeping bag on the floor of a warehouse, not in her comfortable bedroom. Justin looked so peaceful asleep. She could hear others stirring, and decided to get up and dress before waking up Justin.

She smelled coffee while she pulled on her jeans and shirt. She hovered over Justin and squeezed his shoulder. "Wakey-wakey. Coffee brewing."

He opened his eyes and stretched. "That was better than I expected. Last I remember was somebody snoring, then boom."

"Well, good thing is we're still here and there aren't any troops outside." She waited for him to dress then they walked by some still-sleeping people before joining Bubna in the office, pouring the coffee into paper cups.

"Thought I would get things started," Bubna said. "We should check the news and do a little gateway peeking outside to be sure the coast is clear, then send somebody out for food."

"We've got all this freeze-dried stuff, and water, and a microwave," Justin said. "If we have to, we can lay low and eat from stores."

"I'd rather eat real food when I can," Sam said. "We'll be stuck with space food for awhile until we find a better way to supply ourselves.

Why start until we have to?"

Steve came in and grabbed a coffee. Justin said, "We need to check the news and find out if we've been identified. And see what's happening on campus."

"I took a look at campus," Steve said. "Lots of military vehicles, lots of officials standing around drinking coffee and talking, media trucks around the perimeter. Nothing actually happening since the fires are out and there's no obvious move to go in yet."

"It will probably take them a few days to plan their search while the Feds get organized."

"Probably so," Steve said. "The news hasn't changed from last night. A press conference scheduled for noon. We aren't mentioned as suspects. Still a likely 'terrorist attack.'"

"Could we check around this neighborhood to see if there's any unusual activity?" Steve said. "I worry that we haven't been careful enough, and that this lab will be too easily found if they try hard enough."

"I'll go survey the area." Steve left and headed for his console. Others were waking up and coming for coffee and biscuits.

They could see the gateway viewpoint changing as Steve joysticked around the neighborhood. Not much stirring, and no military or police presence. Steve looked their way and gave a thumbs-up. Sam and Rasna left for the diner down the street, which looked like a good spot for a take-out breakfast for seven outlaws.

"I don't know how long it will take us to assemble the parts of our camp infrastructure and get a machine up and running there," Steve said. "We have the lab's Vortex-5 but we need to set it up in a controlled environment, with a Dewar 'flask of liquid nitrogen and a solid power supply for the pumps and coils. All of those things are here somewhere in boxes, but how long will it take to set it up over there?" He pointed to the gateway.

Emerson answered. "Set up a tent, install a generator outside and a Dewie of liquid nitrogen inside, attach wires and tubes. A day at most. Send me over and I'll get started."

Justin looked around at the masses of boxes and said, "Why don't we start by moving everything now? Then if they come after us here, we'll have everything for an extended stay while we get the gateway there up and running. Get everything we need out of here now."

Bubna and Emerson nodded. Justin said, "Steve, open the gateway in large form to the camp site, and match the floor edge as closely as you can so we can roll carts over there. Handtrucks and stacked boxes go much faster."

Then Sam and Rasna returned with breakfast, and everything stopped until they had finished their eggs and hash browns. More coffee and talk, and then finally Steve opened the gateway to New Earth and they began moving the boxes of supplies.

And so it happened that Bubna and Emerson's first step onto the new world was rolling handtrucks in. It was just past dawn there, and the light was pink and orange against a deep blue sky, with the sun rising behind a cloud bank to the east. "Which reminds me, " Justin said, "we need to get most of this stuff under cover before it rains. That means put up the tents, move the boxes in but leave the ones we need now out, and otherwise bust our butts."

"I guess we don't have time to appreciate the moment of traveling to a distant star system and experiencing an alien planet," Bubna said.

"Right. One moment of appreciation, now past. Back to pick up another load."

* * * * *

They were done moving the smaller items quickly. The larger items like generators, solar panels, and bundled tents took a bit longer. They had planned for eight large tents to start, and by the time they had cleared the warehouse floor of boxes and bundles, it was noon. This time Bubna went out for barbeque, and afterwards Emerson and Bubna crossed back over to base camp to start the tent building.

Steve was about to switch the gateway to communication mode to start the round of calls to relatives and friends to say goodbye when he realized something. "This is the scary moment," he said. "When I close the gateway to them. If we are interrupted or anything goes wrong, they are trapped there with enough food and supplies for a year, at least, but only we know where they are. We have to succeed and join them."

"Let's not think too much or worry about what might happen," Justin said. "There are many risks, and we have many more to take before it's over."

* * * * *

After dinner the round of gateway calls began. Emerson surprised his friend and neighbor by appearing as a talking head across his kitchen table; his friend seemed to accept the situation quickly and agreed to take on the cat for the duration. Then they opened the gateway in Emerson's apartment, and he retrieved a suitcase of clothes and some special possessions. No one commented on the pipe, or whether there'd be weed supplied off-planet.

Rasna spoke to her parents in Santa Clara. They seemed much more surprised by the appearance of the gateway, and it took several minutes to explain that it was part of the technological breakthrough she was getting involved in, like a startup. She could postpone school and get in on the ground floor. They took that explanation well, but her mother wondered when she would get time to date, and would there be the right kind of boys around?

Samantha operated the joystick for the first time to walk through her parents' house. Everything appeared normal, and she found them together in the kitchen cleaning up after dinner. They heard her first, and turned to see her face through the gateway frame. "Sam! Is that you? How are you doing that?"

"Dad, we've made an amazing discovery at the lab—we've found a way to communicate across long distances." Justin had helped her work on a version of the truth that wouldn't reveal much in case they were questioned. "Justin's here with me." He stuck his head in the frame and waved.

"Hi, Justin! Good to see you," Sam's mother said, and suddenly it was just a family phone call.

"We don't have much time," Samantha said. "I need you to know I'm following our dream, and what we're doing is the right thing. I won't be able to call you very often, but I'll be safe. If anyone comes by to ask questions, you don't know where I am or anything about what we've done. Just keep cool and don't tell them anything."

"That doesn't sound very safe," her father said. "Are you sure you know what you're doing? We heard about the explosion and were worried when you didn't respond to our calls."

"That's one of the things that happened, Dad," Sam said. "Because of the explosion, Homeland Security is arresting all of us, and we're hiding out. We'll be hiding out until it's safe to come back. Which I hope is soon. But I'll try to get messages to you when I can."

"I'm not liking this at all," her dad said. "But you're an adult and we raised you to do what's right. You're going to be with her, Justin?"

"Yes," Justin said, nodding and putting his arm around her. "I will."

Sam's dad nodded and hugged her mother, while her mother looked like she was going to cry, but nodded also. "Good luck," she said.

* * * * *

Steve begged off, saying he would call his family later—they wouldn't expect to hear from him for months anyway. Justin had already warned his parents, but decided to drop in on his grandfather, who lived alone out in the country near the old Marine base. He had stuck with the old house after Justin's grandmother died, resisting all efforts to get him moved into town where he'd be closer to his children and the hospital. Justin wondered if he hadn't inherited a lot of his stubbornness from Grandpa Smith.

Justin stepped around inside the house until he found Gramps, watching TV from the couch. He opened the window in front of the TV. Gramps didn't stir and his eyes were closed. "Gramps," Justin said. He had to repeat it loudly a few times before Gramps' eyes fluttered and he woke up.

"Justin? Is that you?" Gramps still looked woozy.

"Yes, it's me. Calling via a new projection thingie we built."

"You look good. Great picture!" Gramps sat up and leaned forward. "It's like you're really there!"

"Look, we don't have a lot of time to talk. I just wanted to explain to you that I'm going away for awhile, and it will be hard for me to talk to you. It's for a great cause and I've already told Mom and Dad."

"An adventure? And your dad approved? I guess he's grown up some. He used to be a worrier. You're smarter than we ever were, and I trust you know what you're doing. I just wish I could go on an adventure, but those days are over for me."

"No, they're not," Justin said. "You just have to keep them shorter and easier."

"I wish I could go with you. There's not much left that I can do here. I've let the garden go, and the house needs painting, but I can't do it."

"I've gotta go, Gramps. I'll be back. And don't let me forget this," Justin said, dropping a bundle of bills through the gateway. "Just hide that someplace safe and I'll be back for it."

Gramps just stared at the money on the carpet in front of him. "How did you do that?"

"Don't worry about it. If anybody comes asking around about me, you haven't seen me, you don't know where I am, and you're a confused old man with a bad memory."

"I think I can act that part without breaking a sweat."

＊ ＊ ＊ ＊

When the calls were done, they opened the gateway to New Earth and retrieved Bubna and Emerson Wilding, who had put up most of the tents and started work on setting up the Vortex-5 there. They were tired and hungry since they had not stopped to rest, and even though the sun was still high in the sky on New Earth, their body clocks told them to sleep.

Steve set the Vortex-5 up as a listening post again, to record sound and video from Gao's office as well as the Oval Office and Chief of Staff's office, then they all went to bed.

Oval Office

Morning came, and news reports still did not report any clues as to who the "terrorists" might be. Steve and Justin listened to the recordings of morning activity at Gao's office and the White House.

Steve took off his headphones and called everyone together. "This meeting happened in the Oval Office about ten AM DC time," he said, and then he played the file back.

The sound was not perfect, but the President's voice was distinctive: "Send them in."

"Good morning, Madame President."

"Good morning. I've read your memo and the background. I agree that these people present a clear and present danger to the security of the United States."

"So you will sign the proposed orders?"

"Yes. I'm a bit unhappy that I wasn't informed of these developments at an earlier stage, Ms. Immerman."

"It did not appear to warrant your involvement until the existence of a breakthrough with national security implications had been confirmed. We get stories like this all the time that turn out to be hyped for attention."

"Nevertheless, I would like to have been briefed. Your strategic threats officer—McDonald?—may have mishandled this. Foster should be pursued and secured."

"We're working on it, Ma'am. The tail lost him and he hasn't turned up or used his phone in days, but we have positive ID on him as the person seen in security videos stepping out of thin air to steal gold bars from a sealed vault. We searched his home and computers and have found evidence of recent erasures, so he was there after the explosion. But so far we haven't been able to recover anything useful. And most of the conspirators have gone to ground. We have custody of the professor who ran the project, but he seems to know nothing useful, and the student we picked up has resisted questioning."

"Persuade him—bring them to the secure facility here, where we have the tools. And this Prof. Wilson you have been holding—use him, train him. Those implants weren't cheap and he has an in with these people you can use."

"Yes, Ma'am. That's part of the plan. And the kill orders?"

"'By any means necessary.' We want what they know, or we want them eliminated. It's too dangerous to have Chinese spies sniffing around who might find them before we do."

Another voice spoke. "We've got sigint searching for any clue as to their whereabouts. Once we have a location, anyone there will go on the list, and the drones are ready."

"I want to approve the location before you use drones in an inhabited area. Wilderness is one thing, but if there are large numbers of civilians who get to the scene before we do, we can't hide what has happened. Much preferable to surround and arrest them."

"Yes, Ma'am. That is SOP. Drones will be used only if we have no other way of getting to the scene before they move again."

"All right. I didn't like the bad publicity from that Idaho incident."

Steve stopped the playback. They all stood silently for a moment, considering their new status.

"That makes hiding on New Earth a lot more appealing," Samantha said. "And 'Foster'?" She looked stricken. "Could that possibly have been Dylan?"

"What other Foster would have been able to break into the lab and operate the gateway?" Justin said. "That explains a lot—"

"And what was that about the Chinese?" Bubna said. "Where did that come from?"

"We've tried to keep the existence of the gateway technology secret, but it looks like there have been leaks," Justin said. "Probably Dylan. I'm wondering how he could have operated the gateway software without knowing one of our logins." He looked around; no one looked guilty.

"I think he might have been snooping in my phone at one point," Samantha said. "He knew too much at times, and I did give him the passcode once. But I didn't expect him to remember it."

"Well, it's too late to worry about it," Justin said. "The government—and maybe the Chinese, too—are after us for the gateway. We have to stop worrying about them finding out, and start thinking of what we can do to protect ourselves. And that implant bit—we need to find and rescue Prof. Wilding."

"We should do what we can to stop them from following us using a similar device," Bubna said. "I know we ordered a Vortex-6 with another eightfold increase in qubits, and the fab may have started on it. And there are probably more Vortex-5s in the pipeline. Collecting those should be a high priority, before they realize they want them."

"I agree," Justin said, "that should be the first thing we do after we get people over and safe. Like today. And then find Ben and Friedman, and Prof. Wilson. And on that I have some news: I've been listening to the recordings from Gao's office, and it looks like they're holding Ben and Prof. Friedman in that building. Let's look at the directory and floor plan on the first floor...."

Steve directed the one-way gateway view to Gao's office, then changed some coordinates to get the view to the ground floor, where he joysticked around the lobby until he found the directory. There wasn't much there—no information about Homeland Security's floors. He moved the view up to the lowest floor of the HomeSec floors and joysticked down toward an EXIT sign, where a floor plan was posted. "Aha," Steve said, "this block of tiny rooms looks promising."

He joysticked down the hall, at one point passing through a woman— they got a brief flash of her innards in cross-section. The view settled in front of the first door with a small security window; several others appeared on that side of the hall. Steve moved the view through the door—empty. As was the next, and the next; each room had a bed and toilet, and little else. On the fourth try, they saw a man sitting on the edge of the bed—"Prof. Friedman," Steve said. "Still here; it doesn't look like they keep people here long. What should we do?"

"He doesn't know anything, and if we take him, they will know and the alarms will go off," Justin said. "Our original reasons for keeping him out of this still stand—family and career."

"I'm not sure I would have chosen to join this myself," Bubna said, "if I had known it would come to this so quickly. Not that I'm not happy to be part of it, but I would have thought a lot more before deciding. Leave him there—they'll let him go when it's clear he's not involved."

"I hope so," Samantha said. "He looks unhappy. And bored."

Steve looked around. "I guess leaving him is the consensus. Moving on." He moved the view directly through the wall to the next cell, where Ben lay asleep on the bed. "Okay, what about Ben? He knows everything and they have been working him over—he looks tired."

"We rescue him now while no one's around," Justin said.

Steve widened the gateway and positioned it directly in front of Ben's sleeping form. "The camera on that side can already see some darkening from the photons we're stealing, but when I switch it to matter transfer, it will look a bit into this room, so everybody move away from that side. And Justin, get ready to shout at him to jump through as soon as I open it. Best you not show yourself."

Justin positioned himself right in front of the gateway, and when Steve hit the switch, shouted, "Ben! Wake up! Time to go!"

Ben's eyes opened and he started to sit up. "What?" He blinked a few times and focused on what he could see through the gateway. "Oh!" And with that, he stood up and stepped over the threshold and into Justin's arms.

Steve flicked the gateway closed, but not before they heard a faint alarm from the cell left behind. He moved the view through the remaining two cells, but they were empty.

"Buddy," Justin said, hugging Ben. "How are you?"

"Very, very happy to see you," Ben said. "They've been asking me questions for days, and wouldn't let me sleep much. I'm in bad shape."

Justin walked him to the office, where he sat in one of the few chairs while he talked. "At first they wanted mostly to know where all of you were. Then they started asking about the lab and the Vortex-5 project. Oh, and they have been intercepting messages and calls on our new phones—I have no idea how they did that, so we shouldn't use them again. But they didn't know much and they hadn't been able to decrypt any of the traffic through the Grey Tribe app, so that's good."

"Anything about Dylan?" Samantha asked.

"They wanted to know where he was, too, but I told them I had not seen him for a month—which is true."

"We listened in on a meeting with the President," Justin said. "Dylan was the one who opened the gateway and blew up the lab. He stole some gold and got himself caught on tape doing it. And they think the Chinese are after us as well."

"Really? The President? The Chinese?—none of that was mentioned. Mostly endless questions about you guys, why was I conspiring against my country, that kind of thing. I tried not to get drawn into talking and just stopped answering after awhile. They finally let me sleep."

"And I guess we should let you sleep," Justin said. "There's a cubbyhole in back with a sleeping bag for you."

Chapter Sixteen: Exodus

Talisman

Steve set the gateway back to looking through the two fab warehouses for partly-finished pieces of the rumored new Vortex-5s, as well as the new design Vortex-6 they had ordered up. They discovered two additional crates had appeared where they had left the empty ones a week earlier; they were a bit larger and had the right labels to be the grid plates for the Vortex-6 design. "The improvements this time shrank the scale of the grid to half the width per element," Steve said. "So the plates are just a little larger, but there are four times as many qubits."

They repeated their earlier theft and put the empty crates back in place. But they found no evidence of extra Vortex-5s in either warehouse.

"At least we have the makings of the most powerful machine ever," Justin said. "Now we have to come up with plans to prevent anyone from repeating the work. Like by subtly sabotaging the fabs, and keeping an eye on other quantum computers they may be cooking up."

Bubna looked worried. "And I wonder if leaving this warehouse machine here is a good idea; once we are set up with working machines over there, wouldn't it be safest to take this one with us? They will find this place eventually."

Justin looked at Bubna, then at Emerson. "He's right. Once we know we can do everything we need to do from camp, we need to dismantle this place and take the machine with us. Sorry, Emerson, we kid-napped you for just a few weeks of security."

"I don't mind," Emerson replied. "I am totally loving this. It's a lot more interesting than my usual life."

"Lets hope it doesn't get too much more interesting!" Justin said. "We don't have enough people to use the gateway to defend ourselves very well. There are a million destructive things we could do that would slow them down, but we can't damage too much or let our activities become public knowledge, or there'll be a panic and a crackdown to make the State of Emergency look like good times. We have to con-sider our strategy very carefully. It's easy to destroy, hard to build a new way of life."

Ben had woken up and joined them. "I should take a phone and go somewhere to check the Grey Tribe messages and tell them what's happened. I'll probably have ten minutes to operate the phone before anyone could arrive to arrest me, so I'll keep it short and come back quickly."

"Put the battery in, send, take the battery out," Steve said. "Move a mile or two. Put the battery in, get messages, take the battery out. And so on. Don't give them time to find you and follow you back here."

"They will catch on quickly to that," Ben said. "So I think we should ask Michael McCulloch for his coordinates for a face-to-face chat. From now on, we need to talk to them via the only secure method, the gateway itself."

Justin and Steve looked at each other. "Of course," Justin said. "We don't need encrypted channels if we know where people we want to talk to are."

"And I've got an idea for a system to find people wherever they may be," Steve said. "We can't scan in or specify DNA yet, though in the long run we should try to get that capability. But what we can do is make unique physical tokens, using 3-D printing of a block of plastic with an embedded filament of carbon thread. This would be simple to specify in the program space we have for queries, yet complex enough that no other object in the universe would match it. Embed it in a person, or wear it, and you can always find them using the gateway."

"That sounds like something we could do fairly quickly. Like a dog tag for each of us." Justin said.

"But even better—when we have enough program space, we can have a subprogram always listening to the area around the talisman," Steve said. "We could have it activate a gateway near that spot on a verbal command from the person with the ID block."

"So, like a magic talisman. If you had it, you could move around freely then leave via gateway whenever you wanted to."

"That would be the idea," Steve said. "Depending on how complicated the voice commands can be made, you could specify where you want to go, or what you want the gateway to do—sizing, transparency, photons-only, etc."

"Another project for our overloaded research department," Justin said. "Which is you, plus a little bit of help from me. We need more programmers and physicists."

They viewed the neighborhood again before Ben left, just to be careful; they watched through the gateway as he took off in Sam's car. When he returned a half-hour later, he had written down the precise longitude and latitude of Michael McCulloch's mountain cottage in

Switzerland.

Grey Leader

Michael McCulloch wasn't surprised when a window opened in front of him as he relaxed on his couch with a glass of wine. It was after ten PM, and he was tired. But it was thrilling to see what Prof. Wilson's California kids had cooked up.

Two young men looked out at him through the gateway; behind them, he could see other people, and it was very bright. One of the two young men said, "I'm Justin Smith, Prof. Wilson's student, and this is Ben, who you've been in contact with earlier."

"Nice to see you. This is better than the Internet."

Steve stuck his head in the frame. "In 3-D and stereo sound!"

"Well, kids," McCulloch said, wondering if that was condescending— but they were so *young*—"we've been at this battle for years and things are only looking worse for freedom. After the Russian war, Europe is a mess, the US is a fascist state much like China, and together they are turning the whole world into their shared police state. It's not clear how much longer I will be safe here. So you come to me with this news at the right time. It scares me, but it's the only way."

"We've started the base on New Earth. When we have the machines set up and working there, we can safely take this machine with us and do all our guerrilla work from there."

"Ben described your plans. You are thinking big, but we need to think bigger. We've set up a special comm network for recruits willing to leave their current locations to join a big rebel effort—they're ready to go when we give them the word to assemble at the various collection points. So far we have hundreds of people, mostly meeting your requirements for programmers and scientists. They've also been told what to bring with them."

Samantha stepped forward. "I'm Samantha West, also with Students for Liberty. One of the things we are worried about is keeping out the spies, the power-hungry, and the psychopaths. One of our members, who I admit used to be my boyfriend—bad judgment on my part— has already caused a lot of damage and revealed some of the gateway's abilities to Homeland Security. What assurance do we have that your people are good?"

"The most we can say is that each of them were willing to take the risk to oppose their governments to maintain some privacy and space for individual freedom online. I can't promise you none of them will cause trouble or try to gain power over others. But I would say they are a most reliable group, since we have had almost no leaks or security issues with any of them. Though a sleeper agent is always possible."

"So trust, but not too much," Samantha said. "We'll keep access to the gateways restricted to a few to be sure. We still don't know how Dylan —my traitorous boyfriend—did it."

Steve stepped in again. "I'm got that fixed already. Extra security layer. Could add biometric IDs, I suppose."

"We can worry about that later," McCulloch said. "I'm ready to go. I have some work left here, wiping machines and removing evidence, but I've already packed most of what I need, and in here—" he held up a memory stick, "—is everything I need to set up anywhere. How long until we can get a safe network connection from there?"

"Almost immediately. The machine is almost ready," Steve said, looking questioningly at Bubna, who nodded, "—and the program for hopping wifi nodes is ready. We should be on the net tomorrow."

Escape to New Earth

And so the exodus began.

They reopened the gateway to New Earth, and moved the supplies that had been delivered in the last few days over. Then Bubna and Emerson went over to continue setting up the Vortex-5. When they came back to the gateway and confirmed the machine was operating and the computers were set up, Steve crossed over to do tests and be sure it was safe to rely on it; he took the mice in the cage along, just in case.

Justin and Samantha hid behind a partition to get a bit of privacy. "I'd rather be going with you guys," Justin said, "but I have to stay a few more days to work with Wendy and line up suppliers. If by some chance I get arrested, you guys should come get me."

"Of course," Sam said. "But that won't happen. How many days?"

"I'm thinking two or three. Just a bit more setting up and some expected deliveries, and we can handle everything else through agents. I need to visit one of Wendy's suggested agents here to give him more money and be sure we can trust him. This guy is in the industry and has the connections to have parts made in neutral Europe, something Wendy was pretty sure she couldn't pull off."

"Risky having a mercenary knowing our business."

"It's always risky," Justin said, "but you keep him well-paid and never give him any information the bad guys don't already know, and our losses are minimized in case he goes to the government. He's paid not to ask questions or worry about where these parts are going. I might drop clues that we are arms dealers, a story that he will understand."

"Just don't take any risks. Take cabs, pay cash, come straight back. We need to get everybody out."

"Yes, ma'am. I wouldn't want to be away from you for very long."

A gateway opened on the other side of the room, and Steve stepped through it. "Up and tested. Time to go," he announced. He went to the console and changed the coordinates back to Michael McCulloch's living room.

McCulloch moved into the field of view. "Ready?" he said.

"If you don't mind roughing it," Steve said. "Camp is a bit raw yet."

"I'll need to sleep since it's two AM my time, but I have everything boxed and ready." McCulloch pointed to a stack of boxes and a row of suitcases.

"Bring 'em on through," Steve said.

Justin stood just inside the gateway and took each box as McCulloch handed them over. Then McCulloch came through and handed Steve a memory stick. "Coordinates for the rest of the pickups. I've sent messages out confirming the times tomorrow morning."

"We'll handle that from New Earth, along with pickup of the campus contingent," Steve said, closing the gateway to Switzerland. "We should all get back to camp. Justin, when you're done here, Emerson will come back over to help you dismantle this machine so we can retrieve it."

"Two days, I expect," Justin said. He hugged Sam one more time, then Rasna, then Steve. "I'll see all of you soon."

Justin watched as the rest walked through the far gateway, and waved back as Steve went to the console there and closed it. The gateway vanished.

It was very quiet in the empty warehouse.

Purchasing Dept.

Justin had a lengthy list of parts and supplies needed. He had gone over it with Bubna and identified alternate sources in Europe for most of the items; they had also added a variety of decoy goods they would talk about to make it less obvious what they were really doing.

He closed up at the warehouse and left. Making his way to a main street, he hailed a cab after waiting ten minutes—without a phone, he was reduced to antiquated methods. He had the cab drop him off a few blocks from Wendy's place and made his way to her apartment.

"How is this going to work?" Justin said, after she got him coffee and they sat at her kitchen table.

"You work with Quinn," Wendy said. "Quinn works with the other agents. They order things under one of our corporate names—there are six now—and they are delivered to a warehouse space we've rented north of Stockholm. We've contracted for a temp worker who will log in all the shipments. He's being told someone else comes by once a week to pick up items after hours, so he won't realize we're just gatewaying in to take them away."

"Did you get the new phones?"

"Yes. Dumb phones for old people, and I paid cash for prepaid time, so they should be safe. No Grey Tribe app because I suspect they are watching for that. Just be sure you don't use any keywords, even in voice calls. Use it to call me mostly, and it should stay safe."

"Okay," Justin said, taking the phone. "We won't need phones for much longer—when Steve gets his talisman system set up, we'll be able to call up and talk securely over mini-gateways."

"And someday we'll have flying cars. Let's move along, I'm supposed to be getting on a plane to Atlanta in two hours., so I need to leave."

"I should go see Quinn now. Our biggest hurdle is getting the CAD files for the gallium arsenide grids to the new fabs without it being obvious they were taken from our project. Steve has worked the files over and tried to hide the origins, but if anyone compares the masks, it'll be obvious where they come from. I've got them on a memory stick."

"The worst that can happen is our order is intercepted and the Swedish warehouse is compromised," Wendy said. "Then we abandon the shells we used to order and pay for everything related to that, but we can always start again."

"If it gets to that point, we'll have to find a new way to make the machines, because there won't be any fabs left who aren't alerted."

"I find paying extra for silence usually does wonders. In Europe, they're used to secretive orders and shadowy clients. The manufacturers know if the order is cut off by state action, the lucrative business stops completely. I'm pretty sure they won't look too closely. In the last round, they sold parts to the Iranians, and even after what happened there, they haven't really changed their ways."

Part Three: Betrayal

Chapter Seventeen: Sellout

Dylan

Burned and wounded by his encounter with the gateway, Dylan Foster had dragged his backpack full of gold to the basement level, then out a fire exit to the back of the building. He dragged the backpack down the service alley a block, then behind some bushes and threw mulch chips over it to disguise it. Then he limped back to his apartment and got his car to pick it up. The sirens warned him to approach carefully, but he was able to get to the spot and back out without being noticed by the campus cops who were already on scene. Then he drove himself to the medical center ER, where they took one look at his face and rushed him forward for treatment.

"What happened to you, honey?" The admitting nurse dabbed carefully at his eye. "This looks bad but it's hard to tell until we clean you up a little."

"I was cleaning out a grill with gasoline and it must have exploded. Something cut my shoulder and I can barely see out of that eye," Dylan said.

She tsked. "You should know better than that."

"I didn't have anything else," he shrugged.

The nurse helped him get his shirt off and slapped on a temporary dressing. "That looks deep. We're going to have to clean that out. The doctor will be along in a minute."

He waited on the examining table for some time. When the doctor came, she didn't ask him any questions, but tutted when she saw how deep the cut was. "Almost to bone. What did this?"

He shrugged. "Don't know. Flying glass, maybe."

"I don't see anything in there that needs to come out. Antiseptic rinse and stitches should fix you right up. But no activity with the arm for a few days, and take it very slow after."

It was an hour before they were done with him, and it was nearing midnight. His right eye had been burned, so he had an antibiotic salve to put in, and an eye patch to wear. He was told to check with his regular physician in a few days for followup.

He paid cash for the copay.

✳ ✳ ✳ ✳ ✳

Dylan went back to his apartment to get his laptop and wipe the files on his desktop. He pulled out his phone and started to use it when he remembered his worry that he was being tracked, so he left it. He packed suitcases and got out as quickly as he could, then drove to a sleazy motel where he could pay cash and they didn't ask for ID. The front desk clerk paused for a moment when she saw his burned face and eyepatch, but took his money without comment. The room was clean, at least. He showered what parts of him he could and felt better. He was going to have to focus and plan his strategy for negotiating.

He slept on the top sheet, just to be safe.

＊ ＊ ＊ ＊ ＊

Dylan spent the next day charting out the possibilities from his motel room. He knew his car was a liability, since they could scan his license plate number at many of the major intersections with cameras. The news reports didn't mention that they were looking for anyone, but then they wouldn't. He would have to leverage what he now knew to get a deal from the Feds, and that would be tricky. For now, he was safe if he stayed put.

He went to the diner next door for dinner, and when he got back started working on a flow chart of the possibilities. The local news station on the radio hadn't changed what they were reporting on the explosion, but then the flow of canned programming was interrupted: "We've just heard that there has been a building collapse on the university campus, that same building where an explosion happened last night…"

He switched on the TV, and the local channel showed regular programming for a few minutes while the radio news kept repeating the story with no additional details. Then the TV station broke into the show in progress with a "Special Report," and the view from their helicopter of the collapsed buildings and fires told him that he had more leverage than he had known. The only reason to trash the IT building as well as the lab was to destroy the backups of the group's programs. And he had copied them all onto a memory stick.

The gold, it turned out, was really not important. He had something far more valuable to trade to the Feds.

Gao and Dylan

At his Homeland Security office downtown, Andrew Gao's intercom buzzed. "What is it?" he said.

"A Dylan Foster here to see you."

"Send him up." Gao picked up the phone and called Security. "Gao here. I'm expecting a Dylan Foster here from reception, check the videos. Post someone at reception to make sure he can't leave, and send two men up here in case we need to arrest him. Have them stay outside my door until I come out. Alert McDonald so he can jump in if he wants." Another minute passed before Dylan arrived.

"Dylan," Gao said, "Good to see you again. Looks like you've had a bad time lately. Sit. Can I get you anything?"

"No, I'm fine. I'm just here to make a deal."

"We know you were involved in that explosion on campus. Frankly we've wanted to arrest you, but we couldn't find you."

"I made sure of that. But you won't need to arrest me. I have something you're going to need badly—the source code for the quantum computer they've turned into a teleportation device. They obviously wanted all copies destroyed, or they wouldn't have trashed the IT building."

"You have the source code," Gao said carefully. "Where is it?"

"In a safe place, encrypted, and if I don't come back to retrieve it personally in an hour, it gets destroyed."

"Okay. So what do you want for it?"

"I want full credit for the discovery, and principal author status on all papers that may result. I want a public announcement that I'm being appointed head of a new national research lab with photo ops with the President and Congress, so you can't easily get rid of me. I get to keep the gold I retrieved—"

"Stole. From the Federal Reserve Bank, but actually owned by Treasury. The people's gold."

"The people owe me. And I want an additional ten million a year in consulting fees, tax-free. A fully-staffed lab with no budget limitations and free choice of personnel. I was able to make the machine work, and I can develop it further."

Another voice broke in. "Foster, this is Jim McDonald, Advanced Threat Assessment in DC. We've re-evaluated our position in light of these new developments, and we'll give you what you want. I'll have to clear some details with my superiors, but they are now very interested in bringing you in to manage this problem."

"Good," Dylan said. "Now that we all know what we're talking about, it only makes sense."

"We can't give you a completely free hand—you'll have to answer to a White House liaison, like we all do—and we will want to see half the source code up-front to be sure you have it. But then we'll set you up as you ask. And then we'll want results, and you'll deposit the source code with us."

"That sounds fair. I'll still know more than anyone about it, and without me you'd still take a lot longer to understand how it works."

"Get results and we'll be happy," McDonald said. "If you fuck up, I can make no promises."

"Now I need to leave. And I want you to stop following me, and tapping my phone. I want to be free to go home. Immediately."

"Gao, you want to handle that?" McDonald said.

"I can do that. You are free to go, Dylan. Because there are other actors in play, though, you'll want our people keeping watch on you. You could end up kidnapped by a foreign power."

"What?" Dylan said. "Who?"

"The Chinese, possibly. Or others. In fact, we need to get you to a safe house now, because even these offices aren't safe."

"Oh," Dylan said. "Oh. I see."

"We've had prisoners disappear from locked cells," McDonald said. "Your friends are finding new ways to cause trouble. You need us to protect you."

"That does make going home sound like a bad idea. Okay, I accept your protection. But I still need to go back to retrieve the source code and my things."

"See to it, Gao," McDonald said. "I'll take this upstairs for feedback."

* * * * *

After the security detail escorted Dylan out, Gao said, "Still there?"

"Yes," McDonald's voice replied. "He's a weasel. But word came down from the Oval Office itself that I am considered a fuckup for not bringing him in in the first place—hindsight being so easy from up there. So we give him what he wants—it's nothing compared to the military implications of this. When we have the source code, if he's not useful we dump him. Let him try taking us to court with that agreement. Most likely we can hold him forever for national security reasons and confiscate whatever we've paid him, because he's already a felon many times over. And who knows, maybe he's just the man to run the show."

"He's just a grad student," Gao said.

"But he's brilliant, and comes equipped with the right instincts to survive in our wonderful government. Greed, dishonesty, and a willingness to sell out his friends. Or am I too cynical?"

"You are, boss," Gao replied.

"I'm going to fly out there to handle this in person. I'll send you the details—have someone meet me at the airport."

Chapter Eighteen: Justin's Deal

Justin and Quinn

Justin got out of a cab at the downtown office building where Quinn had his office. Hiding the thick roll of bills he carried, he pulled one out and said, "Keep the change."

The building was a 1960s glass-and-steel tower that had seen better days. The lobby directory had a listing for "Quinn Trading, LLC," on an upper floor, so he took the elevator. The office door was frosted glass, and when he knocked there was no answer. Opening the door, he could see the reception desk was empty.

"Oh, hello," said an older bald man stepping out from the only doorway leading back. "You must be the person 'Wanda' told me to expect. I'm Quinn, and I don't need to know your name, just like I didn't need to know hers." He stuck out his hand and they shook.

"I was expecting more people," Justin said.

"I sent the receptionist to lunch. Better no one knows you were here. And it has been quiet here in recent years—business has been really slow. I'm thinking of giving up the office and working from home, since I had to let everyone else go a year ago. But I've been here almost twenty years, so it's hard to break old habits."

"I'm sorry to hear that. The economy sucks."

"Many things suck, young man. Now why don't we get to the business at hand? *That* doesn't suck." Quinn led Justin into his office. "Sit down. Need anything?"

"I'm fine. But thanks."

"So Wanda has filled me in on most of what you expect from me as an agent. I understand discretion is very important and your interests are planning to be a good customer for a long time, all music to my ears."

"We need a lot of parts and equipment delivered, and we need them to be routed through neutral countries wherever possible."

"I'm familiar with the arms control regimes of this country and a variety of other jurisdictions," Quinn said. "For anything not related to nuclear weapons or missiles, we can get it for you, though of course there will be additional expenses related to the discretion required."

"I fully understand that. We'll expect you to bargain as you may, but in the end price is not our chief concern."

"Did Wanda tell you about my retainer policy? She paid that, but I'd advise paying into your account here as much as you intend to spend on your first orders. We need the money before the orders go out."

"She mentioned that. I've brought enough for our first orders." Justin slid a paper bag across the desk. "Half a million in hundreds."

"From a safe source? Bills not in order? My banker is cooperative, but they have to be untraced."

"Older bills from banks, not serialized. I didn't actually check." Justin opened the bag and riffled through a bundle. "Random."

"So outline the kinds of things you are looking for."

"Wire, tubing, cables, computers. Pumps and valves. Medical equipment. Scientific instruments. Prefab buildings. Generators. Liquid gases like nitrogen. And it's critical we establish relationships with the two fabs in Germany capable of making specialized gallium arsenide circuits to our design. The CAD files for what we want are in this," he said, pushing the memory stick across Quinn's desk toward him.

"I don't know too much about CAD files, but I know people who do. We'll put them in a secure place and transfer them to the fabs when it's time."

"It's critical that these remain secret," Justin said. "Tell them if there are any leaks, they lose all our business. And we intend to be regular customers. I'm told we will be spending millions on these."

"You want me to approach both of them?"

"Approach but don't reveal. Pick one based on price and quality, then reveal the full specs to only the one. It's better to use only one for production, and not leave the one we leave out with any information that might leak."

"I get it," Quinn said, scribbling a note. "I will have to get someone who knows a lot more than I do about fabs to help me with this and talk the right talk. Which will cost extra."

"As I said, we want it done carefully, with the highest quality and secrecy, not cheaply."

"Okay, then. How will you communicate with me?"

"I will visit personally until we've established a secure alternative."

Justin got up to leave. "It was nice to meet you. However it might look to you because of our secrecy, we're working for a better world. In case that matters to you."

"Everyone who comes in here thinks they're working for a better world. It's just that people disagree about what that means. I don't judge."

*****

After he left Quinn's building, Justin walked to the corner where he had seen a coffeeshop on the way in. He ordered a cup and a muffin and waited. When his coffee came, he found a table and sat down. He realized how tired he was. The muffin tasted like the best muffin he'd ever had.

When he looked up, the four men had already surrounded him. They all that that security look—dark glasses, fitted shirts, dark jackets. "Come along with us, please," the leader said. "We'd rather not make a scene."

There was no sense fighting; Justin could see they had guns underneath their jackets. He got up and followed the leader out of the coffeeshop, with the other three flanking him. "Not that it matters," Justin said, "but how the hell did you find me?"

"Facial recognition. That cam up there, I believe," said the agent, pointing up at a globe on the light pole at the intersection.

"Ah. I didn't expect that."

"Most people don't," the agent said. "We don't like to talk about it, because it wouldn't work so well if people realized how much we use it."

They walked on in silence until they reached an alley, where a black van waited. Justin felt a needle in his arm and everything went black as they bundled him into the van.

Justin and McDonald

Justin woke up gradually. Lights above him were unpleasant, so he tried to pull the pillow over his head. He remembered being brought here, just barely. Opening his eyes a bit, gray was the color of everything he could see.

There was a stack of his clothing folded on the chair next to the bed, so he sat up and started to dress, because it was cold in the room.

Someone knocked on the door, and it opened. A man in gray coveralls brought him a tray; breakfast, with coffee. "Enjoy your breakfast, sir," the man said cheerfully, and left.

Justin sorted through what he remembered. Wendy, then Quinn, then the coffeeshop and the men who took him away. So this was a jail of some sort. He sat down and started to eat. Cold runny scrambled eggs, cold dry toast. At least the coffee was warm.

After he finished eating and used the toilet, he tried to gather clues from what he could see of the room. No windows, armored door. The furniture had bar-coded inventory control stickers, but no writing. He sat on the edge of the bed and thought.

Someone knocked, and as before they opened the door immediately without waiting for him to say anything. Two men came in and motioned for him to come with them. Outside the door, the hall looked like an ordinary office building's, but there were hints of military use—Air Force posters and pictures along the hall of people in uniform. They escorted him down the hall to a room with a conference table, where two other men in suits waited, and held a chair for him to sit in.

"Justin," the younger Asian man said. "I'm Andrew Gao, investigator for Homeland Security here. This is my boss Jim McDonald, chief of Advanced Threat Assessment, out from DC."

He didn't really feel like shaking their hands. He remembered Gao and his voice well.

"We understand you're not in a mood to talk," McDonald said. "But you can help yourself and your friends more by cooperating with us sooner rather than later."

"I don't have to answer any questions," Justin said. "I have the right to remain silent until I have an attorney present."

McDonald laughed. "Kid, that might work if we were talking about a standard criminal offense here. But you are involved in a terrorist conspiracy, and the law gives us power to ignore all those niceties. Counterterrorism is war, and you are a terrorist. You've already caused millions of dollars of property damage."

"But no deaths," Justin said, hoping it was true.

"Lucky accident," Gao said. "One of our guys was hit by falling concrete and spent a few days in the hospital. You couldn't have been sure everyone was clear of the building when you brought it down. Right?"

Justin had no answer for that.

"Every national security agency is crapping their pants over what we've seen you kids do with that computer," McDonald continued. "Memos re-evaluating physical security for all installations are being written as we speak. All of our assumptions about barriers and access control are being questioned, if you can enter any room or steal anything you want."

"We're not out to do anyone harm," Justin said.

"But you have created a major ruckus and apparently attracted the attention of the Chinese and who knows who else," McDonald said. "We can't allow you to control the technology even if you are harmless, because someone else who isn't might get hold of it. You understand this is a matter of national survival."

"So because there are dangerous people in the world, you have to ignore the Constitution and become just like the barbarians. Because the ends justify the means."

McDonald looked at Gao and paused before speaking. "What you have is so dangerous that the Commander in Chief, acting under her constitutional authority to make life-and-death decisions when there is a clear and present danger, has authorized us to gain control of this technology—or destroy it—by *any means necessary*. And you and your friends are also in grave danger from other powers."

"My friends are safe," Justin said.

"Look, we are not the barbarians," Gao said. "But others may not be so civilized as to leave your loved ones alone. What would you do if the Chinese kidnapped your family and told you they'd be killed if you didn't do what they say?"

"I guess that's a danger," Justin said. "But if they try that, they also know we can come after them and take out their military facilities in a day. So I'd say they will try not to make us mad."

"You've got a point there," McDonald said. "But that doesn't stop terrorists with nothing to lose."

"If there are agencies writing memos," Justin said, "it's because you told too many people about it."

"That," McDonald said wearily, "was not my decision. Your stunt with the buildings made it impossible to keep the political people above us satisfied. And they chose to push the panic button."

"So tell us why you did it," Gao said.

"I think I should listen to myself and not say a thing."

"We've compiled a complete dossier on you and all the others," McDonald said. "Gao here has had his people interviewing your families and searching records for days. I've only had time to read yours completely, but I expect the others are similar—there's no reason why you should be angry at your country. Your life has been comfortable, more than most. Your families think the world of you. Idealistic and naïve, maybe, but not terrorists."

Justin sat silent and looked away.

"Your grandfather sounds like a great guy—he was combative," McDonald said. "Your father was trying to protect you without letting it show. Your mother would not talk to us at all."

"I should warn you," Gao said, "that if you do not cooperate now, we've been ordered to transfer you to our secure facility back East, and there they have a variety of tools—drugs and devices—that can induce a more helpful attitude."

Justin stayed silent.

McDonald looked at Gao. "Andy, leave me alone with him for awhile. I have a feeling I can turn him around, but I need a free hand. If he doesn't listen, you can do whatever you need to."

"You're the boss," Gao said, and left.

"Okay, now we're alone and I can level with you," McDonald said, looking into Justin's eyes. He turned to look at a picture on the wall. "Guys, I am going to have to discuss highly sensitive information. Stop the recording."

After a moment, a tinny voice said, "Yessir. Recording off."

"Now we're really alone," McDonald said. "Here's the thing. What you don't know is that we've been able to bring in Dylan Foster, and he says he has the source code for all of your programs, which he will give us in return for certain considerations. We know he was able to operate your machine because we have video of him stealing gold from a sealed bank vault in New York. I can't control what will happen from here on out, because of the pressure from on high to give him anything he wants in return for duplicating your work."

"Okay," Justin said. He tried not to show how much this news disturbed him. "Dylan doesn't know anything much, and he's a mathematical physicist in a different area. So I don't think he can catch up with us that easily."

"He'll have the help of the best theorists and technologists we can find. Imagine the Manhattan Project, but all aimed at finding and destroying your friends. It will only be a matter of time before they succeed."

"But we will be making progress, too. And we can disrupt any efforts they start."

"You willing to bet on that? How many people will you have working on it? The government can overwhelm you with numbers. In World War II, the German factories and railroads were being bombed day after day for months, and yet their output of arms and ammunition was only marginally affected."

Justin had no answer for that. He thought about what a scenario of constant whack-a-mole efforts to stop the US government would lead to. "I don't know. But I know we have to try."

"You can't win and there will be a lot of damage, and maybe deaths. The chaos could spread in ways neither of us can imagine. So why not stop all that before it starts? The government will have this technology sooner or later. Help us negotiate with your friends. If you help us bring them in, we can keep the technology secret and avoid disrupting everything. You all could be back to you old life in a few days. We'll look the other way on all of the charges we might file. I see in your file that you have a new relationship—" McDonald looked through the dossier. "With a 'Samantha.' She's pretty and obviously brilliant. Why not let us handle it, and go make a real life with her?"

"The reason we can't, and we won't, give it to you," Justin said, "is that we no longer believe our government is run for any goal except increasing the power and status of the people running it. We think this regime would abuse this technology just as badly as the Chinese or any terrorist organization, because it already has. It has rigged elections and insured that only Unity candidates are elected. It has droned civilians whose only crime was to speak freely. It has throttled freedom of thought by making people's livelihoods dependent on the favor of politicians and pressure groups. It has corrupted education through central control of funding, and forced poor children into schools that don't educate, but train them to be victims dependent on the state. It has imprisoned millions of young men for victimless crimes and built a staggering number of prisons that both support and train criminals."

"I can see you've thought about this. But the people did elect this government, because they were afraid. If you help us, you could become a player and have a good chance of changing things. I've been in Washington quite a few years, and I can tell you that none of the people in charge want to harm anyone. They are afraid, too, and they try to keep the people who support them happy by using government power to help them."

"With the result that people who don't support them are extra-taxed or jailed or droned, and the 'help' is just more government employees interfering with business, writing reports no one reads, and going to conferences. Where they plan new prisons and weapons and dream about their retirements."

"Let me ask you this," McDonald said. "What do you suppose would happen if you kids got your way? How would you reorder the world to make it better? If you don't have a plan, then you can't say we should risk disrupting the complex systems of government and business that we have now. Doing nothing might be better than uncontrolled chaos."

"We're not sure yet," Justin replied. "But we do know if the technology gets out, there will be chaos and warfare anyway. Our primary problem is finding a way to allow its use for good, like colonizing other planets, while making sure it is not used for destruction—and we don't know how to do that yet, but we will! The secondary problem is reforming Earth governments to allow their people more freedom. Corrupt and micromanaging government is not going to be consistent with human advancement and expansion. We want an end to surveillance and control, and a return to true freedom of speech, and the full Bill of Rights. We want real elections with candidates that have diverse ideas, not the party hacks you have limited us to. Restoration of the right of every person to succeed or fail based on their merits and hard work, not on connections with the government."

"Most people are just trying to live normal lives with their families— harming them to change things as you propose is hurting the innocent. You shouldn't destroy their livelihoods and wreck their lives for some ideal of freedom you have. You have a responsibility to do as little damage as possible."

"The same argument was made in 1776," Justin said. "We're taking a risk. But the conditions have become intolerable, and the system doesn't allow the people to reform it. Like the frog slowly boiled in a pot, the gradual erosion of our freedoms never seemed all that bad, because each little loss was tolerable, trading for 'security.' But now we are individually not safe from our own government, and it gets steadily worse. We will be as careful as we can to not injure or disrupt normal people's lives, but for their good and their children's good, we have to do something. And we are responsible people."

McDonald tapped his finger on the dossier, and appeared lost in thought. Then he got up and walked to where his back was to the camera in the wall. He mouthed the words, "They are still watching."

Justin raised his eyebrows, but said nothing.

McDonald left the room, saying something to the guards posted on either side of the door. A few minutes later, a door at the other end of the conference room opened. McDonald entered, and said, "I've spoken to Gao and the security officer monitoring. I told them I was done for now and going to lunch with a friend, so they should get their lunch fast and be back by one for the next session. That gives me time to talk to you freely."

"What am I missing? Why do you need to?"

"Because," McDonald said, "I'm letting you go. This is part of the Air Force base—they had to work hard to find a secure facility that your friends would be unlikely to spy on, and this was close. But it's not really secure—walk slowly off the base and no one will challenge you."

"But why?"

"I've been meaning to really retire," McDonald said, "and some of what I've had to do lately just reminds me why I should. I see your idealism and it reminds me what we've lost. My own kids are climbing the ladder, but even as a proud dad, I can see the only one who's doing well is just brown-nosing his way to the top. And it stinks. I've always done my job and followed orders, even when I didn't understand the reasons—and sometimes when I was pretty sure they were wrong. But this old soldier has had enough."

"Won't they come after you?" Justin said.

"I'm already on the outs because of this case, and—if you don't get caught—I have the perfect excuse: your friends spirited you away into thin air while we were eating lunch. They must be wizards to have found you here! Anyway, I will take the risk. I need to sleep at night."

"I hope it goes well for you. You won't regret it."

"I'd better not. The government is a dumb beast, but the people at the top aren't dumb. If you threaten their power, they'll come after you. And if you threaten our people, *I'll* come after you. Be very careful not to antagonize the government further, and they may start to forget about you."

"What about Prof. Wilson?"

"That was one of the last straws, what they are doing with him." McDonald said. "They're experimenting with conditioning people directly with brain implants. For your own good, they will make you docile and agreeable when you get a government directive. You'll feel what they want you to feel. So far just a few, but I'm pretty sure they plan to install more and more of them in key civilians. The implant itself is harmless, but it can be controlled by radio signals."

"Every paranoid schizophrenic's delusions made real. Can it be removed?"

"By simple brain surgery! The tricky bit is he doesn't even know he has it. You should rescue him before they get much chance to program his feelings—he's being held in Homeland Security's secure facility at Ft. Meade, which you can find on old maps as the Kimbrough Army Hospital. New wing to the south, third floor. Got that?"

"Ft. Meade, Kimbrough Hospital, south wing, third floor," Justin recited.

"Right. Now this door goes to the next conference room, which has a door to the parallel hall that way," McDonald said, pointing. "Go right and a few doors down there's an exit stairway door. Go down to the exit door. Turn right and head straight up the road to the main gate; there's a pedestrian exit turnstile. Act like an employee going to lunch."

McDonald got up and held the door open for him. "Exit that way, turn right, down stairs to exit, turn right."

"Thanks," Justin said, holding out his hand to shake.

McDonald pulled him into a bear hug and said, "Good luck. Let's go."

They walked through the door, with McDonald pausing to lock it behind them.

McDonald listened at the door opposite. "No one out there. You leave first, and go right to the exit stair. I'll go left in a few minutes. Now, git."

Chapter Nineteen: The Struggle

ALife Simulation, Model 8: Organism 2998102359041171

Since the war ended, funding for his physics lab at the university had declined. But this freed his team from researching weapons. Now they could go after the tantalizing clues in pre-war experiments showing asymmetries in fundamental interactions of matter and energy, and one experiment in particular he wanted to duplicate—it had shown the speed of light to be almost (but not quite) constant no matter which direction it was going, which conflicted with some of the theories about a medium, or "ether," which any wave must require to propagate. It would be strange if this medium was somehow tethered to the planet, which was known to be traveling at great speed in its orbit around the sun, and the speed of any normal wave in a medium would appear to vary depending on its direction if the medium itself was in motion.

His team did a tremendous job of improving the apparatus with flatter mirrors and carefully isolated it from vibration, sound, and air inside a sealed jar floating on a pool of liquid metal, since it was thought some of those disturbing factors might have caused the slight anomalies seen in the interference patterns in previous experiments.

The day finally arrived when the experiment could be run; the two beams of light split from a single source, traveling crosswise to each other, reflected back and forth several times to increase any differences found, then merged on a screen where interference patterns would change if there was any difference in travel times between the two orthogonal paths.

They did one run and found some variation in the interference patterns, but it was small and might have been due to temperature differences creating slight expansion of some parts of the apparatus. They tried several temperature-control methods and the anomalous pattern remained. The more they ran the experiment, the more obvious it was that light traveled slightly faster in two directions, orthogonal to each other, so the beam speeds matched every quarter-turn of the apparatus; and further experiments confirmed there were three dimensions, x, y, and z, where light traveled slightly faster, which of course rotated as the earth did so they remained at rest relative to the universe. Whatever that meant, since the finding created a burst of new theorizing in the physics community about exactly what light was and what the medium could possibly be....

Prof. Wilson

Walter Wilson was getting used to the routine. They woke him early, fed him, and took him to a lab where he was strapped to a chair and watched movies. Some were full-length films, some short clips. Sometimes he wept for no reason, and other times he was thrilled and excited by the stories. They were surprisingly involving, and he found himself looking forward to the sessions.

Then they fed him again and let him exercise. And after that he was left alone for the rest of the day. They had stopped forcing him to take so many pills, and his head had cleared enough in a few days to start to feel bored. He asked for books and wrote in the notebooks they had given him, but since he had no idea who might end up reading them, he stuck to thoughts on his projects and lists of things to be done when they let him get back to work.

The days passed. He remembered someone had told him while he was fuzzy that he would be released soon. "Soon" seemed to be a long time.

The Interrogation

One day, the routine changed. Prof. Wilson expected to be led to the lab for movies, but instead they escorted him to a featureless room and strapped him to a chair, then left him to wait.

A woman entered; her silver hair was cropped short, and she wore a severe gray suit with a blue scarf that matched her eyes. She stood in front of him with arms crossed, and said, "Prof. Wilson. I'm Christine Immerman, taking over from Jim McDonald, who has been relieved of this case by order of the President. You realize you are very important to us."

Wilson looked up at her, puzzled. "Important? You seem to have forgotten I'm here."

"Some of your students have given us a scare, and apparently got themselves involved with the Grey Tribe, who were our initial target in this investigation. But you don't seem to know very much about what they were up to. And now they've blown up some buildings and disappeared."

"I wouldn't know anything about that," Wilson said. *You fuckers kidnapped me.* "But my students are a bright group, and they know right from wrong. Are you sure you do?"

"Your government is responsible for defending the United States and its people from enemies, both foreign and domestic. And with the Unity government, we've had an opportunity to finally remove the racist and sexist elements that have oppressed so many for so long. The one percenters are no longer running everything for their benefit."

"It seems to me that you have only changed the favored one percent to be a different group. And they are accumulating the wealth to qualify. Of course there's much less wealth to go around now, since you reward the connected, not the productive."

"We have had to compromise and take the long view. We need the cooperation of business to lift up the people. We help them, business supports us. By implementing complete equality in employment and pay, and hiring the disadvantaged first, they have helped bring us to a more socially just society."

"But by helping some businesses, you lock out others. By helping some people, you hurt others. And you have taken away the incentive to try harder, to be conscientious, to manage carefully. Now most businesses are more like government bureaus, and work as efficiently."

"There have been some necessary adjustments," Immerman said. "Reparations have a cost to those who amassed great wealth on the backs of others. But enough about that—this is a matter of national security; we don't have time to waste talking about your obsolete notions. Your students and their friends have come up with a tech-nology that could let them destroy anything and anyone, anywhere. It's too dangerous to be used by anyone but our government; it's more dangerous than a nuclear device. If they had a nuke, we'd be justified in taking any measures necessary to get it under our control… and this is in some ways worse."

"I know nothing about it. I had a student doing some work at the quantum computing lab, but just simulated evolution. No weapons possibilities at all," Wilson said. He noticed he was oddly comfortable in her presence; she was really very striking… *her eyes are so beautiful,* he thought.

"Since they know and trust you, though, we're going to ask you to help us bring them in and prevent the disaster that could happen if they let anyone else get control of that technology."

"Why should I do that? You kidnapped me." Wilson felt a chill. He really did not like being rude to this pleasant creature.

"You of all people should support us. I've read our file—you are gay and HIV positive, and we are the ones who gave you equal rights of marriage and protection from discrimination. We're fighting the same backward prejudices that kept you down and made you a second-class citizen."

"You didn't 'give' us equal rights and marriage, we persuaded the people and they responded out of a native sense of fairness. Your candidates resisted until the moment the polls showed the majority of the population favored it, and even then nothing happened until the wealthiest gay donors threatened to cut you off.' And what did one of your people say? 'You never want a serious crisis to go to waste.' You lied and you bribed and you used the State of Emergency to force the only opposition party to merge or die. Which meant there was no one left to question your new laws and regulations."

"But you can see all the progress we've made. Racism and sexism are on the way out. Misogyny is not just offensive now, it's illegal. Once we have a few generations brought up free of prejudice—"

"The need for control will fall away, and the New Man[10]—or Woman—will create paradise on earth. I've heard that story before. Millions died." The pain was stronger this time. Why was he making trouble?

"Don't be ridiculous," Immerman said. "No one is dying! We have the best minds at work on organizing a fairer society. Where everyone gets good medical care, housing, and education."

"You think fairness is about distributing a fixed pie of benefits to everyone equally. You fail to understand that good things are the result of applied intelligence and hard work, not just the automatic result of combining generic capital and labor. Most of the wealthy in this country made it themselves, by providing a useful new product or service in a new way. You think of equality in materialistic terms, and project those feelings onto the successful—but true greed is wanting *unearned* wealth, and taking from others to get it. Equal distribution of the bounties of hard work and intelligence means there is no reward for taking a risk or going against the herd to try something new. And telling entire classes of people that they are victims owed compensation is robbing them of the dignity of making their own lives on their own terms. You keep them down by treating them like children. You're shrinking the pie, and you are wasting their lives in needless contention over scraps when they could be creating their own futures."

"So we are sacrificing growth—so what? The planet could not take more people, more growth, more emissions. We have to control development, reduce consumption, and direct technology toward human needs. The carrying capacity of the Earth has already been exceeded, and our only hope is managing down the population and resource use. What use is freedom and progress if only the few can benefit, and the planet dies? We work for a more humane society, like a family, that will treat everyone equally, and leave no one behind."

"Which guarantees we will all be poorer, and the poorest in the world will starve," Wilson said. "Economic growth leads to cleaner air and water, and 'carrying capacity' without considering improving technology and trade, which your government has slowed, is a meaningless concept. Malthus was wrong then, and he's wrong now. The most polluted lands, and the poorest, are those run by authoritarian governments." More pain in his stomach. Something did seem to be wrong, but he was intent on making his point.

"We are doing our best, and we have programs for rewarding the most environmentally responsible companies. It's hard when we share the planet with the Chinese, who are still trying to outrun the growth paradox. But we're making progress with them. And with the gateway technology, we could start bringing the rest of the world under more enlightened management."

That sounded very hopeful. 'Enlightened' was a good word; they really did mean well. All the best intentions. Perhaps he could persuade them by sounding like he might work with them. "I still don't know how I could help you, even if I wanted to."

"We'll be talking about that over the next few days," Immerman said. "I will visit every day, and my assistant will coach you on what we want you to do. We'll get you back to campus, to your normal life, where presumably you'll be contacted by your friends."

And suddenly he felt awash in warm feelings....

Chapter Twenty: On New Earth

Beehive of Activity

Justin walked briskly to the main gate of the air base. It was chilly, and he kept his hands in his pockets, but it was warm enough in the sun that no one would think it unusual that he didn't have a jacket. He made it through the pedestrian turnstile and resisted an urge to walk faster. It seemed like a long time before he had turned a corner and the guard post was out of sight.

He had no money or ID, so he walked all the way into town by back streets and then to the warehouse lab, where he had to break a window to get in. It was then he realized that the warehouse key they had taken from him was a clue that they might be able to use to find the warehouse—they should have installed a code lock. *Too late now,* he thought.

He logged in to the console and set up the gateway for New Earth. When it opened, he saw a field of tents and activity, with people and carts moving along the packed earth paths between them. He stepped through, and a blond-haired girl—Amy, he remembered, from those Students for Freedom meetings that seemed like they happened years ago—saw him and shouted, "It's Justin! He's back!"

Amy ran towards him, and Justin said, "Hi, Amy. I need to find Emerson to help me shut down the machine back home and help me move it. Any idea where he is?"

She shouted, "Emmmmerson! Emerson! Justin neeeeeds you!" and beamed at him.

"I really could have done that myself," Justin said. "But—here he comes. And could you go find Samantha and tell her I'm back?"

Emerson and Steve came out of the nearest tent. "How'd it go?" Steve said.

"I mostly got everything set up. But then I was arrested and held by Homeland Security. It was looking grim—I knew you guys would have no way of finding me—but the head guy decided to let me go. I've been worried that it was a trick to follow me and find us, but no sign of that so far. But just to be safe, let's shut down the home machine and move it here. Leave them nothing in the lab in case they find it."

"Okay," Steve said. "I'll go open the gateway to there big enough to move the machine. You and Emerson go back and dismantle it for the move. Bring all the equipment and computers, too."

He led Emerson back through the gateway to the lab, and they quickly unplugged and got the machine ready to move. The other gateway was waiting for them, with Steve and Samantha watching from the other side. They rolled the Vortex-5 across, then went back for the pumps and equipment.

"Get the desks, too," Steve said. "We need more of those." And so they did.

When they were done, little but trash remained, and Justin looked through that, wondering if there were any tell-tale clues. He decided it was safer to just bring that along, too, and so they spent a few more minutes bringing trash to the new world.

Finally Steve closed the gateway, and they were safe. For now.

Justin hugged Samantha and looked around inside the tent they had arrived in. People he didn't know were taking the items they had brought over away. He turned to Steve and said, "One more thing. I have Prof. Wilson's location, or almost do. We need to look for an old hospital—Kimborough? Something like that—on the grounds of Ft. Meade. New south wing, third floor. Can we start looking?"

Prof. Wilson

For Prof. Wilson, it was another day like the others—talk with Immerman or her assistant until he was tired, eat lunch, and then an escort back to his room for exercise. He got off the exercycle and was rather pleased with himself—ten miles in forty-five minutes. He was feeling better every day.

He went to the toilet to take a leak, and was surprised to see someone else's face—Justin's—in the mirror. Justin spoke quietly: "Prof. Wilson! Time to leave. Get anything you want to keep and come back into the bathroom. We'll open the gateway for you."

Whispering seemed wise. "I want to know everything, but that can wait. Give me thirty seconds." He left the bathroom and went to his desk, where he casually picked up the journal book he had been writing in, and his reading glasses. When Justin saw him returning to the bathroom, he gestured to someone out of sight, and a door to somewhere else opened in front of the sink. He stepped through, and Justin hugged him.

"It's really good to see you," Prof. Wilson said. "They have been trying to turn me, and I swear it was starting to work—I wanted to please that woman and give her whatever she wanted. Some kind of Stockholm syndrome."[11]

"We'll talk about that later," Justin said. "For now, let's get you set up with a tour of camp and a bunk. You'll never guess where we are…."

The Founders

Steve and Justin broke for lunch and walked toward the mess hall. Someone had put up a hand-lettered sign: "GALT'S GULCH." Justin laughed, then sighed. "That's pretty funny, but we need to take it down."

"Why? I don't know what it means," Steve said.

"It's from a controversial old novel which presented a romantic and oversimplified version of individualist thought, and most people in the US—even our type of people—have been taught to disparage it. Collectivists are very successful at trashing the images of people who fight them. If you don't want to spend all your time correcting false ideas planted in people's heads, you avoid trying to rehabilitate images and symbols and move on to address reality."

"Whatever you say. This is not part of my culture," Steve said.

Justin pulled the sign down and tucked it inside the nearest tent. "I hate to be a censor, but it would only have caused trouble."

They were getting lunch in the mess hall when Ben came in. "Mind if I join you?" he said, and they sat at one of the trestle tables toward the back. There were clusters of campus people—he saw Redshirts leader Zach Lee Donner holding forth at a table of Redshirts and a few older Grey Tribe types, who aside from their age, seemed to fit right in.

Steve nodded toward that table. "There are a few Grey Tribe people who program in English, but hardly speak it. They seem to be getting along, but I wonder how long it will be before our little tribes merge and get to know each other."

"Not too long, I think," Justin said, eyes following Grey Leader

Michael McCulloch and the bubbly blond student, Amy, as they walked by. She was giggling at something McCulloch had said, and blushed pink. *Okay, I didn't see that one coming,* he thought. Which reminded him of the rumor that Emerson the lab tech had been seen canoodling with one of the Grey Tribe programmers, which seemed less surprising; Emerson had already smuggled in some marijuana plants and was trying to grow more in New Earth soil. Meanwhile, Rasna seemed to have made looking after Steve Duong her job, despite his obsessive focus on his work.

Samantha saw them after going through the line and came over with her tray. Ben made room for her to sit next to Justin.

"I just checked in with Wendy," Samantha said, giving Justin's forearm a squeeze. "She's still laying low with cousins in Atlanta. No sign her cover has been blown and no inquiries about her back in California, so she plans to go back to campus and manage our finances while finishing up her degree."

"Wendy is smarter than all of us, in some ways," Justin said. "She gets the commissions, sets herself up in business, and gets to stay home and live a normal life."

"Though there's always the risk that they'll trace something back to her and bust her," Ben said. "In which case we mount another rescue. It will be better when we have the communications set up and can run everything from here."

"We've been working with some Grey Tribe wizards to set up better communications," Steve said. "We've figured out how to get one of the Vortex-5s to open dozens of tiny radio-photon windows at a time, which should let us borrow wifi and 5G connections from multiple sites in neutral countries. They've brought over all the gear we need, and we can automate the finding and rotation between connection locations, to keep them from figuring it out. So, we have Internet. And therefore we'll have phone service, from a series of VoIP vendors."

"And the same idea for surveillance," Justin added. "We can spy on dozens of places at once and record them all. Our limit now is finding people to listen to them."

"There are some personnel issues," Ben said. "There are seven of us original members. And thirty more from the campus cells. Grey Tribe has recruited over a hundred already, and more are on the way. Do we worry about that? And we have to retain control over the gateways and communications. We can't risk a spy or a homesick person sending email."

"I'm not too worried," Justin said. "Those people were already involved and taking risks, and there are thousands of them in trusted groups. We need the people. If only to help with surveillance! And there is all the logistics of supplying us here. Which reminds me, where did we get the porta-potties?"

Ben smiled. "We hauled them over from a storage yard while you were gone, since digging latrines seemed like a bad way to spend our time. We'll need something better soon, so we need to find out who knows about digging septic fields and setting up indoor plumbing."

"Which is the kind of problem you forget about when you live in an advanced civilization with division of labor," Justin said. "Somebody took care of all that, and I took it for granted. Now we have to do it ourselves. We need a list of all the things we need to do."

"I've been working with McCulloch and Justin on plans for long-term programs," Steve said. "An exploratory program, to map New Earth and some other suitable worlds and find resources we can use. We're stealing for now, but we won't always have to. We could mine gold and cast the bars here. In the longer term, I want to start matter assembly and duplication."

"While you're doing that, work out a way to get that implant out of Prof. Wilson's head," Justin said. "It's not doing any harm, but I don't like the idea of its being there."

"I've actually thought about that," Steve said. "The gateway is the perfect scanner and surgical device—detect and find the boundaries of what you want removed, and replace it with something harmless. It's a 'mere matter of programming' away."

Ben slurped loudly on his noodles. "Any chance of getting some Grey Tribe folk up to speed on helping with the programming?"

"Some of them are far better programmers than I could ever dream of being," Steve said, "but I want to wait awhile before giving them any instruction on it, until things have settled down and we know we can trust them."

"So what's on your list of software projects that only you can do?" said Samantha, pointing at Steve with a spoon full of yogurt.

"First we need those ID cubes, the 'talismans,' so we can have an always-on program watching them for requests to open gateways or communications wherever a person is," Steve said. "We need those talismans now, and Justin will help with the 3-D printer. DNA scanning and searching would be better, but that will take more time and program space than we will have for awhile."

"There are several bioinformatics types in the Grey Tribe crew," Justin said. "Should we get them started on that?"

"We still have to set up the extra machines, but then we can let them have one to use, with supervision. But that's just the start of the medical uses—it should be possible to go through the body knocking out a certain disease organism, or cancer cell type. But we focus first on survival strategies. Keeping Earth governments from using the technology is our first priority."

"You mentioned generating power before," Justin said.

"There are two approaches to that," Steve said. "Steal power from Earth by intercepting electron pressure in mains, or just search for high electrical currents in nature and intercept those. The stealing option is more tractable, but the power flow in nature is vastly greater, and would avoid any possibility of detection."

"That could get tricky," Justin said. "'Always turn off the power before touching the wiring.' Experimenting with large power flows could be very dangerous."

"I'm aware of that," Steve said. "Then there is the matter specification and assembly problem. Duplication first, then digital specification of assembles, like our grid boards—which would let us manufacture everything we need. Then there's the problem of software to discover connected objects—to find all particles in a solid matter object and transport them all at once, replacing it with matter similar to the surrounding medium—usually air. Then we can just click on something we're viewing and have it where we want it, without having to physically move it through a gateway plane."

"That would save us a lot of schlepping," Samantha observed. "Shoplifting would be so much easier, too." Justin gave her a look. "Just kidding. Carry on, Steve."

"Then there are weapons. Destruction is easy: open a gateway from the heart of a neutron star aimed toward whatever. Instant destruction, scour the planet in a few days. Slightly less damaging; a solar plasma gun. With the talisman, a user could just point and say 'zap!' and dissolve anything. Long-term ideas."

"One hopes," Ben said, eyebrows raised, "it never gets used for planet-wiping. That's a horrible idea."

"If I can think it," Steve said, "someone else will, too. The hardest problem of all is finding a way to guard the technology so it's only used for good. For that, I need to solve two big problems: making programs substrate-resident so they can operate without the computer, and building benevolent AIs to guard use of the gateways on behalf of humanity. I'm thinking an always-resident kernel we put up which runs forever, and loads programs we present to it; those would be the apps. And the AIs. Someday we'll figure out how to upload ourselves as well."

"The biggest 'mere matter of programming' of all," Ben said. "If you're going to dream, dream big, I suppose."

"You have any ideas for engineering a government structure to deal with the technology?" Justin asked, looking at Ben.

"Well, I started by considering the analogy with nuclear weapons," Ben said. "Mutual assured destruction between a limited number of nuclear states seems to have prevented all-out war, though we know now there were many near-misses—the Soviets had a doomsday machine[12] that could easily have been triggered accidentally and started a massive missile exchange. The US was not much more careful until more safeguards were put into place. The strategy breaks down when the technology is simple enough to be duplicated by groups without a state to lose, as we saw with the New York bomb. The perpetrators were scattered and no direct reprisal was possible."

"So in their desire to do *something,* governments simply repressed their own populations," Justin said.

"If you can't control the real problem, do something to pretend you are, and gain control of bigger budgets and more minions." Ben said. "We're human, and even individuals lie to themselves to feel more secure."

"So what can we do?" Steve asked.

"I can think of some options to reduce the power of governments and contention over resources. Once people know we exist, we announce we're opening gateways to great colony planets, specifying what colonists will need to bring with them. Open the gateways in the poorest and most overpopulated parts of the Earth, where taking a chance on a new land will seem better than staying. Step back and watch as attitudes change and people escape poverty and corrupt governments."

"There must be many planets like this one," Steve said, "where there's little competing animal life, and soils that support Earth crops."

"You know what will happen?" Samantha said. "Governments will try to stop people from leaving. The greens will forbid colonization that might displace native life. They will spread fear about alien plagues and dangers from living on a planet you weren't evolved for—like the twenty-six-hour day here, which in theory could screw up our circadian rhythms."

"But seriously," Steve asked, "what do we do *right now* to keep the technology from being used for destruction and control?"

"Until you build those benevolent AIs," Ben said, "the only strategy I can think of is strict control of the technology by the only people we can trust—us. We seek out and destroy every effort to duplicate Steve's work. We find Dylan and arrest him—not sure how we're going to deal with criminals and punishment; maybe the Coventry model of transporting them to a wilderness would be best. Which reminds me, we need to find him and that source code before it's given over to the government."

"It might already be too late," Justin said. "McDonald made it sound like a deal was imminent."

Samantha sighed and said, "Is it too late to talk to him? I could try to persuade him to give it up and join us."

"And what would we do with him?" Justin said. "He can't be trusted. The first thing we'd do is transport him to Coventry, to be prudent."

"That's all right with me," Sam said. "It would get the source code back, though."

"The first of many bad things we may be forced to do, for the greater good." Ben said. "And that's how it starts."

Back on Earth

TRANSCRIPT

Meeting of the Unity Security Committee, White House Situation Room.

Identified Attendees:

President Elizabeth Howard Stanton
Defense Secretary Sheila Edwards
Homeland Security Secretary Lewis Jackson
Homeland Security Advanced Threat Assessment
Liaison Christine Immerman
NSA Liaison [name unknown]
Joint Chiefs of Staff Liaison Vincent Cardone
[Two unidentified voices]

PRESIDENT: Gentlemen. You've all seen the briefings. We have a threat and we need a more pro-active plan.

HOMESEC SEC: We have a team working on a crash program to duplicate their technology, with Mr. Foster's help. We've ordered fabs to build more machines on a crash basis, since they stole the ones in progress.

PRESIDENT: I didn't relish appointing Foster and sending out the photos. Get what you can from him, but give him no opportunity to build contacts. Everything through the liaison.

HOMESEC SEC: Yes, Ma'am.

HOMESEC LIAISON: Since they can penetrate any
level of security, every effort must be
secret. Even the workers should not know their
location.

NSA: We have filters in place looking for
patterns of communication and commerce they
would make in seeking out certain speciality
goods—thanks to Homeland Security staff for
the lists. So far nothing but noise, but we
investigate each one.

DEFENSE SEC: We are installing equipment in
our new buried fab, which will be ready in
months. A secure supply of critical chips was
always a good idea, but until recently the
industry was progressing too fast—whatever we
did, we couldn't keep up. That has changed, so
we started this project two years ago. If
they're smart, they will be watching all the
known fabs that can do this kind of work, and
steal or destroy anything we do there. So,
Lewis, don't be surprised if your machines
disappear from the factories.

JCS LIAISON: We presented the issue as a theoretical problem to staff. The consensus strategy was to duplicate and weaponize as quickly
as possible, but with no actions against the
rebels until we are ready to strike. If they

don't bother us, we should not provoke them
until we have overwhelming strength. Pretend
we've forgotten about them. Right now they
could destroy us, but their actions so far
have been limited in size and scope.

PRESIDENT: I see no choice. Keep their existence a secret, do nothing and hope they make
no demands, until we can eliminate them in one
blow.

Prof. Wilson's Journal

It has been interesting being the oldest person on the planet, and a kind of mascot for the kids—actually many of them are so young they could be my grand-kids, if I had ever had children. They treat me with a certain reverence, though of course it's Steve Duong who should really be honored for giving us this chance. But I have gray hair and whiskers and no other role, so the kids are solicitous. Perhaps it's pity....

Samantha helped me use the gateway to find the anti-retrovirals I need. I've wished I could go back, but Justin reminds me that enemies lie in wait. I miss my office and the routines of my old life. Justin promises to give me an office and students soon. I need to work!

Every day there are more tents, and now they are bringing in prefab buildings. The weather has so far been mild, but Steve says there are likely to be seasonal storms. The camp grows too large and the paths too crowded. But these are the problems of success.

Of course we are afraid. We know they will come after us sometime, more likely sooner than later. But I trust the kids to be faster and more clever, and stop them before they can. I may not live to see the day, but I believe in them, and I know they will find a way to release humanity from the limits of Earth and its rulers.

Jim McDonald

Jim McDonald, retired! It had been six months since he had been eased out at his insistence, but it still seemed strange after so many years of being on-call and scheduled. McDonald sipped his coffee and started his day reading news on his pad computer—that hadn't changed.

The end had not been too bad. He knew they suspected him, but there was no way of proving it had not been just bad luck that he had dropped the ball several times in the Grey Tribe investigation, code-name "Neutral Armor." The bureaucracy gave him his pension and benefits, and he moved south to a mountain town in North Carolina where life was cheaper and easier. He decided not to put up a picture of his wife as in the old place, because it had been a long time and he wasn't going to spend any more time missing her laugh and the teasing way she kept him honest. And his kids were neglectful, or busy with the day-to-day problems of their own families. It had been weeks since anyone had called him, and he didn't feel like being a pest himself.

He took another sip and started reading a story about the skirmishes in the Middle East.

With a faint pop, a window opened in the air beyond his pad. The kid from the case—Justin—looked out at him.

"Mr. McDonald," Justin said. "We found you."

"So you have. And call me Jim. I'm not official any more, just Jim."

"That's why I'm calling. We are running a pretty successful operation here. We have a ground-floor opportunity for a security specialist."

"See the world. Join the Army!" McDonald said. "I remember when that sounded good. I'm a bit old for a new posting."

"We need someone like you. And you can make a real difference in whether we succeed or fail at getting our rights and freedoms back. There is nothing more important. You're just gonna fly-fish, or something?"

"Actually I've been cataloging my collection of military ephemera. But your point is well-taken."

"So get your stuff together and join us," Justin said.

"Give me some time to think about it. Come back in an hour and I'll either be ready or say no."

"Fair enough," Justin said. "Over and out." And the window vanished.

McDonald finished his coffee. He already knew he would go, he just didn't want to be rushed.

ALife Simulation, Model 9: Evaluation

The conclave of intelligences gathered near the end times of the ancient universe continued their great work collecting and ordering the knowledge of Humanity and the other civilizations that had come before and since. Reconstructing the earliest evolution of each civilization from the fragmentary records remaining was an enormous field of study for vast numbers of students and researchers.

The researchers studying Earth stored the state of the latest simulation for the archives and evaluated the results, but kept the simulation running despite the resources required, since all life was to be nurtured and respected.

They had come so very close to reproducing the evolution of the early baseline humans, despite obvious failures to match in every detail the physics and chemistry of the true universe. Discussions began on how to improve the simulation on a more sophisticated substrate, to prevent the simulated humans from discovering so quickly that their universe was a simulation. Bigger and better substrate cores were needed, and several galactic masses would be required to construct them, to support a finer-grained model. Until then, there were eons of archived history to be analyzed.

Part Four: Appendices

Coming in Substrate Wars, Book 2

I have started work on the rest of the Substrate Wars series, but finishing those depends on getting a reasonably warm reception and good readership for this one. So if you enjoyed this book and want to see more, please take the time and review this book at Amazon and other online sites and recommend it to your friends. It's very important and much appreciated.

In the next installment, Earth governments strike and New Earth defends itself. Steve Duong, Justin Smith, Samantha West, and Ben Ramirez take on the world, with help from some new friends. And new enemies appear—those mysterious Chinese spies are just the tip of a power-hungry iceberg.

In the meantime, follow news on my progress and postings by signing up for email notification at substratewars.com.

Notes on Politics

What is fascism?

From Wikipedia, where the definition focuses on the 1930s fascisms seen in Italy, Germany, and Spain:

> Fascists sought to unify their nation through an authoritarian state that promoted the mass mobilization of the national community and were characterized by having leadership that initiated a revolutionary political movement aiming to reorganize the nation along principles according to fascist ideology.[13]

The Wikipedia definition goes on to list other characteristics, notably that fascism of that day "replaced socialism's focus on class conflict with a focus on conflict between nations and races."

As Mark Twain noted, "History doesn't repeat itself, but it does rhyme." The fascism of Substrate Wars is built on exploiting tribal divisions, but not between states so as much as between races and the sexes, and between an anointed class of academic and government-class progressives ("the Clerisy") and the private economy. The scapegoating of some groups and relentless attacks on them as manipulators who are harming the oppressed and stealing from the common people is aimed at different groups, but the basic mechanism remains.

We see this today in schizophrenic demonization of the wealthy "one-percenters" at the same time there is continuing support by many of the same politicians of Wall Street's artificially high share of the economy. The Federal Reserve's efforts to limit the stock market crash of 2000 and the 9/11 panic produced a real estate bubble and ensuing debt crisis, but instead of reforming the systemic problems that caused the crash and paying down the bad debts, the world's central banks and politicians have tried to artificially reflate the economy with even more debt, and as of this writing the US debt has climbed to $18 trillion. When actuarially sound and realistic accounting is applied to pension and Medicare obligations of state and federal governments, future taxes to pay the debts down at more realistic interest rates would have to rise to over 50% of incomes, closing on 100% in some states, a level so high it would depress actual tax revenues collected. Meaning some sort of debt repudiation—either hyperinflating it away or default—is likely.

And in the US, the two parties are deeply entrenched in local and state politics and election supervision, and the law is written to discourage any new parties or independent candidates. The increasing partisan warfare has set people of good will who largely agree on most matters against each other, with the worst behavior of each party presented as entertainment to partisans of the other. The hatred and obsessive preoccupation with demonization of the other party disguises an important fact: if it were not for that party you hate so much, full of stupid, evil, and ignorant people you disdain, your party would become as corrupt as it is in those states where one party dominates. And the chances of governments run by one party investigating and reforming themselves is low. Some pundits admire China, where one party rules and Gets Things Done; but corruption is an enormous problem there, and will likely bring them down eventually. So, partisans, be grateful for those jerks in the other party—*they keep your people honest.*

I have many friends who work for government agencies—teachers, scientists, managers. They tell me they work hard and do valuable work, and I know they are conscientious and well-meaning. But when they spend much of their time in meetings and fighting other parts of the bureaucracy; when they write thousands of pages of reports and laws that no one reads; when their function is not essential to defense, law enforcement, or some other core function only government can handle, it's a tax-funded, permanent bureaucracy that squeezes out private alternatives and ensures that competition can never improve efficiency. I salute my hard-working friends who are public servants—but most of their time is actually spent serving the interests of the state and not the people.

In the sectors of the economy that aren't run or heavily regulated by governments, efficiencies constantly increase as competition and innovation combine. In sectors run by politicized regulation or directly by governments, innovation is very slow and relative costs of services continue to rise. Examples: education, medical services, defense, social services. Student loan debt is breaking the backs of young people; college administrators are higher-paid than ever, and there are more of them. Hospitals expand and merge and pay administrators huge salaries while charging astronomical fees for simple services. Military contracting is padded and turned into pork for Congressional districts. The space shuttle boosters blew up because they had to be made in segments to allow the contracts to be spread across districts. *These are all consequences of politicized decisionmaking processes.*

A notable example is universal public schooling. No one thinks education is a bad idea, and local public and private schools competed in the US until the mid-1800s. Then states began to take more control, aiming to raise standards and make the curriculum more uniform, on a Prussian model which viewed children as raw material to be molded into good workers and citizens with allegiance to the state.

The public education system evolved, and local control was reduced. Families found themselves taxed heavily to pay for the public system, which was "free" to them, and naturally chose not to pay twice to get education that was more directly tailored to their children's needs or family desires. Thus an important link between parental concern and schools was broken—schools, like all other institutions, ultimately serve the concerns of those who fund them, not their clients. In many school districts now, parents are given lip service but opposed whenever they try to support reforms.

And schools beholden to politicians and unions of their workers can be both expensive and truly awful. The worst result of this is that children are now learning very little history, economics, or science, and rigor has suffered. The least damaging solution is vouchers—give every student the money now being spent on their education to spend on any school their parents deem fit that passes reasonable standards. Public schools would have to compete with private and charter schools, and all would benefit—except possibly overpaid public school administrators. Resistance to this idea is fierce, of course.

So that was a key mistake which allowed the population to be programmed with the idea that more government is the solution for every problem. Fixing it will take time, and the system will most likely crash before rebooting.

And as recent graduates of this political indoctrination system have taken most of the positions in government, academia, and mass media, the commitment to truth has suffered. An entire society has been dumbed down.

Visit substratewars.com or jebkinnison.com for more material on politics, economics, education, and civilization.

Notes on Science

If you're a theoretical physicist, you'll note I am taking liberties with the science. But only a little—and the plot is very much real science. Steve Duong discovers something unexpected, creates a new hypothesis which explains his anomalous results, then confirms his hypothesis by further experimentation. I don't personally believe we live in a universe where giant quasiparticles can talk to every other particle in the universe and ask them to attach to new partners, but *it could be so*. We are always just one experiment away from a revolution in understanding. And it will likely be something equally unexpected that allows us to travel to the stars.

I have the Grey Tribe communicating by using encrypted messages embedded in public web site photo streams. For a similar app available now, see Crypstagram.[14] There are several messaging apps that are encrypted currently, for example Whatsapp.[15] But in this future State of Emergency, standard encryption of messages and email has been outlawed, and phone companies and apps are not allowed to secure user data against surveillance. There are high officials in the US government at this writing asking that all phones be searchable for law enforcement purposes, and we can expect more efforts to outlaw encryption. "When encryption is outlawed, only outlaws will have encryption!"

On the attempts to find a cellular automaton model that explains quantum physics, this is the abstract of one interesting paper: "Quantum Field as a Quantum Cellular Automaton I: The Dirac free evolution in one dimension":

It is shown how a quantum cellular automaton can describe very precisely the Dirac evolution, without requiring Lorentz covariance. The automaton is derived with the only assumptions of minimal dimension and parity and time-reversal invariance. The automaton extends the Dirac field theory to the Planck and ultra-relativistic scales. The Dirac equation is recovered in the usual particle physics scale of inertial mass and momenta. In this first paper the simplest case of one space dimension is analyzed. We provide a technique to derive an analytical approximation of the evolution of the automaton in terms of a momentum-dependent Schrödinger equation. Such approximation works very well in all regimes, including ultrarelativistic and Planckian, for the typical smooth quantum states of field theory with limited bandwidth in momentum. Finally we discuss some thought experiments for falsifying the existence of the automaton at the Planck scale.[16]

Real quantum computing is still in its infancy. Efforts so far have been plagued by noise and the small number of qubits available—the current state of the art is 4! Researchers—and especially outside evaluations—find it hard to tell whether current quantum computers are actually doing quantum computation. This is an area where many discoveries are likely to clarify quantum phenomenon, and perhaps, as in this story, open up completely new vistas on how the universe is organized.

If you are already familiar with the basics of quantum phenomena and want to learn more about quantum computing, the Wikipedia articles[17] on the field are excellent places to start.

Artificial Life is a kind of computational model of the biology of life as we know it. Starting with very simple worlds,[18] models have become more and more sophisticated to the point where significant discoveries about emergent features are being made. Larger, faster simulations feature co-evolving organisms in ecosystems and environments that have been molded by biological processes. Wikipedia is a good place to start learning about the field.[19]

The abstract of a current paper, "Indefinitely Scalable Computing = Artificial Life Engineering," by David H. Ackley and Trent R. Smallon, on the state of research and ideas on applying ALife concepts to general computer architecture:

> The traditional CPU/RAM computer architecture is increasingly unscalable, presenting a challenge for the industry—and is too fragile to be securable even at its current scale, presenting a challenge for society as well. This paper argues that new architectures and computational models, designed around software-based artificial life, can offer radical solutions to both problems. The challenge for the soft alife research community is to harness the dynamics of life and complexity in service of robust, scalable computations— and in many ways, we can keep doing what we are doing, if we use indefinitely scalable computational models to do so. This paper reviews the argument for robustness in scalability, delivers that challenge to the soft alife community, and summarizes recent progress in architecture and program design for indefinitely scalable computing via artificial life engineering.[20]

The Red Queen hypothesis is one of the key concepts of modern evolutionary biology.[21]

Quotes from Golden Age Science Fiction

I learned much of what I know by reading science fiction. For my younger readers, many of the quoted titles and authors below will be unfamiliar, but they are still worth seeking out and reading from a time when anything seemed possible. The long tradition of social tolerance and advanced thinking in science fiction has been under attack by ignorant academics who want to turn all entertainment into propaganda for their idea of progressive thought. Read widely and route around the schools and libraries who want to program your thinking by restricting what they offer you to read.

These quotes seemed especially suited to the themes of this story:

Gully Foyle is my name
And Terra is my nation
Deep space is my dwelling place
The stars my destination
—Alfred Bester, *The Stars My Destination*, 1956

In brightest day, in blackest night,
No evil shall escape my sight.
Let those who worship evil's might,
Beware my power, Green Lantern's light!
—Alfred Bester, writing for *Green Lantern*, c. 1945

Every law that was ever written opened up a new way to graft.
—Robert Heinlein, *Red Planet,* 1949

How anybody expects a man to stay in business with every two-bit wowser in the country claiming a veto over what we can say and can't say and what we can show and what we can't show—it's enough to make you throw up. The whole principle is wrong; it's like demanding that grown men live on skim milk because the baby can't eat steak.
—Robert Heinlein, *The Man Who Sold the Moon,* 1950

Reason is poor propaganda when opposed by the yammering, unceasing lies of shrewd and evil and self-serving men.
—Robert Heinlein, *Assignment in Eternity,* 1953

I also think there are prices too high to pay to save the United States. Conscription is one of them. Conscription is slavery, and I don't think that any people or nation has a right to save itself at the price of slavery for anyone, no matter what name it is called. We have had the draft for twenty years now; I think this is shameful. If a country can't save itself through the volunteer service of its own free people, then I say : Let the damned thing go down the drain!
—Robert Heinlein, speech at World Science Fiction Convention, 1961

I believe in—I am proud to belong to—the United States. Despite shortcomings, from lynchings to bad faith in high places, our nation has had the most decent and kindly internal practices and foreign policies to be found anywhere in history.

And finally, I believe in my whole race. Yellow, white, black, red, brown—in the honesty, courage, intelligence, durability ... and goodness ... of the overwhelming majority of my brothers and sisters everywhere on this planet. I am proud to be a human being. I believe that we have come this far by the skin of our teeth, that we always

make it just by the skin of our teeth—but that we will always make it … survive … endure. I believe that this hairless embryo with the aching, oversize brain case and the opposable thumb, this animal barely up from the apes, will endure—will endure longer than his home planet, will spread out to the other planets, to the stars, and beyond, carrying with him his honesty, his insatiable curiosity, his unlimited courage—and his noble essential decency. This I believe with all my heart.
—Robert Heinlein, "This I Believe," 1952

The future is better than the past. Despite the crepehangers, romanticists, and anti-intellectuals, the world steadily grows better because the human mind, applying itself to environment, makes it better. With hands...with tools...with horse sense and science and engineering.
—Robert Heinlein, *The Door Into Summer*, 1957

"…They have no art and only the most primitive of science, yet such is their violent nature that even with so little knowledge they are now energetically using it to exterminate each other, tribe against tribe. Their driving will is such that they may succeed. But if by some unlucky chance they fail, they will inevitably, in time, reach other stars. It is this possibility which must be calculated: how soon they will reach us, if they live, and what their potentialities will be then."

The voice continued to us: "This is the indictment against you—your own savagery, combined with superior intelligence. What have you to say in your defense?"….

"—you say we have no art. Have you seen the Parthenon?"

"Blown up in one of your wars."

"Better see it before you rotate us—or you'll be missing something.

Have you read our poetry? 'Our revels now are ended: these our actors, as I foretold you, were all spirits, and are melted into air, into thin air: And, like the baseless fabric of this vision, the cloud-capped towers, the gorgeous palaces, the solemn temples, the great globe itself... Itself—yea—all which it ... Inherit—shall dissolve—"

I broke down. I heard Peewee sobbing beside me. I don't know why I picked that one-but they say the subconscious mind never does things "accidentally." I guess it had to be that one.

"As it well may," commented the merciless voice.
—Robert Heinlein, *Have Space Suit—Will Travel*, 1958

"My mother said violence never solves anything." "So?" Mr. Dubois looked at her bleakly. "I'm sure the city fathers of Carthage would be glad to know that."
—Robert Heinlein, *Starship Troopers*, 1959

Must be a yearning deep in human heart to stop other people from doing as they please. Rules, laws—always for other fellow. A murky part of us, something we had before we came down out of trees, and failed to shuck when we stood up. Because not one of those people said: Please pass this so that I won't be able to do something I know I should stop. Nyet, tovarishchee, was always something they hated to see neighbors doing. Stop them for their own good.
— Robert Heinlein, *The Moon is a Harsh Mistress*, 1966

I began to sense faintly that secrecy is the keystone of all tyranny. Not force, but secrecy...censorship. When any government, or any church for that matter, undertakes to say to its subjects, "This you may not read, this you must not see, this you are forbidden to know," the end result is tyranny and oppression, no matter how holy the motives. Mighty little force is needed to control a man whose mind has been hoodwinked; contrariwise, no amount of force can control a free

man, a man whose mind is free. No, not the rack, not fission bombs, not anything — you can't conquer a free man; the most you can do is kill him.
—Robert Heinlein, *If This Goes On—*, 1940

First they junked the concept of "justice." Examined semantically "justice" has no referent—there is no observable phenomenon in the space-time-matter continuum to which one can point, and say, "This is justice." Science can deal only with that which can be observed and measured. Justice is not such a matter; therefore it can never have the same meaning to one as to another; any "noises" said about it will only add to confusion.

But damage, physical or economic, can be pointed to and measured. Citizens were forbidden by the Covenant to damage another. Any act not leading to damage, physical or economic, to some particular person, they declared to be lawful.
—Robert Heinlein, *Coventry*, 1940

Sure, ninety percent of science fiction is crud. That's because ninety percent of everything is crud.
—Theodore Sturgeon, 1951

Here, too, was the guide, the beacon, for such times as humanity might be in danger; here was the Guardian of Whom all humans knew—not an exterior force, nor an awesome Watcher in the sky, but a laughing thing with a human heart and a reverence for its human origins, smelling of sweat and new-turned earth rather than suffused with the pale odor of sanctity.
—Theodore Sturgeon, *More Than Human*, 1953

Earth keeps a solemn festival at the meadows of Hack and Sack, through whose blue arch came first death, and then life.
—Theodore Sturgeon, "The Incubi of Parallel X," Planet Stories, 1951

The fall of Empire, gentlemen, is a massive thing, however, and not easily fought. It is dictated by a rising bureaucracy, a receding initiative, a freezing of caste, a damming of curiosity—a hundred other factors. It has been going on, as I have said, for centuries, and it is too majestic and massive a movement to stop.

—Isaac Asimov, *Foundation*, 1951

Quotes about Government

Some ideas are so stupid that only an intellectual could believe them. —Either George Orwell or Michael Levine

The whole aim of practical politics is to keep the populace alarmed (and hence clamourous to be led to safety) by menacing it with an endless series of hobgoblins, all of them imaginary. —H.L. Mencken

Love your country, but never trust its government. —Robert A. Heinlein

The most dangerous man to any government is the man who is able to think things out for himself, without regard to the prevailing superstitions and taboos. Almost inevitably he comes to the conclusion that the government he lives under is dishonest, insane and intolerable, and so, if he is romantic, he tries to change it. And even if he is not romantic personally he is very apt to spread discontent among those who are. —H.L. Mencken, from "The Smart Set" (December 1919)

Of such sort are the young wizards who now sweat to save the plain people from the degradations of capitalism, which is to say, from the degradations of working hard, saving their money, and paying their way. This is what the New Deal and its Planned Economy come to in practice—a series of furious and irrational raids upon the taxpayer, planned casually by professional do-gooders lolling in smoking cars, and executed by professional politicians bent only upon building up an irresistible machine. This is the *Führer's* inspired substitute for constitutional government and common sense. —H.L. Mencken, "The New Deal," 1935

[The aim of public education is not] to fill the young of the species with knowledge and awaken their intelligence. ... Nothing could be further from the truth. The aim ... is simply to reduce as many individuals as possible to the same safe level, to breed and train a standardized citizenry, to put down dissent and originality. That is its aim in the United States... and that is its aim everywhere else. —H.L. Mencken, *The American Mercury,* April 1924

How did we evolve from a country whose founding statesmen were adamant about the dangers of armed, standing government forces—a country that enshrined the Fourth Amendment in the Bill of Rights and revered and protected the age-old notion that the home is a place of privacy and sanctuary—to a country where it has become acceptable for armed government agents dressed in battle garb to storm private homes in the middle of the night—not to apprehend violent fugitives or thwart terrorist attacks, but to enforce laws against nonviolent, consensual activities? —Radley Balko, *Rise of the Warrior Cop: The Militarization of America's Police Forces,* 2013

Socialism, like the ancient ideas from which it springs, confuses the distinction between government and society. As a result of this, every time we object to a thing being done by government, the socialists conclude that we object to its being done at all. We disapprove of state education. Then the socialists say that we are opposed to any education. We object to a state religion. Then the socialists say that we want no religion at all. And so on, and so on. It is as if the socialists were to accuse us of not wanting persons to eat because we do not want the state to raise grain. —Frédéric Bastiat, *The Law,* 1850

[The socialists declare] that the State owes subsistence, well-being, and education to all its citizens; that it should be generous, charitable, involved in everything, devoted to everybody; ...that it should intervene directly to relieve all suffering, satisfy and anticipate all wants, furnish capital to all enterprises, enlightenment to all minds, balm for all wounds, asylums for all the unfortunate, and even aid to the point of shedding French blood, for all oppressed people on the face of the earth.

Who would not like to see all these benefits flow forth upon the world from the law, as from an inexhaustible source? ... But is it possible? ... Whence does [the State] draw those resources that it is urged to dispense by way of benefits to individuals? Is it not from the individuals themselves? How, then, can these resources be increased by passing through the hands of a parasitic and voracious intermediary?

...Finally...we shall see the entire people transformed into petitioners. Landed property, agriculture, industry, commerce, shipping, industrial companies, all will bestir themselves to claim favors from the State. The public treasury will be literally pillaged. Everyone will have good reasons to prove that legal fraternity should be interpreted in this sense: "Let me have the benefits, and let others pay the costs." Everyone's effort will be directed toward snatching a scrap of fraternal privilege from the legislature. The suffering classes, although having the greatest claim, will not always have the greatest success. —Frédéric Bastiat, *Justice and Fraternity,* 1848

The world in which we Westerners live today has grave faults and dangers, but when compared to the countries and times in which democracy is smothered it has a tremendous advantage: everyone can know everything about everything. Information today is the "fourth estate." In an authoritarian state it is not like this. There is only one Truth, proclaimed from above. The newspapers are all alike; they all repeat the same one truth. Propaganda is substituted for information. It is clear that under these conditions it becomes possible (though not always easy: it is never quite easy to do deep violence to human nature) to erase quite large chunks of reality. —Primo Levi

The more men know, the smaller the share of all that knowledge becomes that any one mind can absorb. The more civilized we become, the more relatively ignorant must each individual be of the facts on which the working of his civilization depends. The very division of knowledge increases the necessary ignorance of the individual of most of this knowledge. —F.A. Hayek, *The Constitution of Liberty*, 1960

Once definitely done with our adolescent longing for the Absolute, we would find this world valuable after all, and poignantly valuable precisely because it is not eternal. Doomed to extinction, our loves, our work, our friendships, our tastes are all painfully precious. We look about us, on the streets and in the subways, and discover that we are beautiful because we are mortal, priceless because we are so rare in the universe and so fleeting. Whatever we are, whatever we make of ourselves: that is all we will ever have—and that, in its profound simplicity, is the meaning of life. —Philip Appleman, *The Labyrinth: God, Darwin, and the Meaning of Life*, 2014

Further Reading

Online Resources

You'll find updates on the next book in the series at SubstrateWars.com, where you can sign up for email notification of the latest news on the books and postings on science and technology and topics from my other books.

Email me at JebKinnison@gmail.com if you have questions or comments. I try to answer every email.

Please visit the updated list of online resources at SubstrateWars.com.

Prof. Wilson's *Starspark* poster episode is based on the real-life *Firefly* poster episode at the University of Wisconsin-Stout, where FIRE was able to assist in getting the administration to back down.

FIRE (The Foundation for Individual Rights in Education at www.thefire.org) has been fighting for campus freedom of speech and thought for many years. If you're a student and have a problem with an administration that tries to stifle speech or too easily accedes to the demands of Social Justice Warriors to limit debate on important issues, they're the people to talk to.

And it so happens that the fictional Students for Liberty (StudentsForLiberty.org) is mirrored in real life. Join while it's still legal!

Reason.com is the online presence of *Reason* magazine, the magazine of "free minds and free markets," presenting news and essays free of the talking points of political parties. They're not even sure they agree with libertarians! Call them classical liberals....

The Foundation for Economic Education (FEE at fee.org) is one of the oldest free-market organizations in the United States. Their site is well worth your time.

The Cato Institute at www.cato.org is a "public policy research organization—a think tank–dedicated to the principles of individual liberty, limited government, free markets and peace."

Recommended Books

In recent years, classic science fiction ideas have been echoed in so much popular entertainment that many seem familiar. But the original mind-stretching quality is poorly duplicated in movies like the Matrix series, and for really expansive looks at the future, you can't beat some of these originals. And meanwhile, the decline of legacy publishing and its dominance by academics has produced a crop of "socially relevant" science fiction that is short on optimism and technical imagination, and values story less than political content. So try some of these to get an idea of true diversity....

The best Heinlein juveniles, perfect for that 10- to 16-year-old who likes adventure:

Have Spacesuit, Will Travel
Tunnel in the Sky
Citizen of the Galaxy

For more mature adolescents (and adults, too):

Door Into Summer
Starship Troopers
The Moon is a Harsh Mistress

Alice Mary Norton, writing as Andre Norton, wrote numerous adventure science fiction books of interest to younger readers that are still good reading, and cheap in Kindle form: see, for example, *The Andre Norton Megapack: 15 Classic Novels and Short Stories*.

Other selected adult science fiction classics that are still relevant:

Foundation, Isaac Asimov
The Stars My Destination, Alfred Bester

Shards of Honor (Vorkosigan Saga Book 2), Lois McMaster Bujold
Childhood's End, Arthur C. Clarke
The City and the Stars, Arthur C. Clarke
Neuromancer, William Gibson
The Forever War, Joe Haldemann
Dune, Frank Herbert
Ringworld, Larry Niven
The Mote in God's Eye, Larry Niven and Jerry Pournelle
Snow Crash, Neal Stephenson
Lord of Light, Roger Zelazny

… That should be enough to get a new reader started. And also explore Greg Bear, Harlan Ellison, C.J. Cherryh, David Gerrold, Philip K. Dick, Dan Simmons, Neal Asher, Iain Banks, Walter Jon Williams, Vernor and Joan Vinge….—there are too many great writers to list!

For more recommended books, go to jebkinnison.com/curriculum/.

About the Author

I grew up in the Midwest, child of a schizophrenic father and a hardworking single mother. I read everything I could in the school and town library, and discovered science fiction in second grade, starting with Tom Swift books and quickly moving to Heinlein juveniles and adult science fiction.

When I was twelve, I discovered the collection of city telephone books in my local library. I pretended I was doing a paper and called Isaac Asimov; we spoke for a long time, and he sent me a postcard encouraging me to write. So thank you, Isaac, wherever you are, for being so kind and generous with your time. Robert Silverberg had no time for that kind of nonsense...

I studied computer and cognitive science at MIT, and wrote programs modeling the behavior of simulated stock traders and the population dynamics of economic agents. Later I did supercomputer work at a think tank that developed parts of the early Internet (where the engineer who decided on '@' as the separator for email addresses worked down the hall.) Since then I have had several careers—real estate development, financial advising, and counselling.

I retired from financial advising a few years ago and have done some work in energy conservation (ask me about two-stage evaporative coolers!) and relationship issues. My books on attachment theory have done well enough to try fiction again, and the Substrate Wars series is the result.

I recently visited the Mormon genealogical web site, which shows me as a descendant of Eleanor of Aquitaine, Edward I Plantagenet (King of England!), William the Conqueror (who you might remember from such historical events as the Norman Conquest of 1066), and Rollo the Viking. It appears that my ancestors in between lost track of their money, lands, and power, so I was brought up in "reduced circumstances."

Visit my web site at JebKinnison.com for more: rail guns, Nazi scientists, the wreck of the Edmund Fitzgerald, the 1980s AI bubble, and current research in relationships, attachment types, diet, and health.

Visit the Substrate Wars website at SubstrateWars.com for more on upcoming books, physics, and the politics of the future.

Acknowledgements

I'd like to thank my gamma and beta readers, especially Paul Perrotta, Mike Cunningham, and David Friedman. For inspiration, I'll point to Charlie Martin and Sarah Hoyt for their activities in promoting a more inspiring, freedom-oriented variety of science fiction, and of course all those science fiction authors whose work I absorbed from childhood on. Thanks to all of the writers and editors at *Reason* who have remained reality-based through decades of spin by political party propagandists of all flavors, and to Walter Olson of Over-lawyered.com and the Cato Institute for his encouragement. And thanks to Prof. James Miller, Browncoat-at-large at the University of Wisconsin-Stout, for fighting the good fight and inspiring the academic setting.

I'm also grateful to the readers who wrote me about my first two books on relationship issues and expressed their appreciation.

------

[1] "[The] Grey Tribe [is] typified by libertarian political beliefs, Dawkins-style atheism, vague annoyance that the question of gay rights even comes up, eating paleo, drinking Soylent, calling in rides on Uber, reading lots of blogs... [and] getting conspicuously upset about the War on Drugs and the NSA..." —Scott Alexander, "I Can Tolerate Anything Except the Outgroup," SlateStarCodex.com.
http://slatestarcodex.com/2014/09/30/i-can-tolerate-anything-except-the-outgroup/

[2] Red Guards (China). Wikipedia. Retrieved 04:38, December 9, 2014, from http://en.wikipedia.org/w/index.php?title=Red_Guards_(China)&oldid=628885735

[3] Von Neumann architecture. (2014, December 4). Wikipedia. Retrieved 06:38, December 9, 2014, from http://en.wikipedia.org/w/index.php?title=Von_Neumann_architecture&oldid=636564959

[4] Cellular automaton. (2014, November 13). Wikipedia. Retrieved 19:18, December 7, 2014, from http://en.wikipedia.org/w/index.php?title=Cellular_automaton&oldid=633699187

[5] Conway's Game of Life. (2014, December 3). Wikipedia. Retrieved 19:20, December 7, 2014, from http://en.wikipedia.org/w/index.php?title=Conway%27s_Game_of_Life&oldid=636502416

[6] Red Queen hypothesis. (2014, November 26). In Wikipedia, The Free Encyclopedia. Retrieved 05:02, December 9, 2014, from http://en.wikipedia.org/w/index.php?title=Red_Queen_hypothesis&oldid=635485906

[7] Xyzzy (computing). (2014, December 2). Wikipedia. Retrieved 05:04, December 9, 2014, from http://en.wikipedia.org/w/index.php?title=Xyzzy_(computing)&oldid=636291662

[8] Vacuum flask. (2014, December 6). In Wikipedia, The Free Encyclopedia. Retrieved 05:06, December 9, 2014, from http://en.wikipedia.org/w/index.php?title=Vacuum_flask&oldid=636843980

[9] Democrats won election victories with support of wealthy gay donors, but dragged their feet in supporting gay rights until the donors gave them an ultimatum. See, for example, http://news.firedoglake.com/2012/05/08/gay-donors-begin-boycotting-obama-campaign-over-anti-discrimination-executive-order/

[10] New Man (utopian concept). (2014, October 21). In Wikipedia, The Free Encyclopedia. Retrieved 05:07, December 9, 2014, from http://en.wikipedia.org/w/index.php?title=New_Man_(utopian_concept)&oldid=630483507

[11] Stockholm syndrome. (2014, December 2). In *Wikipedia, The Free Encyclopedia*. Retrieved 05:21, December 4, 2014, from http://en.wikipedia.org/w/index.php?title=Stockholm_syndrome&oldid=636329805

[12] Dead Hand (nuclear war). (2014, November 24). In Wikipedia, The Free Encyclopedia. Retrieved 05:08, December 9, 2014, from http://en.wikipedia.org/w/index.php?title=Dead_Hand_(nuclear_war)&oldid=635188058

[13] Fascism. (2014, December 6). Wikipedia. Retrieved 19:15, December 6, 2014, from http://en.wikipedia.org/w/index.php?title=Fascism&oldid=636909721

[14] http://www.wired.co.uk/news/archive/2013-10/10/cryptstagram

[15] http://www.theguardian.com/technology/2014/nov/19/whatsapp-messaging-encryption-android-ios

[16] "Quantum Field as a Quantum Cellular Automaton I: The Dirac free evolution in one dimension," by Alessandro Bisio, Giacomo Mauro D'Ariano, and Alessandro Tosini, Dipartimento di Fisica dell'Universit`a di Pavia, via Bassi 6, 27100 Pavia and Istituto Nazionale di Fisica Nucleare, Gruppo IV, via Bassi 6, 27100 Pavia. http://arxiv.org/pdf/1212.2839v1.pdf PACS numbers: 11.10.-z,03.70.+k,03.67.Ac,03.67.-a,04.60.Kz

[17] Quantum computer. (2014, December 2). Wikipedia. Retrieved 22:57, December 5, 2014, from http://en.wikipedia.org/w/index.php?title=Quantum_computer&oldid=636297961

Topological quantum computer. (2014, December 4). Wikipedia. Retrieved 23:00, December 5, 2014, from http://en.wikipedia.org/w/index.php?title=Topological_quantum_computer&oldid=636644002

[18] Tierra. (2014, June 16). Wikipedia. Retrieved 23:29, December 5, 2014, from http://en.wikipedia.org/w/index.php?title=Tierra&oldid=613111195

[19] Artificial life. (2014, December 5). Wikipedia. Retrieved 23:09, December 5, 2014, from http://en.wikipedia.org/w/index.php?title=Artificial_life&oldid=636808124

[20] "Indefinitely Scalable Computing = Artificial Life Engineering," by David H. Ackley, Trent R. Small. From *Artificial Life 14: Proceedings of the Fourteenth International Conference on the Synthesis and Simulation of Living Systems,* MIT Press, July 2014. http://mitpress.mit.edu/sites/default/files/titles/content/alife14/ch098.html

[21] Red Queen hypothesis. (2014, November 26). Wikipedia. Retrieved 23:28, December 5, 2014, from http://en.wikipedia.org/w/index.php?title=Red_Queen_hypothesis&oldid=635485906